Steele Influence
Kimberly Amato

Little Crown Media, LLC

Copyright © 2024 by Little Crown Media, LLC

Cover Art by Deranged Doctor Design

All rights reserved

This book is protected under the copyright laws. Any reproduction or other unauthorized use of the material or artwork herein is prohibited.

This ebook is licensed for your personal enjoyment only. This ebook may not be resold or given away to other people. If you would like to share this book with another person, please purchase an additional copy for each recipient. Thank you for respecting the hard work of this author.

Disclaimer: The persons, places, things, and otherwise animate or inanimate objects mentioned in this novel are figments of the author's imagination. Any resemblance to anything or anyone is unintentional.

SI.BK6.03.2024

Dedication

For those who persevere through the evil thrust upon them.

Contents

Foreword	1
Chapter One	3
Chapter Two	10
Chapter Three	22
Chapter Four	38
Chapter Five	51
Chapter Six	63
Chapter Seven	79
Chapter Eight	90
Chapter Nine	105
Chapter Ten	114
Chapter Eleven	119
Chapter Twelve	125
Chapter Thirteen	134
Chapter Fourteen	141
Chapter Fifteen	146
Chapter Sixteen	156
About Author	165
Also By Kimberly Amato	166

Foreword

Two years that should have felt like growth turned into a consistent nightmare I could not escape. Ambulances screaming at the top of their lungs all hours of the day, every day for months. As time rolled on, it lessened, but the counts did not. They continued to climb as ineptitude, greed, and ego took the place of policy, hope, and compassion.

I miss the routine of my old life. The simplicity of going to work, catching criminals, and then coming home to my family. Even the warmth of their hugs before the door swung shut behind me feels so far away. Everything felt perfectly in place. That comfort has been missing for a long time. In my head, all I hear are the muffled cries of family members on the other side of the plexiglass shield as their loved one struggles to breathe. All I see is the fear on the faces of victims of domestic violence who truly have no refuge from their daily torment. That was my daily life at work.

Coming home was a chore. Once in the door, my body dragged along the floor to the disinfection procedure. The cracked skin on my hands, a reminder of the multiple washes a day in antiseptic, burned incessantly as the hot water poured over me. It was inevitable given my exposure to a deadly disease touted as nothing worse than the flu. When I fell ill, isolation did nothing for my mental state. Two weeks trapped between four walls with a small bathroom. They delivered food to the door like I was in prison for life. It felt overwhelming, and it silenced me. How can one share their thoughts when no one is around to talk to?

My relationships outside of work are hanging on by a thread. My marriage, once the most stable thing in my world, shaken. Chase, my poor nephew, was terrified every time I walked out the door. No one made it out of this unscathed. Shot or no shot, we have all suffered its effects.

The world I knew has irreparably changed. Gone is the innocence, replaced by the vitriol hidden deep below the surface. This world allowed it all to travel free from repercussions under the guise of democracy. Lies trickled down from the highest levels and eventually found their way into my nephew's mouth. His repetitive denials of reality were the spark that lit a fire that erupted out of me like I was a crazed lunatic. My inability to keep my cool when confronting the teenager was the step too far. I'm relegated to the basement couch since my outburst.

It feels like I'm back where it all began. Silence is once again the most terrifying sound I've ever heard.

Chapter One

Two years ago, Hadley Moreno, one of my best friends and Chase's aunt, left to promote her new film. The death of her fiancé, Logan Pevy, was fuel for social media and news outlets alike. Those willing to label her an accessory to murder made her desire to hide away even more enticing. Several hashtags calling for the end of her career filled the trending pages almost daily. The assumption that she could control a stalker was as plausible as a human being teleported across the world. But the unregulated internet ran with the story alongside news organizations and papers. The once honorable press pushed forth a narrative they knew would sell, get likes or ratings with no ramifications for their actions.

Hadley spent more of her lockdown in Berlin, learning a new language and culture. She refused to do interviews and only spoke to those she truly trusted. We all felt guilty about our thanks for the pandemic taking over the news broadcasts. When things popped up again, the election cycle came along, and no one brought it up. Sadly, Hadley informed us all every time she does anything in the future, these lies will come to the forefront. It's disturbing.

During all of this, Hadley remained in constant contact with us. Every week, she and Chase video chatted without fail. They'd talk about her new movie shooting in Montana or a video game they both played. It gave him some normalcy in an ever-changing landscape of daily tough decisions that still rages outside the window.

We have an unspoken agreement to not discuss Logan. Until Hadley is open to discussing it freely, we don't press. Our job is to support her and , above all else, be the family she needs. She and I haven't spoken since my outburst with Chase. He leans on her not only as an aunt but also as his best friend. I'm sure she knows everything from his perspective. It might just be easier for her to not partake in the drama. She has her own heart and mind to repair.

Chase has grown literally and figuratively, his shorter stature lost in a sea of gangly limbs and shaggy hair. Remote learning and the ability to take his classes in his underwear was a bit too much for my eyes to handle. Frankie never seemed to mind. He took part in each of the school's designated periods at his desk in his room and always wore a nice shirt. She was thankful he wasn't pushing more boundaries.

"He'll be a teenager soon. We'll have our hands full then. Let me just save my energy for when that happens," she would tell me. How could one argue with her sound logic?

Besides, Chase was never far away from his three-legged best friend. Hank ran around the house like it was his personal playground. While shoes were safe, our dirty laundry was not. Somehow, the dog would manage to knock over the hamper and rifle through it. I would get text messages weekly with a picture of a pug with a bra or some other item on his head.

He's more a part of this family than I ever thought possible. From licking Chase's tears when Logan died to snoring by the basement door while I was in quarantine, Hank made us feel less alone. Since the episode that landed me on the couch, he seems to be the only one comforting me. He still rushes to the door but doesn't jump up anymore. After I'm out of the shower, I'd sit on the floor, and we'd play for a bit. He'll kiss me on the face if I let him. Then Chase calls from upstairs, and the pup dashes off to bed. I found it hard to sleep when his napping noises were missing from the emptiness of my dungeon.

Things have been difficult with Frankie and me. Even though she's back in her office, she still sees some clients remotely. Her patient numbers have increased exponentially since the pandemic began, but we expected that. The crisis pushed her to the limit outside of work as well. As essential personnel, I had to work all the time. She was running a business, helping a child learn when he would rather play video games, taking care of Hank, and trying to fit in some time with me. It was enough to push her to the brink of insanity.

Our combined stress has led us to an inability to communicate. I couldn't be there for her, and I'm sure she understood that, but it never eased the pressure. When work pushed me to my limits, familial responsibilities rushed over Frankie like a rogue wave. I concealed my emotions behind a façade. It was easier than processing everything. It also allowed anger to fester within me. I know why neither one of us was available to the other, but it doesn't help me deal with the fissures that seem to have formed in our marriage. We've talked about therapy, but the world hasn't stopped long enough for us to breathe. Once shots were in people's arms, the world wanted to go back to normal as quickly, and irresponsibly, as possible. But how could it? How can one just magically remove over a year of trauma and distrust?

"What time will you be home?" Frankie shakes me from my thoughts.

"Barring any issues, five," I answer, not looking in her direction.

"Okay. Text Chase if you'll be late."

"What about you? Maybe we can have a phone call during lunch?" I ask, hoping for an affirmative answer.

"I can't. Tomorrow is that all day conference that I put on our family calendar. I have a lot of things to finish before then." Frankie was in her morning mode. The way she deftly picked up her briefcase, keys, and morning coffee. It was precise, emotionless.

"Oh, okay. I can pick up Chase—"

"I'll pick him up on my way home today. He has a game tomorrow afternoon."

"Cool, okay. If I can get away, maybe I can make it." Defeated, the words fall out of my mouth weakly.

"If you do, let me know." She turned around and walked a few steps away before my words stopped her.

"I love you." She stood there, her arms hung at her sides as if frozen in place. "I know I've been . . . distant, but I love you. I hope you know that."

"I do," she whispered. "But this isn't about you, Jasmine. It's about each of us and what we've all experienced. You can't just fix that with an 'I love you.' We all need time." She slipped out of the kitchen with a light click of the door. This is how my marriage ends, not with a bang but with a whimper, rolled through my mind.

"Sleeping together in our bed might be a start." I threw out to no one as the emptiness of the room swallowed my words. A small cry brings my attention to the floor. "Hey, Hank. You take care of them while I'm gone, okay? Same thing as always. You do a good job and I'll bring you a treat."

He smiles as I scratch behind his ears. If only human relationships were as easy to maintain.

***

In the flickering, old fluorescent lights of the basement, the all-encompassing chill from the dampness brings an odd feeling of relief. With everything changing outside the door, to have a constant, ever reliable pain in the ass . . . it's nice.

The people sitting at the desks, however, tell a very different story. Will got the call to assist in the pandemic response. He made the tough decision to leave Mia and his daughters behind to fight another war. Once things settled down, West Point called. He's been on leave teaching and training up north. I thought it was a temporary assignment, but seeing his family move up there supports my gut instincts. While we all laughed as each box went into the truck, there was a sadness too. It's a forgone conclusion I won't be working with my friend again, but I dread the actual confirmation. Change keeps rapping at my chamber door, but

I don't want to answer. Maybe I'm the stick-in-the-mud. Everyone around me moves, but I stay still.

His departure left a gaping hole in the team, let alone my little chosen family. It feels as if time and life crept in when we weren't looking to push us apart. Between Will finding a third career and Sydney being promoted to the tech floor, taking over Logan's position, our ragtag team is left with two official members. Poor Agent Karina Marlow and I simply live in the dungeon, awaiting horror to befall on someone.

"Staring at their desks won't magically make them appear," Karina says. She drags her boots along the floor and drops her bag on the desk. Her mask, covered with superheroes from Hadley's latest movie, brings a smirk to my face. "Don't go there, Steele. My kids begged my mother to make them. She bought too much fabric, and now we all have them. Double lining, carbon filter . . . the woman is a mask-making machine. Now if I could only get her to follow a different football team. Traveling to Buffalo in the cold is just too much for one daughter to handle. Don't get me started on my boys jumping through inflatable tables. It's insane."

"I don't think you're going to change her mind. Frankie still believes the Broncos are the be-all and end-all of football. I've been trying to get her on my side for years," I laugh.

"This coming from a Dolphins fan who lives in New York and who has only stepped foot in Miami for a tennis tournament," she retorts, dropping her bag on the desk.

"Yeah, yeah." It's nice to laugh about mundane things again. "How are they handling the kids being back in school full time?" I ask. Since Frankie and I have been distant, I don't know how she's processing Chase going back to school. Personally, it's been an odd feeling for me. I'm thankful for the stability and routine he's had in these last few months being back in a physical building. I'm also scared. Kids are petri dishes of disease.

"They're happy to have some downtime, but I think they miss them during the day. Got used to all the noise, you know?"

"Yeah, I guess."

"You talk to Frankie or Chase about it? How do they feel about the whole thing?"

"I assume they're doing okay. Frankie has a conference tomorrow, and the kid has a game. Would you believe he's graduating from middle school this year? Feels like we've lost so much time that I'll never get back. I need to catch as many moments as I can before he's married with kids of his own, or just hates me. Who am I kidding? He already does, but you get the point."

"He doesn't hate you, Steele. He's a kid. They screw around, annoy the hell out of you, make you feel like the worst mother on the planet, and then suddenly love you again. Parenthood feels like a roller coaster you didn't ask to be on, you have a full stomach of junk food, and the loops make you want to evacuate everything within you. Even with all of that, you stay on that ride forever, because every drop comes with the lift on the other side. Those times when they look at you like you hang the moon, they're worth the free fall when you hit the top." She laughs as her fingers graze her mask. "You'll never be the sun, though. That's reserved for their partner. That person will be the center of our kid's universe with us on the outskirts looking in. Close enough to reach and giving them the consistency they need without being overwhelming. I'm rambling, but the point is, be patient. Tides shift. The ride slows in spots. Chase doesn't agree with you right now. In time, he'll change his tune."

The sound advice makes me uncomfortable. Like any other serious conversation, I find myself deflecting with humor. "You do realize I hate roller coasters, right? I passed out on one in Florida once. Freaked Frankie out. Oh, and I left my lunch on my dad's pants after one in New Jersey. Needless to say, the metaphor kinda falls flat."

"You're crazy, Steele." My partner laughs again as her cell phone shrills through the air. "Damn kids changed my ringtone again." A professional façade falls over her facial features as her eyes land upon the caller identification. "Agent Marlow."

Her tone, serious, cold, and lifeless, reaches my ears. It's unnerving. Her entire body becomes almost rigid, as if in rigor mortis. Her arms lock in place. One hand firmly rests on her hip, the other presses the phone to her ear. The muffled chatter continues with Karina giving a noise of understanding.

"Yes, sir. We'll be right over." She ends the call and exhales as she leans back in her chair. "Looks like a day of filing out requisition forms has to wait. F.M.L."

"Acronyms of FBI moms everywhere. That is definitely an underrated tweet," I mumble.

"Underrated? What the hell are you talking about? You do not tweet or have any form of social media," she presses, and I feel my body coil into itself.

"I may have some. Sydney has been helping me understand the platforms better. Besides, Frankie let Chase have Twitter and some other one with brief video clips." The truth is, I want to be aware of what he's getting into. He lied about his age and had full adult access to all social media out there.

"So, you're spying," she says dryly. Karina stands, fixes her outfit, and begins packing up some items from her desk.

"No, just observing secretly so I don't lose touch with my kid's life."

"Sure, as a mom, I call it spying. Necessary, but if you haven't already, better give your wife a heads-up." She exhales, slips her bag over her shoulder, walks to the elevator, and hits the up button. "Remember that time you asked if the FBI was ever going to trust us with a case?"

"Yes. I also remember you telling me when they have a crappy, unsolvable, want-to-dump-it-on-someone-else case, then and only then would they call."

"Yeah, they called."

"Well, shit."

The elevator dings, notifying us of its arrival. I scramble to grab my things and slip into my jacket before she leaves me behind. The two of us enter the box before the doors rattle shut. Reaching into my pocket, I grab my filter mask and wrap it around my poor ears.

"Please tell me you have something more professional than that vampire mask?" she says as I shrug in reply. "Seriously, Steele, you need a new one."

"I have too many at this point."

"And you chose to wear that one?"

"It's an icebreaker. We had that one domestic with the young boy. He loved it. Got him to open up while discussing his favorite vampire films."

"Arguing with a ten-year-old over the *Twilight Saga* does not mean it is an appropriate mask for work."

"It's the only fun we get to have, Karina. Besides, you're wearing a superhero mask."

"True, but mine doesn't have blood dripping off a K9. Yours is against regulation," she counters.

"You think they care what the depressed lone detective working in the forgotten bowels of the precinct does? Even Captain Zeile hasn't spoken to me in months. Cases haven't hit our desk for a reason, my friend. The writing is on the wall. The experiment went sideways, and when the budget comes up, they'll cut it. You'll be sent back to the feds, and I'll have a new partner who lives by the pages of a manual."

"First, when this task force was formed, we were told only specific cases would come our way. A blessing and a curse. Second, they'd put you behind a desk for the rest of your time there. Who'd want to work with you? Hell, I get hazard pay." A smirk breaks free from her stone-cold expression.

"Okay, that was harsh. God, could you imagine me behind a desk for the rest of my twenty? Still, it's all better than the alternative, right? I mean, everyone second-guessing everything I do sucks, but we're not in a pine box yet. A day above ground in pseudo-hell is always better than dead."

Karina looks on with sympathy but says nothing. The last few years, we've experienced things that are hard to explain to anyone who hasn't been through it. So, we both keep things inside, packed away in the trunks of our mind's memory. We've talked to one another, mostly in code, about the things we did. It might be an echo chamber of sorts, but we can't unsee all that death. We both know how close we were to it . . . to welcoming it in. But it didn't take us like it took others in our precinct.

    Guilt, rage, acceptance. It's nice to finally be to the third stage in all of this. But knowing we're finally working with the FBI puts me on edge. It feels like the calm before the storm. The overwhelming tension rolling off Karina is stifling. It's like I'm standing at the base of a volcano rumbling all around my feet, with an explosion around the corner. I just don't know if or when it will happen.

Chapter Two

The number of cars within the small confines of Manhattan continues to amaze me. If there is a sliver of pavement, a vehicle will find a way to squeeze into it. Of course, that means our sirens blare into the void with little to no movement from the people in front of us. The tedious commute, the people yelling at the top of their lungs to move, the honking, and pedestrians walking with phones occupying their attention used to irritate me. Now, it's a refreshing reminder that life continues to return to some semblance of normalcy around here.

"Do you not hear the siren?!" Karina slams on the horn again as the cars remain still in front of us. "What?"

"Nothing."

"Steele, you're silent staring is adding lighter fluid to my smoldering headache. Speak." Karina switches lanes with a jerk of the steering wheel.

"Right now, I'm hoping my breakfast remains in my stomach. You going to tell me where we're headed?"

"Crime scene." Karina cuts the wheel again, sending us into the far left lane. My hand flies to the dashboard and door panels to prevent my head from hitting the window. The traffic ahead moves a bit, probably afraid of the crazy car behind them.

"You know this isn't a go-kart, right? You hit something, car and bodily harm is a distinct possibility." My stomach continues to roll as she swerves back and forth with practiced ease.

"Distractions help prevent getting sick. Tell me about the Frankie situation," she tries to deflect.

"No, let's not do that," I fire back. "I'd like to know why my partner is driving like a madwoman on the packed streets of the city. I know it's important we get there soon, but this isn't like you."

"I didn't expect them to call." It's then I notice the small beads of sweat gracing her brow. The tires squeal as she forces the cruiser to turn right. "After Seattle . . . after my ex-husband turned out to be the Seattle Slayer, I've been on thin ice with the Bureau. Before you say anything, yes, I was cleared of any wrongdoing or connection to his case. I wouldn't be working with you if I wasn't, but perception is everything. I was the lead on the Seattle Slayer file for so long without coming close to capturing him. He was always one step ahead of me because he knew my schedule, patterns, and what not. Still, some people think I helped him. You'll see when we get there. I apologize in advance for the side-eye stares, distrust flowing off them in the presence of a demon, namely me."

"You're not a demon, though you're driving like one . . . but I can forgive you this one time." I swallow the bile as Karina presses the gas to pass another car. We're almost out of the Midtown mess. "You were cleared, and they caught him. They should be happy you had all that evidence. Hell, you painstakingly collected and organized everything to prosecute the man. If you were helping him, he'd still be free today with a much higher body count."

"I understand that, Steele. But people within the organization just don't care. They sent me here hoping I'd resign. Once their confidence in you is shaken, it's almost impossible to get it back. They sent me to the task force to keep me out of the main office. I don't even know if they truly believed in the unit or if it was a perfect excuse to dump me off somewhere. If we're being honest, I doubt the NYPD was all gung-ho for it either. Your team made one hell of a public relations nightmare back in the day. Maybe we're both just castoffs being given cases to warrant our paychecks. We had to fill out a ridiculous number of requisition forms just to get better lighting in our basement lined with mold. Not to mention your . . . issues. It's just not a fun time to be working down there."

"Look, we both caught COVID in the early days. Thank heavens you don't seem effected by it. Me, I still get some brain fog, headaches, and some minor things. I passed all the recertification tests, so let's not pretend this is all on me here. Are we screwed? Probably. Could they make me a scapegoat for whatever they have planned because of my symptoms? Sure. But what do you want me to do about it?" I say between deep breaths. "I don't know what to tell you, Karina. I can tell you it sucks. I understand the department would rather I stand tall and be the picture-perfect officer, but that's not me. I'm human. I screw up. I learn from it and move on. But that's not what matters anymore. Big, cold, unsolvable—I don't care. Those cases have families attached to them. They have victim's names in bold print asking for help. It's not up to us to pick and choose what happens. We do our best and we follow the evidence. That's all we can do."

The words hang in the air as the car continues, finally free of the gridlock. I believe everything I said, but Karina isn't far from the truth. We've both discussed this at great length. It doesn't change the inevitable or how we do our jobs.

"Sorry, I didn't mean to just go off. I'm managing everything with my shrink and the captain. I wouldn't be out here if I couldn't handle the job," I finish.

"While that might be true, Special Agent Chalet does not just ring your phone for a chat. He's in charge of the Criminal Division of the New York office, and saying he is a tough man to work with is an understatement. We worked together on a case when I was green around the ears. He was intent on teaching and mentoring me in an almost militant style. My failure to capture the Seattle Slayer before more women died, knowing who he turned out to be . . . Chalet never looked at me the same way. It shamed him, especially since he recommended me for the position in the Seattle office. Director Toby is the only reason I'm even working in this city. He's taking a risk and I can't afford to mess it up. If I do, my career is over. Hell, I won't be able to be an adjunct professor for a criminal justice class. They'd blacklist me nationwide."

"Perfection is impossible, Karina. You're going to make a ton more mistakes before you retire." I say flatly. "Before you get angry, just accept you're going to mess up. That misstep might cost someone their life. I can lie and sugarcoat it, but that's not reality. You're my partner. We need to be honest and keep our heads on straight. From experience, obsession about every little thing you do will only lead you down a rabbit hole that is dark and lonely. It's not a fun place to live."

She pulls the car to a stop near the police barricade. I wait for her to turn the car off before opening the door to exit. I struggle for balance, and immediately flashbulbs blind me. My thoughts rush to the headlines hitting the public soon. I wonder if they'll say I'm drunk or unfit. Maybe we didn't get here fast enough, or they'll bring up my wife and somehow twist the connection. It's irritating to see the same reporters with cameras who routinely put out false information. There could be reputable ones in the crowd, but we always remember the bad before the good.

"You okay?"

"Yeah, I'm good."

"Got your kit? I have a spare in the glovebox if you need it."

"Nah, I'm good," I answer, patting my blazer pocket. God, I hate this new forced dress code. More camera clicks hit my ears, but this time I can't hold in a slight chuckle. All the photos will have my vampire mask front and center. The rebel in me cheers.

Pedestrians badger police officers manning the barricades. Most need to walk through to the next avenue. Others say they live on the block, and some just want to know what's going on. Cell phone cameras pop up as Karina and I walk by. Maybe they're hoping we'll say something or the body's coming out soon. Either way, it's a sick addiction that plagues every crime scene since the cell phone camera was in the public's hands. We flash our badges and continue to the shorter building in the middle of the block.

Officers by the boundary and the front door verify our credentials before we head into the complex. They wave to the door on the right leading to the stairs.

Descending into the depths, the smell of garbage hits my nostrils before anything else. The paint flaking off the cement walls shows the age of the pre-World War II building. The flickering lights above us give the aura of a horror film. The pipes above clank and rattle each time water is called for from the upper floors. If any part of the crime happened in this area, the evidence would be useless.

An old elevator with the classic circular window opening pulls my attention. Several officers congregate near it, some holding it open. I doubt the coroner would use it, considering it's a small, square box. They'd use a freight elevator, if this building even has one.

"Excuse me," a resident from a dark cavern of a hallway says to my right. "I was curious if I could get my laundry? It's just around the corner."

"It's a crime scene, ma'am," one of the officers replies.

"I understand that, but did it happen in the hallway or the laundry room?"

"No, ma'am, but we need to ensure a safe perimeter."

"Officer, holding the elevator and hanging out in the corridor doesn't protect the scene. You're all just milling about, stomping all over whatever evidence could have been here. So, I ask again, can I go around the corner, down the hallway next to the elevator, and get my laundry?"

The officer doesn't answer but leads her through the small crowd of blue. The woman huffs as she enters the small room. I can hear her complaining about someone else removing her clothes from the dryer. I remember those days. Somewhere in the ether of left sock world is my favorite Tigger sock. Frankie lost it when someone took out her laundry and dumped it in a bin. I try to work it into conversations even now.

"Detective, Agent Marlow, over here." A young-looking officer waves us over.

We approach the bright-yellow painted door with fingerprint powder on it. They must have pulled a few sets before we got here.

"What have we got?" Marlow asks, sliding past the tech and into the room.

"Sorry you got called down for this one," a man in an oversized suit says to Karina. "Looks like a trick gone wrong. Studio apartment, victims on the bed. Crime Scene Unit is documenting whatever evidence it can dig up."

"It's not an issue, Isaac. Chalet asked us to take a look. We won't step on your toes."

"Oh, I know. He called to let me know you two were the leads. Don't know why, though. Like I said, seems like a pretty simple case."

"If Feds are involved, it's never simple," Karina says softly. "How many officers have been inside?"

"A few."

"Can you break it down?" She stares at the blank walls of the apartment while Isaac answers.

"Police got an anonymous tip about the vic. Maintenance let the officers and paramedics into the apartment. After medical personnel called it, they notified dispatch. The coroner was informed he had a pickup, and next thing I know, Chalet calls me cause I'm in close proximity. I was told to hold the fort until you and Detective Steele arrived. Since then, only the two members of the forensic team and myself have been inside."

Karina nods her head as she looks around the entire apartment. I can see the wheels turning as she tries to figure out the victim by what is, or more accurately, what isn't visible. Flashes from the CSIs documenting the body brighten up the studio. The room feels rather claustrophobic with the five of us and a full-sized bed with a body lying on it. A closet is to my left, followed by the bathroom. To the right is a small kitchen with an opening in the wall, looking out into the living area. There's nothing fancy or spectacular about the layout. The only thing making it feel more livable is the higher-than-average ceilings.

Karina and Isaac continue their conversation while I slip into the kitchen. Two glasses rest right next to the sink. The towel they lay upon, long since dried, has reddish stains on them. Red wine? Could this have been a date gone wrong instead? I don't know if a sex worker would offer high-end refreshments.

I quickly snap on a set of protective gloves before opening the cabinets. Every single one of them is empty. Nothing but dust and what appears to be mouse droppings. The wall with the opening has a small shelf for eating. There, two plates sit next to a plastic cup holding two forks, two knives, and two spoons. All of it cleaned and stacked just waiting for the next meal. But there's no cooking supplies or evidence of a human being truly living here.

The refrigerator tells a different story. Inside is copious amounts of alcohol and one large Brita water filter. There's a ton of cheap beer, several hard seltzers and wine coolers, but no wine. They must not have a corkscrew, either. All the items are twist off or snap tabs. This place was used strictly for hosting.

The living area is more of the same. The bed sits in the corner, one side against the back wall and under the two small slits that serve as windows. I assume the image of feet walking by was all you would see all day. There doesn't appear to be any curtains blocking the outside world from peeking in. Stepping a bit closer, the telltale boxes of blinds come into view. Were they ever used? Did the victim take them down, or did the perp remove them to ensure people could see their handywork?

Across from the bed is a small desk. A laptop sits open in the middle. Two small computer cameras on stands connect to a small hub to the system. A battery backup power supply rests on the floor.

"So, you didn't live here," I say to the victim. Opening the left side of my blazer, I pull out a small notepad and pen. I sketch out the room, adding notes where I think it's necessary. Anything to ensure I don't miss something important. It's procedure now for anyone recovering from the damn disease that spread everywhere. We need to log all our notes, see a psychiatrist and specific milestone doctor's appointments. The union backed it, but it added another step in an already arduous process.

"What gave it away? The lack of furniture? The wall of plastic bins?" Isaac laughs.

Karina jumps in to defend me. "Stop being an ass. Steele has her methods, and it hasn't failed her before." She knows these procedures are brand-new, but I appreciate her taking the heat off me a bit. I'm embarrassed by it, but I have to do it to keep my job.

I glance over at the wall of storage containers. I wonder what the victim could have kept in them. Could all the kitchen supplies be in there? Was she moving out or maybe just moved in? The questions form a picture which makes me rethink my initial assessment.

"There's no food in the kitchen; only drinks in the fridge." The clear plastic bins on the wall draw my attention but offer little insight. "Doesn't look like there are any clothes in here either. One container's labeled *Toy Box* with fuzzy cuffs and some other... appendages."

"Vengeful ex-client or jealous ex-lover?" Karina adds to the conversation. "Might explain the *Paid in Full* stamped on her forehead."

"If she's an online entertainer, it's a possible outcome. Her partner finds out about the side business and feels slighted. Kills her in a fit of passion." My hand flies across my notepad. I pray I can read the chicken scratches when I transcribe all of this back at the office.

The female victim lies on her back, nylons wrapped around her neck. Her head hangs over the edge, staring at the computer desk upside down. Her milky-white eyes just stare into the darkness of the monitor. Into oblivion. Her arms dangle, knuckles resting on the floor. The white lab coat barely covers her breasts, but not much more.

If she ran a sexual fantasy website, I assume the desire to gain subscribers for a higher income would be a top priority. One would assume that would include looking directly into the cameras, or at least playing to them to entice her audience. Yet, her dead stare was at the computer monitor. It's then I notice a small red light on the side of each camera. They might be live.

Without waiting for confirmation, I slam the laptop shut and yank the power cables out of the peripherals.

"What the hell are you doing, Steele? You could fry the thing," Karina admonishes in front of her colleague.

I ignore her and whisper to the CSI next to me. They slip the computer into a plastic evidence bag, seal it, and place it within a case. Karina's stare burns into the back of my head as I inform the tech team to take the evidence outside into the truck. They'll need to have an officer guard it in case the perpetrator had intentions of claiming the equipment.

"Want to explain that?"

"I could be imagining it, but the red lights were on. That usually means it's recording or it's live. Since the screen wasn't lit up and I' not computer savvy, I just closed it and told tech to get it outside. No camera. No microphone. No hearing the information we've collected on the case."

My partner is quiet for a moment, then nods. We didn't need another issue with a perpetrator having access to the case files. It wouldn't matter the reason; Karina knew we couldn't afford to risk it.

"You think it was live?"

"She could have been streaming to anyone or anywhere in the world. You know what Sydney said about these things."

"That adds a new wrinkle to the possibilities."

"Did someone pay to have her killed on air? If so, there should be some trace of it online. Maybe on the dark web or on a streaming site with specific logins. Sydney's going to have to dig into it all."

Karina grabs the tech who handled the laptop for me. "Take all the equipment and head down to Detective Sydney Locke's office. Tell her this is a priority. If she needs to speak to me, she has my number." She turns to Isaac. "Could you please take him to the precinct? He'll give you directions if necessary."

"I know the way," he mutters before the two men leave.

"Don't think he was thrilled to be dismissed like that."

"What man does?" Karina looks over the doorway and the investigative powder. "Door shows no signs of forced entry. So that leaves us with someone she knew, had an appointment with, or the building managers who have a key."

I kneel alongside of the bed, taking in the body and how the blankets are arranged. The struggle definitely occurred on the mattress. Something under the bed pulls my attention. The handle of a purse barely peeks out against the white sheets.

The expensive-looking, black leather bag has a metal plate with the designer's name on it. Within it are some tampons, a travel-sized hand sanitizer bottle, spare surgical masks, and buried beneath all of that, a cell phone and wallet. It takes only a few moments to pull the license out with the victim's image and full name on it.

"Her name's Dierdre Boxletter." I hold up the license for Karina to scan. In the billfold, a piece of white plastic sticks out a bit. Upon further inspection, I see it's another piece of identification. Our victim was a pediatric doctor.

"Oh man, this just opens even more possibilities. Angry parents, business associates who knew about her evening activities . . . I'd prefer a smaller pool of candidates."

"Different address on the license. We should check it out. Maybe get a better idea of who Ms. Boxletter really was. A roommate, spouse, or significant other would really be beneficial." Each item in the purse gets its own bag, sealed and signed for. Her medical card hangs in my hand as I will it to speak to me.

"Could it be possible she was moving to this apartment slowly? Somewhere where she could run her business and her day job?"

"I don't know much about the situation, but I know those webcams are newer models. Chase has been begging me to get him one since they launched. They cost a lot for a kid who just wants to stream himself playing video games. The computer doesn't look that old either. No dust on the power supply or cables. Feels like this whole setup is new or newer."

"True. Not sure about the tech, but no dust could just be cleanliness for work? You wouldn't subscribe or log into a live feed in a dirty landscape." Karina stares at the victim, her mind lost in thought for a few moments. Normally, we'd have some sort of plan of attack. But she seems off. As if everything is another question with no solution. "No matter what we think, the FBI is taking the lead on the investigation. I'm not willing to commit to any theory or plan of action until we're sure of a solid path. Until then, we let CSI finish up and release the body to the coroner."

This does not sound like the confident partner I've had for the last few years. She continues looking around the room, talking to techs and officers while pointing to items around the area.

Deidre looks peaceful. Even with the bruising around her neck, there's a calmness that comes with death. The suffering is over. Her skin is almost perfectly pristine beyond those obvious marks. So many things run through my head as I stare at her body. For someone who cared so much about the tiny humans of the world, I wonder if anyone really cared about her. Was she alone? That thought twists my guts around.

Victor comes in with an assistant and calmly moves the body into a more suitable position. The cracking makes my upset stomach rear its ugly head. I try to remove myself from a scene before the coroner begins cracking a full rigor corpse into a bag. I wish Karina would stop talking so we could leave.

A voice in the hallway echoes into the apartment. "Ever wonder why women get into this industry? It's not for the money, unless you go it alone. Makes you think they're just asking for something like this to happen. I mean, if you can't respect yourself, you shouldn't expect another human being to either. Look at that outfit. I don't know how many of us would stop when that's in our face!" A sudden wave of icy anger washes over me.

My fists clench at the idiotic comments reaching my ears. The hand on my shoulder signals my partner's attempt to keep me away from confrontation. It fails. Two full strides into the hallway and the grotesque comments connect to an officer leaning against the cinder block. His right leg bent, foot on the wall, right thumb hooked into his utility belt with a snake oiled salesman smirk on his face. A stereotypical look for an evil villain in every movie I've ever seen.

"So, she deserves to die because she had a good body?"

"Oh, come on, detective. You know what I mean," he counters.

His face brings a recent memory to the forefront. He was vile during the pandemic, putting his personal beliefs above the needs of citizens. Earlier this year, he bragged about his month in a charity calendar being voted the hottest by the online masses. Lord knows he lives and dies by his narcissistic endeavors. Either that or he enlisted people to vote for him to bolster his ego. I don't care. I can't stand him as a person or an officer.

"By your own logic, I should be able to gut you like a fish for representing the month of August. You did take your shirt off and flex in nothing but your hat and unbuckled pants."

"You wouldn't get a chance. Besides, I don't play mind games. I see what I want, turn into a charmer, and claim what's mine. Women love it, detective. Women like the vic can't handle it when someone cashes in on what they're selling."

"That, by your own words, is a crime. Someone murdered this woman, officer. Maybe you should read the law before you attempt to enforce it."

"No need to get touchy, detective. Just saying what the media is gonna be printing all over the place." He shrugs as if it was obvious.

"What the media should print is a woman was murdered in her own apartment. Someone she trusted came in and removed her life from this Earth. It doesn't matter what her vocation or side hustle was. They should focus on who she was as a human being instead of what her body looked like, what she was wearing... whatever. We should be thinking of her family. She was a daughter to someone. Maybe a wife or a mother. What if the victim was your mother? How would you respond then?" I step closer to the officer.

"Detective, you're really pressing the wrong buttons now. You live in the basement. You have no backing here. Go run back to the captain and tell him whatever you want. Nothing will come of it. I've got people backing me. You're on your own. You and that . . . accomplice of a partner."

That line lands hard. News of Karina's past must have made the rounds, and we missed it or ignored it. I don't know which. All I know is her hand is clenching my arm with a force I didn't know she had.

"Officer, do you understand the type of person it takes to strangle someone? The determination and evil flowing through their veins as they pull the nylon in opposite directions, cutting off the flow of oxygen and blood to the brain. The sheer strength it takes to physically do this is only surpassed by the emotional disconnect from the act itself. This person could be a teacher looking at your child in a new way. Maybe staring at your wife with a new fondness. They would be coy, lure her in, and snuff her out before you could call for backup. All because she wore a skirt to work that morning." Karina's tone forces goose bumps to erupt on my skin. We've dealt with these kinds of killers and spoken to them at length. This officer would shit himself before he sat down for an interview.

"My wife and daughter wouldn't flaunt themselves like that, Agent Marlow."

"Are you on their social media accounts? Do you check their feeds? Remember, you're only looking for a few hours a day. It only takes one creep to see an image and decide which victim fits their desire. Then poof... they're gone."

The dripping sound of a leaky water pipe bounces off the walls as the officers all fall into silence. It's one thing to push me, but another when going toe to toe with a trained FBI agent. They're all silent, but defiant.

Victor pushes his way through the crowd, and they lift the body up the stairs.

"Officer, why don't you follow the coroner out of the building and give him an escort to the morgue. This case is the highest priority, and time is of the essence."

He pushes off the wall but stops by the base of the stairs. "Better watch your backs. You wouldn't want to be all over the press again. They're already over the NYPD's darling duo. Could turn at any time." He smirks as he stomps up the staircase.

I finish writing all the notes from my encounter with the officer. His name, badge number, threats, and more all litter the pages. I should hand it all to Captain Zeile and let him handle it, but I know Mr. August is right. Nothing will be done. In fact, I wonder if the opposite would be true. Would my boss think I was losing control? Would he place me on desk duty for the rest of my career? Force me to retire? If they think I'm out of control, anything is possible. All I can think is how the mighty Detective Steele has fallen.

✷✷✷

The drive back is quiet and disconcerting. The lack of conversation leaves a hollow feeling that I desperately want to fill. Since Will's leave of absence, Karina and I have fallen into a calm working partnership. We talk through most cases step by step. She's been instrumental in finding new ways to help me work through my predicament.

Back in our office, several electrical cables hang from the ceiling, but the new LED lights flicker to life. The new illumination slices through the cold feel of the room. In some way, it makes it feel more inviting, but in another, it shows how empty the office has become.

Along with the new lights, a robust whiteboard hangs on the far wall. Karina slides open a drawer and tosses me the black marker. She dumps her items on her chair and sits on her desk.

"What do your notes say?"

"You're not going to reprimand me?"

"No. You're struggling. I get that. Besides, I was out of line as well."

"But you have to let Zeile know."

"You know I do. No matter what happens, Mr. August was out of line. I'll be writing an official complaint against him. Maybe coming from me, it will mean something. As for your work capabilities, Captain Zeile set the terms of your reinstatement. I've followed them to the letter thus far, and you know I won't deviate from it. You keep doing what you're doing, all good. You stumble, no more field work. But I'm not letting some hothead try to push us to screw up. If it happens, it'll be on us. Not the other way around. You know?"

I simply nod in response because words are meaningless. I know we'd love to go out on our own terms, in control over our errors, but that isn't always possible. If it happens though, I'm torn as to my response. If I walked away, I'd have to explain to my wife why our benefits are no longer guaranteed. Our financial plan would burn to a crisp.

If I was staffing the desk or demoted, she'd notice immediately. My demeanor would probably change, I wouldn't discuss cases with her on a professional level, and my uniform would be reinstated. Either way, I couldn't hide any change from Frankie. She'd know the minute my eyes connected with hers.

With all that noise rolling around in my brain, I take out my notes and jot down basic information onto the whiteboard. I add a pathetic drawing of the crime scene, complete with a stick figure body. One page at a time, I transfer it over to bring the larger picture to life.

I start to add questions on the right side of the board, each one more annoyingly complicated than the last. This was part of my new routine. Getting all the information down several times committed it to memory and made me feel more confident in my analysis. It also allowed me to see patterns I might not otherwise notice. There's something to be said for old-school detective work.

Once completed, I stood next to Karina staring at the board, willing it to speak to us. She moves forward and adds some thoughts of her own—some additional details and Isaac's name as the first agent on scene.

"It's not much to work with." She leans back on the desk next to me. "We can assume cause of death, but until Victor processes everything, we have to be careful."

"Hopefully he can find something the naked eye missed." My eyes scan the board again and again. Everything is there, but it is so vague. "Sydney has all the tech stuff. Maybe she'll dig up something."

"I'll send her a message and ask for a full workup, including financials, criminal record, and associates."

"The work ID was from Pediatrics Medical. Might be worth heading over there to see if we can get some more information."

"Notifying her workplace of her death before family . . . it's wrong."

"We need something, Karina. We could go to the other address on the license, but I'd like to have some paperwork to back our entry in case someone else lives there. Right now, this is the only play I see as an option."

"We don't know if they'll even entertain the idea of a friendly conversation."

"Maybe not, but it's worth a shot. We need a warrant for any records, but we might get a hint of a clue. Might lead us to investigating an angry client or staff member. Anything to get us started."

"You do have a gift at making people talk, even when they should really shut up."

Sadly, that statement is very accurate. I can get most people to talk for whatever reason. People open up and tell me their demons, troubles, and doubts without any prompting. Yet, when it comes to speaking my truth, or being my best advocate, the words fail me. That's why I prefer to speak for those unable or struggling to speak for themselves.

Chapter Three

Cartoon characters cover the glass windows of the medical practice. A television plays various animated classics as Karina and I head to the counter to check in. The receptionist slides the plexiglass window open and smirks at the two of us. Even though we know we don't need to wear masks anymore, this is one of the many reasons we choose to. The silly designs lighten the mood of anyone coming across our path.

"Can I help you?"

Karina holds her badge in her right hand. "We'd like to speak to the person in charge."

"One minute, please." She slides the divider back in place and picks up the phone. She hits a few buttons before turning away from us.

Karina slides her badge back inside her interior blazer pocket before those in the waiting room catch a glimpse. Of course, that doesn't stop a young boy pulling on her pant leg. His blue-gray eyes stare up at her and his shark teeth mask looks ready to bite down.

"Well, hello."

"You are too old to be here. Mama said this place is for kids. You have no kids." He waves his arms around as if gesturing to the lack of children by my side.

"Dylan," a woman warns as she grabs his hands and yanks him away from us. "How many times have I told you not to talk to strangers?"

"But you do it all the time on your phone," he replies.

"Ladies, if you'll follow me." The receptionist holds the interior door open for the two of us. "Last door on the right, the elephant."

Karina nods her head and walks down the hallway. Each entryway is identified by a different smiling cartoon animal on it. They designed the entire area like a safari with trees, wildlife, and trucks painted on the walls. It feels like a perfect setup to treat children in a calm environment. It reminds me of my pediatrician. He would draw little creatures on my arm and give the injection as a nose. He once told me if it lasted over three seconds, I could hit him. My little hands smacked him once. He told me two seconds had passed. I sat up straight and told him time was relative. My mom said it once, and my dad listened to her, so I repeated it like a good little parrot. I wish we all had these murals to distract us from the treatments, tears, and fears inside the rooms.

"Doctor Helmut will be in shortly." I'd almost forgotten the receptionist was still behind us.

The small office holds the usual self-aggrandizing information. Frames touting the physician's degrees, photos of their family, articles listing them within the top 100 of their field and more. Everything a parent wants to see to build trust in how the doctor handles their child's care. Other than that, the room is a boring office with no windows, a computer desk with two chairs in front of it. It feels rather claustrophobic.

"Sorry to keep you waiting." A bald, wiry-looking man walks into the room, closes the door, and sits down behind the oak desk. "I understand you wish to speak to me, but I believe I'm at a bit of a loss as to what it's regarding."

"Doctor Helmut, I'm Special Agent Karina Marlow and this is my partner, Detective Jasmine Steele. We were curious about an employee, Doctor Deidre Boxletter. She is employed here, yes?" Karina asks right away.

"Yes, she's a member of this practice." He folds his hands together on the desk and sits ramrod straight, defensively. "Beyond that, I'm afraid you will have to speak to our lawyer."

It always amazes me how quickly everyone tosses out the law firm card. It used to be a red flag for us to investigate further. Now, it's one of the first things mentioned every single time we talk to anyone. I know it's meant to protect their best interests, but sometimes we end up deferred to a paralegal or a friend who watches crime shows or reads a lot of books. Neither ensures the individual will be represented properly or puts their best interests first. I understand the lack of faith in working with us, but sometimes I really wish people would talk to us first.

"Doctor Helmut, we can assure you the practice is not under investigation, nor have we received complaints of criminal activity within these walls. We're just here about your colleague. How long has she worked here?"

He hesitates, and his lip twitches a bit as I assume his brain funnels through the various avenues for a response. "It's been several years. You'll forgive me if I don't have an exact date. Pediatrics Medical is part of the Northeast Medical conglomerate. I can give you the contact information for our human resources department for more details."

"We'd appreciate that," I add, jotting down some notes for myself. "Has anything out of the ordinary happened recently?"

"We're still dealing with the aftereffects of a global pandemic. You might need to be more specific than that."

"Has Doctor Boxletter shown signs of distress other than the obvious?"

"We're doctors trying to convince children and families that health is important. We keep them occupied before we give them a vaccination. Some of our doctors create magical worlds to explain personal hygiene and whatever else we have to do to ensure well-being. Once a patient walks through the door, we leave calm and ordinary in our offices." He leans back in his chair, seemingly more comfortable but still guarded. "While I can't speak to specifics, Deidre seemed to be acting normally during the last few weeks. Nothing stood out to me as abnormal."

"When was her last shift?" My little notepad fills with his comments. Thank God for Chase teaching me texting shorthand. I'd be running out of pages without it.

"Yesterday. We both had full schedules and barely enough time for lunch, let alone paperwork."

"Was this normal?"

"During the pandemic, we had to space everyone out dramatically. We've only recently opened back up to our maximum patient allotment per day. It all depends on what the higher-up guidance says."

"Do you know if Doctor Boxletter had any issues with scheduling? Considering the health concerns for both clients and staff alike, parents must have been unhappy if they couldn't be seen in a timely manner."

"We do our best to accommodate everyone as quickly and efficiently as humanly possible. We can't over-schedule our office to the point of dysfunction to ensure every call gets an appointment when they demand it. Unless it is an emergency, we follow procedure and give people the next available opening. Then we refer them to the emergency rooms." His hand rubs the back of his neck as it audibly cracks. "If you must know, we spend more time doing paperwork and whatever else our bosses want. Sometimes our staff members work an additional twenty hours just to finish patient notes. They're giving us all assistants to type as we go, so we should have time to see more patients. As if taking on more cases is in the best interest of medical care, but I digress."

Doctor Helmut's long-winded answer backs up the darker shading under his eyes. The closer I look, the more I can see the stress taking its toll.

"Has any family complained about lack of access?" I ask.

He inhales deeply before exhaling slowly. Doctor Helmut leans forward and lowers his voice. "I know you legally cannot share with me the details of your investigation. But you're asking a lot about my colleague and that leads me to make my own conclusions. Either she's in the hospital because of an assault, she's been reported missing, or worst-case scenario, she's been murdered."

"We can't—"

"I told you I understood that. What I would like is to cut through the bullshit and get right down to the nitty-gritty. Deidre is an amazing doctor. She's kind, compassionate, and parents rave about her to anyone who will listen. In fact, most of her patients come from referrals. The staff loves her, and yes, patients can be crabby if they had to wait for an appointment. But they've all waited their turn without incident. Beyond her professionalism, she is a dear friend and someone I trust explicitly."

"Is it more than friendly?" Karina presses. "Your relationship with Deidre. Is your partner aware of your devoted friendship with her?" She points to the photos of a woman and three kids on his desk.

His laughter at the comment gives way to a sneer of disgust. "Why is it law enforcement always considers male and female co-workers as sexual partners? Can't they just be friends? Why must it all come down to sex?"

"Doctor Helmut, we're just trying to gain a bigger picture of the situation. We reference the relationship between the two of you because of your insistence that you were close. We're extrapolating data from that remark. If we've offended you, I sincerely apologize," I answer quickly.

"There's a better way to inquire about our connection." He reaches forward and picks up the frame on his desk. "If you must know, this is my baby sister and her children. Not that it's any of your business, but before this gets any more attention than it deserves, Deidre and I are not physically intimate. To further that point, it's common knowledge among those I trust that I have no desire to be romantically involved with anyone. Deidre is fully aware of this and is supportive. She's family, my confidant . . . my best friend."

"There was no room for a misunderstanding?" Based on her line of questioning, I'm sure Karina got the point, but needed to make sure the victim did, too.

"Not at all. I won't discuss her private life, but we are fine."

"Are you aware of her other job?" The question flies out of my mouth as I scan over my notes. Helmut might feel they were close, so maybe he has more information than he's letting on.

"I think I've answered enough of your questions to ask one of my own. Where is Doctor Boxletter?" He places the photo frame back on the edge of his desk. I can feel him build up his walls into a protective force around his emotions. He's probably preparing himself for the worst and praying we give him better news. "If you want more out of me, then I suggest you give me more information to work with."

"We're unable to share any pertinent information regarding an ongoing investigation." The mechanical response makes my stomach ill. It's like a doctor telling you everything is perfectly fine after they find a lump in your breast. It might be fine from a medical standpoint, but the blanket statement does nothing to calm the tornado of emotion that swirls within you. I hate what I said. Every single syllable of it. The more each moment passes, the more I dislike who I've become.

"Can't or won't?" Our silence answers his question perfectly. "I see. Then this conversation is over."

"We could use your help—"

"Yes, you've mentioned that plenty of times already. As I tell our patients' parents, we can only make proper decisions with open communication. You're not willing to do that, and I have shared more than enough for you to . . . do whatever it is you are doing."

He stands and fixes his lab coat and tie. His hands shake with an overwhelming amount of adrenaline or fear. When he notices my attention, he slams them into his pockets.

"We're done here." The crack in his voice betrays his firm exterior. "Take a left out of the office and another left at the end to exit."

I drop my card on his desk. "If you can remember anything, please give us a call."

"Very well, but I have patients to see. If you would please leave." The doctor takes another step forward and opens the door for us.

He follows us out and slips into the giraffe room. His voice is suddenly lighter and friendly as he greets his patients. If the man has a switch to turn on the charm for patients, could he have one for lying to law enforcement? Maybe Sydney can do a deep dive to verify the doctor had no stake in his friend's death.

"Well, that was enlightening," Karina tosses out as we exit the hallway into the waiting room.

The boy from before, Dylan, sees me and squints. I'm sure he was going for a more action hero *I'm watching you look*, but it just looks like he devoured a lemon. It takes a lot to hold in my laughter as we exit the building.

"I think the meeting was exactly what we expected," I finally add to the conversation from the safety of the parking lot. "We know she was a beloved doctor but couldn't see all her patients when they wanted an appointment. Then, you add her evening activities and one has to question if those same parents got wind of it and lost control. You saw them in the waiting room. Too busy on their phones doing whatever to worry about the kids climbing all over those toys. But if one gets hurt, they'll be quick to sue."

"Hey, being a parent isn't a simple job!"

"I know that. When Chase was sick, I would climb the walls screaming at doctors for not getting us in sooner. But they see the bigger picture and might have a patient who's more emergent than we are. I get both sides of the equation here. I just need to talk everything out to ensure I'm not forgetting any options or possibilities."

"I appreciate that, but I don't think it would be a parent." Karina unlocks the car and opens the door. She rests her arms on the roof of the car for a second. "I can see lashing out with words or threats, but actually acting on them takes it to a whole new level. If it was that serious, would they come to a general practitioner? I'd be in a specialist's office screaming my head off."

"Unless they were unaware they needed one. Doesn't hurt if we get a warrant and do some prelim background checks." The shrill of the latest K-Pop song Sydney is obsessed with blares from my jacket pocket. I slide the phone to answer on speaker. "What's going on, Syd? Anything new?"

I slide into the car, and once it's started, I hit the seat warmer. My back has not been happy for the last few days. Then again, since I've been sick, I don't think any part of me has been.

"I'm still digging into the laptop for more details, but nothing is jumping off the page. The lease for the crime scene apartment had two names on it. They also showed up on the primary residence contract as well. Deidre Boxletter and Tazlia Bazana have used both addresses on an off for a little while now. Nothing concrete beyond that. I'll text you the address once I get off the phone with you. You should be able to copy and paste it into a notes app if that helps." Her voice echoes in the car.

"Is Bazana listed as next of kin?" I ignore the last part of Sydney's comments. I know it was meant with love, but I just don't want to deal with it right now.

"From what my team can dig up, yes. Like I said, it's all prelim. Just wanted to give you something to get started, as promised."

"Thanks, Syd. Text either of us if something pops." Karina shifts to reverse and pulls out of the crowded parking lot.

"Sure thing. Just an FYI, captain was in here a little while ago asking about the case. Had some suits with him I hadn't met before. Just figured you should know."

"Appreciate the heads-up. We'll talk soon." The heat from the seat radiates through my sore muscles as the phone disconnects.

"You holding up okay?" Karina tosses my way. I'm sure she's aware of the anxiety ruling my mind at the moment. It always feels like ten steps forward come with twenty in the opposite direction.

"Yeah. I don't like how many cooks are on this case. Makes me nervous for a lot of reasons." The beep of my phone pulls my attention away from the anxiety crawling over my flesh. "Got the address."

My partner rattles off the information to her phone gps app, and zips out into traffic. Another day filled with more questions and even fewer answers. Moments like this always made me wish crime was as easily solved as the television producers make it out to be. Forensics would happen overnight, and there would always be some sort of trail leading them to an assailant. Even when the evidence wasn't physically there, somehow, they would figure it out. It would make it easier to appease the higher-ups and demanding public. But reality is harder to swallow, and demands are never-ending.

So, we take it one step at a time, asking the most mundane questions to get a conclusion we can work with. If Doctor Boxletter was beloved by everyone she met, she'd still be alive. The idea that human beings go through life without creating an enemy on some scale is foolhardy. The internet is rife with lies close enough to the truth to be believable, but false none-the-less. Just existing as she did, living her life, could create a jealousy that ran deeper than respect. Maybe a parent wrote something denigrating the doctor due to how she treated her child. We can blame all the commercials touting drugs to ease our discomforts; just talk to your doctor about it. Doesn't matter if it's beneficial for your case. If the television says it, human beings follow suit.

Doctor Boxletter had a secret life. It was virtually impossible that no one was aware of it. The idea of her clients consisting of married patients rolls around in the back of my head. Hopefully, the district attorney will have more luck getting access to her client list. That might shed more light on the crossover. It's a long shot, though. My faith is with the doctor's roommate. Since their name is on both residences, they could have some information to push this case to a logical conclusion. Otherwise, I fear the murder will become colder than the polar vortex freezing over Niagara Falls.

***

No matter how many times I've notified family members of their relatives' passing, it never gets easier. Any officer that denies its toll would be a liar. The victim's friends and family show you photos of how the person used to be, but all you see is how they ended up. The gruesome scenes of mutilation, pale skin, glazed eyes, and the smell. That one you never fully get used to. Sometimes an image can bring the smell of decomposition back so strong, the urge to empty my stomach is overwhelming.

I've been through a countless number of these processes, and not one response has been the same. Similar, but never the same. Parents are always the hardest to handle. The depth of their wails reverberates around the room and pierce your soul. Some flail their arms, desperately grabbing at stability as the world around them shatters to pieces. We try to shield them from the images and let them assume it was a painless and quick passing. The coroner does their best to cover all signs of a struggle, but in the end, the family members aren't stupid. They read the papers and see the words of others posted around the world. They hear radio personalities or podcast hosts spewing their opinions about their children, who can no longer defend themselves. Right or wrong, that is the blessing and curse of modern society.

The distracted door attendant of the upscale apartment complex waves us through without glancing at our badges. He heartily laughs at a video playing on his cell phone, his attention diverted from our intent and the sign-in sheet on the counter. Karina, understanding my body language means trouble, grabs my elbow and pulls me away from the fool behind the counter. We could be anyone walking in to murder or rob the place, and he just let us float on by as if it was nothing. The privacy and lives of his tenants is worth less than an internet video and some laughs.

"What the hell!" I snap my arm out of Karina's painful grasp.

"It's not worth it."

My partner's words hang in the air as my brain tries to digest them. Why isn't the situation worth my time? Why shouldn't we speak up or let the guard know that what he's doing is inconsistent with his duties? Maybe nothing has happened in this building for some time, but that doesn't negate that it could happen here. Yet somehow, we have forgotten how to politely question people's actions without repercussions. When did we become silent in the face of homegrown delinquencies?

"But it is, Karina. We don't need to belittle the man, but maybe we should ask him if he's seen anything. Maybe he has. Maybe he'll prove the assumptions my brain is screaming about, or maybe I'm wrong."

My feet make it back to the man in question before Karina can stop me. "Excuse me, sir?"

He looks up, his eyes widen as my badge comes into view. "What can I do for you, officer?"

"Would you be able to tell us if anyone visited Deidre Boxletter recently?"

"Umm, I can't give you access to the visitor logs. It's company policy. You'd need a warrant."

"I understand that, and we will look into obtaining one, but you can tell me if you've noticed anyone odd or suspicious going to her apartment."

"No, ma'am. I haven't noticed a thing."

"Would you know if any other security officer reported something out of the ordinary in the last few weeks?" Maybe the person behind the desk hadn't experienced something firsthand, but people talk.

"No, ma'am. Like I said, nothing abnormal has been going on. Now, if you'll excuse me." He leans back and presses play on his phone. Part of me wants to continue pressing the man, but I know it's useless.

Karina points to her watch as if time is running out. "Really, boss?"

The elevator doors open, and we step inside. Karina presses the button for the twentieth floor. The car locks us inside as it rattles upwards.

"Look, our time is better spent upstairs than bothering him. Regardless of whether his actions are right or wrong, it's up to his boss to decide such things. Everyone has to navigate this screwed-up world their way. Best to let them try to figure it out on their own. Understand the consequences of their actions and face them under the law."

The car shakes as it slows down near our destination.

"Condemn the fault and not the actor of it?" I reply.

"That's . . ." Karina pauses, scanning her memory banks for a connection. "Knowing you, it has to be Shakespeare. In my opinion, people will always face the consequences of their actions, whether it be in a court of law, public opinion, or something else. Myths always contain a grain of truth that helped create them. Karma is real."

"But is it? Just look at all the criminals who get to live out their days, never seeing the inside of a courtroom. Money means a unique set of rules. Hell, look at Congress. The hypocrisy that breezes through those halls would make a category five hurricane feel like a summer wind off the ocean. There's a reason every comic book I've ever read gives rise to a vigilante."

The elevator shutters to a stop at our destination. Leaving the claustrophobic box, my eyes land on the door directly in front of us. The number matches the apartment we're looking for.

"We have to believe in what's right, Steele. Otherwise, we lose sight of why we do this job in the first place."

"We never forget the reason, Karina. We're reminded of it every time we get a call." I press the doorbell of the apartment and wait. The silence that follows is bothersome. The possibilities run through my mind: the occupant could be at work, or there could be another body. Karina presses and holds the button this time, the shrill lasting a good four seconds before she releases it.

A deep, sultry voice pierces through the metal door. "Hello? Can I help you?"

"Yes, I'm Special Agent Marlow and this is my—"

"While I appreciate the introduction, can you get to the point? What do you want?" The sharpness of the woman's tone cuts through the pleasantries and puts me on edge.

"Agent Marlow and I were hoping to speak to Tazlia Bazana. Does she live here?" I know her name is on the lease, but you never know if it's a sublet or if someone's visiting.

"And if she does?"

"We were hoping to speak to her regarding her roommate Deidre Boxletter."

"Show me your identification."

Karina holds her badge over the peephole for a few moments before we switch positions. The sounds of the deadbolt flipping open echoes in the hallway. The door pops open a sliver with a metal chain still blocking entry. Her dark brown, inquisitive eyes, scans over the two of us. She looks from my badge to me as if sizing me up. It's unnerving.

"Detective Steele. I've seen you on the news. You're in homicide."

"Agent Marlow and I work in a different department now, ma'am."

"And that is?"

"Ma'am, we'd be happy to discuss all of this inside." Karina wants to stop the conversation from happening so publicly. She's right and following protocol as per usual.

The door closes with a click as we both wait patiently for her to open the door again. If not, I can call the district attorney for a warrant. It will take valuable time away from the case, but if it's necessary, I'll do it. Time ticks by at a crawl as we stand in the hall. In my pocket, my phone buzzes with a call. Removing it, the caller ID shows the department calling, Karina notices the information and shakes her head. I hit the off button, sending the call to voicemail. Whatever it is can wait.

After a few minutes, we hear the chain slide along its track and bounce off the door, signaling its release. A tall, wiry woman with dark brown eyes and long, flowing black hair holds it open, waiting for us to enter.

"Come in." Her clipped tone changes my perception once again. While it seems harsh on the surface, there's an element of fear laced within the simple phrase.

The small entryway leads to a spacious living area. When I fully enter the room, the warmth of the lived-in area envelops me. The blue-gray tones on the wall are inviting, almost calming. The sunlight from the wall of windows bounces off the glass coffee table, reflecting on a wall full of frames. A small hole in the wall behind me leads to a tiny galley kitchen.

The woman waves us over to a table pushed up against the kitchen wall with one side folded down and the other side locked in the upright position. Around it are three chairs. Then I notice the fourth in a corner, hidden under a table with a plant by the windows.

"I'm assuming this conversation will require an infusion of caffeine. May I interest you in some?"

"No, thank you." Karina answers for both of us as she takes a seat.

I find myself perusing the pictures highlighted by the sun. Each one shows Deidre and the woman in front of me exploring various parts of the world—the Coliseum in Rome in one, the two of them scuba diving with a hammerhead shark. But the one on top of a volcano catches my eye.

"Mount Vesuvius," the woman replies from the kitchen.

"I'm sorry?"

"The picture you're staring at." She removes her mug from her Keurig and walks back into the living room. "We hiked Mount Vesuvius after seeing Pompeii. Deidre studied that place since she was a young child. I told her she was obsessed with the idea of the location and not the reality. But she insisted on seeing it in person. We showed up, and she cried every night. Not so much for those who suffered during the event.

No, Deidre's heart was broken by all the stray dogs roaming around in varying states of starvation and pain. It broke her so deeply that she never wanted to step foot in Italy again." She looks longingly over the photos, as if wishing to relive them all. "That's how she is. Always empathetic to every living creature around her. If you counter with a comment about her home country, she says she votes regularly to change the way our country works. She can't fathom hate and lies, winning out over love and compassion. I remember her saying she was a fool until twenty-six. Then she grew up and tried to do better. But it never stopped the past from poking its ugly head."

"How did it?"

"Bringing up old comments, emails, whatever. All shit done after traumatic events or when she thought it was helpful, but it wasn't. Like she said, at twenty-six she started seeing the world differently."

"Is she involved in politics or activism of any kind? "

"Voting, marching and donating, but her schedule prevents more. Plus, she's very in tune with people and sort of takes on their emotions. So it overwhelms her sometimes. She retreats into herself more often than I'd like. But it also showed me a side of humanity I never thought possible. Deidre is a contrarian and loves fiercely. She always puts herself out there and tries to understand the plight of others . . . even if she's been misled at times with false information." The woman moves to the chair opposite Karina and pulls her right knee to her chest. "You didn't come here to hear stories of our adventures. You wanted to talk to me. Here I am. Now, tell me why you're asking about Deidre?"

"Is this Ms. Boxletter's primary residence?" Karina goes directly to the heart of the matter.

"Ahh, you found the main office." She smirks and sips her coffee as her eyes size Karina up. "There's nothing illegal about our side business, Agent Marlow. The city is an expensive place to live, and we have limited time for our looks."

My eyes fall upon an image of a dozen or so nude bodies. It must be an art piece, but it falls flat with me. Then again, I've never been one for modern art. Frankie took me to MOMA once, and I got angry at some pieces. Seeing a piece of scotch tape with scribbled ink on it was the final straw. I left and swore up and down Chase's doodles on our fridge were more impressive.

"Deidre and I were in the back. Tan lines." She answers the question I refused to voice. "It was an exhilarating experience. Then again, having autonomy over one's body usually is."

"Adventurous," I say, finding the two of them and trying to suppress my blush. "As for your office, we never implied illegal activities. If there is something we should know about, now is the time to tell us."

"I assure you, everything that has occurred within those four walls is a legitimate business. The subscription-based model turned out to be a financial success, and before you ask . . . yes, we file our taxes to include this additional income."

"May we inquire about the nature of your business?" Karina doesn't like the remark change her train of thought. Sydney would find out if the woman's comment was accurate. If there was one thing the government never skimps on, it's finding tax dodgers.

"You may . . ." The words hang in the air. "May I also inquire why my girlfriend is being investigated?"

"I know this is a personal question, but both your names are on the two leases, and you mentioned girlfriend—"

"We don't need a marriage license to prove who we are to one another. For all intents and purposes, she's my partner for life. We've got all the prerequisite documentation, power of attorney, and all that fun crap, but marriage has always seemed unnecessary for us. That might not be the answer you desired. Most of our friends don't understand it either, but for us . . . it works."

The images on the wall seem to back up that assessment. Their smiles, the little touches within these snapshots of time, they all show a loving partnership. Knowing they were working together on their side hustle also affirms my feelings about her innocence.

"Has Ms. Boxletter stayed out all night before?"

"Only when she covers the night shift and has an early morning at the clinic. Normally, she comes home."

"I have to ask again, could you please clarify the nature of your business?" Karina comes back to the question we already know the answer to. The evidence at the scene was clear about the work the women take part in, but not the structure of how things take place.

"Agent Marlow, if you found the apartment, you know what we do. The two of us perform for clients on a schedule, sometimes solo, sometimes together. Our subscribers send in what actions they would like to see performed, we put it to a vote, and you can figure out the rest." Tazlia sips her coffee, tilts her head, and takes in the sight of Karina in front of her. "We have a strict set of rules. No one ever sees our faces. We have the right to axe any suggestions we feel are inappropriate. No one can contact us outside of the scheduled screening. If they do, they're banned for life. No excuses."

"Has anyone earned that distinction?"

"Not as of yet. A few sometimes request to see portions of our faces, but a warning regarding the terms and conditions they agreed to when they signed up usually calms them down. They understand the nonnegotiable agreement." She stops as if something comes back to her memory, and her foot falls to the ground as she wraps her hands around her mug.

"We had to add a provision into the agreement. No tagging or location tracking. I don't know how that happened, though, since we only operate online. It's not like we ever logged in with our cell phones. I just know, one day Deidre mentioned it, and the next day it was in there."

"Could we have a look at your client directory?" If she shares it with us it might help narrow down a suspect list or create one. Either way, it would benefit us in the long run.

"No." The harshness of her emphatic answer is off-putting. "You keep prying into our personal lives, and I have been patiently entertaining your questions, but that ends now. I won't answer anything further until you explain to me why you're here. Why are you investigating Deidre?"

Her voice falters a bit at the end, and I feel the terror bubbling up my throat. I truly dread delivering this kind of news, even if we've been cleared to do such a thing. Karina looks determined to keep silent for the time being. I can't do that.

"Deidre Boxletter was found dead this morning in her office."

The wail of pain erupting from Tazlia pierces my chest. Karina's glare burns the side of my head, but my focus is on the grieving woman. She hangs her head between her legs, her breathing shallow as the sobs devour her. I slip to the floor and run my hand up and down her back. Her tears blend into Hadley's in my head. I can see my friend rocking on the floor, begging for reality to be a dream. As Tazlia grasps my arm and holds on for support, I once again feel at a loss for how to help her.

We stay like that for a while as she allows the grief to flow out in her tears. Her body's shivering slows to a twitch here and there. I'm worried she's fallen asleep on me, but the blinking of her eyes allows her eyelashes to tickle the skin on my neck.

"Do you know how it happened?" She whimpers from my shoulder.

"The medical examiner hasn't determined ho yet," Karina answers for me. "Do you think anyone on your list is capable of murder?"

"Isn't every human being? If we get angry enough, what wouldn't we do to destroy the person we thought was responsible for our pain?" Tazlia sniffs and leans back in her chair. I watch as she build a wall of defenses, brick by brick. Denial and anger set in firmly.

"I'm sorry for your loss." The words slip out as I lift myself to the chair next to her.

"We've been together for twenty years. When we met . . . it felt like the world made sense again. Even when we joked about starting this business, it was always a partnership. We never fought over screen time, or client likes or dislikes. We understood this was a means to an end."

Karina opens her mouth to ask another question, but Tazlia raises her hand, stopping the inquiry. She wipes her face and sips her coffee as her breathing calms down to normal levels.

"I know you're both thinking we must have had some shitty relationship. People who strip or perform sexual actions on camera for strangers couldn't have any decent companionship. But we did. It was never about the office. We knew . . . we accepted that side was just about taking control of the narrative already out there. We presented ourselves to the subscribers in a way we felt comfortable and safe. If people disliked how we handled things, we gave them a full refund for the month they were there. With all the other services available online, we were but a small drop in the bucket."

"Did anyone ever ask for a full refund?"

"No. We were surprised too. Every business has its difficulties, but we carved ourselves a small niche into the market. Hell, we even found a perfect work-life balance. We never brought our day job work home, and that extended into evening. Once we left the office, whatever happened within those walls stayed there."

The tears are flowing down Tazlia's face again. Karina pulls a travel pouch of tissues out of her jacket and slides them across the table. The other woman wipes her tears and blows her nose. I feel like I'm watching her crumble into nothing.

"Deidre is so loving and thoughtful. She's... she was my everything. Did you know her patients would request her personally? Her schedule would always end up a mess by lunchtime because she'd do her best to accommodate whoever needed her. She knew her bosses didn't like her putting the clients before profits and taking more time with each one. But she wouldn't sacrifice her patients' care. Some days she'd text me to let me know she'd miss dinner, or I'd have to cover her shift, but she never made me feel less loved or appreciated."

The quick breaths and slight shake in her arms show a woman desperately trying to hold things together.

"You've mentioned your clients agreed to the terms and conditions, but did they include a nondisclosure? Would anyone outside of that list know about your side business? Did Deirdre's boss know?"

Tazlia's hands turn white as she squeezes her coffee mug. "Yes, discretion was part of our agreement. As for anyone else knowing, I guess they will soon enough, right? I can see the trashy tabloid headlines now: 'Sex Working Doctor Murdered: Insiders Say Pediatrician Was a Pedophile.'" She clenches her teeth as anger surges through her body. "They'll say anything to sell a paper, right? Oh God, this is going to be all over social media. There';; be no place I can hide from it."

Karina continues the conversation while I pull out my notebook and jot down some thoughts. There's no sign of discord or an unhappy relationship between the two women. Even the premise behind the business seems to be amicable. While I might not agree with it, they wanted to control the narrative. As long as they followed the legal avenues to host such an entity, who am I to judge? The bigger question is, did someone else? Did her clients feel Deidre was their property because they paid a small monthly fee? Like Tazlia said, anyone is capable of murder if pushed far enough . . . and when opinions and children are involved, there's no filter or barrier strong enough to stop someone.

Tazlia tenses at something Karina asks. Her distrust of us etches on her face, one line at a time. It's a slow process, but I can tell our time here is almost over.

"Every photo you've displayed is just the two of you. Is there a reason for that? No biological or chosen family? Friends?" My words hang there, unanswered, as both women stare at me. Karina looks more displeased at my interjection while Tazlia's eyes darken in what I assume is distaste.

"It was a conscious choice." The chill her words elicit lowers the temperature of the room several degrees. There's more to the story, but it's obvious she won't be sharing that soon.

She abruptly stands and walks to the front door. "If you'll excuse me. I have a funeral to plan."

We both get up and follow the path the way we came in. "I understand and appreciate your time. I have one last question. Did Deidre have a home computer or just the cellphone she had on her person?"

"She has a laptop, yes. However, considering she was a medical professional, I will have to deny you access. I will not risk violating patient confidentiality, regardless of its beneficial nature to the case. You can get a warrant."

Tazlia stands, holding the door open, her back ramrod straight. Her arms wrap around herself as her foot holds the door open.

"Thank you for your time." Karina walks out into the hallway and presses the call button for the elevator.

"I agree with Deidre about Pompeii," I say, staring out into the hallway. "My wife took me there years ago . . . Seeing the dogs broke me too. Being told to ignore something when all it wanted was a bit of love felt so wrong. They could raise the cost to use the bathrooms to open a shelter near the premises, but the guides just told us to walk away. I can't understand it to this day, just throwing away life like that . . . I don't think I ever will."

"You two would have gotten along. She had more compassion in her pinky finger than most have in their entire family lines. But now, they'll only remember her for what we did to get by." She sniffs.

"You control the narrative, Tazlia."

"No, I don't. If I had that power, no one would ever speak ill of her, but they won't see beyond the clips people are bound to share. People want likes, fame, clicks . . . They don't want reality. If they did, we wouldn't have had a lucrative business to begin with."

The elevator dings, announcing its arrival.

"If you remember anything or if you feel it's safe for us to view her devices before a warrant comes through, it would be very helpful." I hold out my card. "Even if you don't, my phone's always on."

"Thank you, but I won't be handing it over without that document."

Tazlia grabs the card out of my hand. My body clears the entryway just before the door slams, echoing down the empty hallway. The sounds of her scream and uncontrollable sobs follow.

Standing in the car with Karina, waiting to hit the ground floor, my head runs at top speed. To love someone so fully that you need to be vulnerable is a tall ask. Yet we humans run to it like a lifeline. Losing that same love opens you up to a pain so relentless it eviscerates your very being. Humans all know we'll face that kind of loss one day. It's the nature of humanity's mortality, but I don't ever want to go through it. It's why Frankie and I joke about dying peacefully in one another's arms in old age.

The likelihood of that is slim, and it makes me want to bury my head in the sand. Because facing reality is hard . . . and I am a coward.

Chapter Four

The ride back to the precinct was quiet. I'm not sure why, but the silence is rather uncomfortable. The two of us have worked together before, faced darker crime scenes, and yet, this one stopped us cold. Construction in the parking garage is the only noise that breaks the unease between us. The jackhammering fills the void, but my confusion over Karina's behavior remains. The elevator doors shake open as if they were on the track of a roller coaster waiting for the first drop. Once inside, Karina presses the button for our main dungeon office. I hit street level.

"Where are you going?" she asks, her tone clipped.

"Need a breather. You?"

"Checking on maintenance's progress. We need a space to work without prying eyes and ears. If they're not done, I'll request a secluded place to function."

While a great idea, we both know it's not possible. We work for New York City; there's always someone listening in to ensure they won't get chopped down because of our ineptitude. Either that, or to take credit. After all, if we succeed, they hired us and take the accolades. If we fail, it's another bullet point on a list of reasons women shouldn't be on the force. In that case, it all falls on us.

My partner leaves, saying nothing further. One more stop and the noise of a busy precinct fills my ears. My hands in my pockets, I move through the crowd, trying to draw little to no attention. Once outside, I exhale a sigh of relief.

The abnormally warm weather rolls over my skin like summer, forcing some beads of sweat to form on my brow. As I get further away from work, I find the crowds on the street recharge my emotional state. Their laughter, stress . . . whatever it is reminds me over and over again why we do this job.

The throngs of people are unaware of the crimes they are just feet away from at any given moment. Blissfully unaware of a murderer that might strike again in this very section. But for how long? Sure, the news will display headlines, the internet will have their own theories, but when will it truly sink in? How many bodies will it take before fear or vilification pours out in droves? Where is that line, and what happens when we cross it?

This is where my job has expanded beyond the academy books. We've drifted into the ever-changing landscape of reality. We find the twisted tales of misinformation and spin it again in a way the people can swallow it without choking on the truth. It's disgusting, and I despise every moment. We try to stay ahead of it, but 'we're always chasing the latest false narrative.

What's worse, the reality of what I see in photos or at a crime scene would make most human beings question humanity in general. Then there are those few who delight in true crime. They share photos of a family's worst nightmare, as if it is a social media post about their dinner. Complete disregard for common decency. The police department tries to fight the dissemination of these images, but it's an uphill battle. Between these two newly added parts of my job description, I don't know which worries me more, or if it's that they're related to the bigger issue at hand—people's belief in everything they read online.

My feet carry me up the stairs to the coroner's building. The cool air-conditioning hits my body, forcing a chill down my spine. Flashing my badge, I slip past the security station they installed after threats during the worst part of the pandemic. The crowded elevator is enough to divert me to the stairs and the basement.

Victor stands by the autopsy table in his usual protective gear. The N95 mask under his face shield replaces the old surgical ones he used to use. During the worst of the pandemic, he lived in his office. Lillian would drop by with whatever takeout he was in the mood for that night. But like Frankie and me, they needed to stay apart until the vaccine became readily available.

The doors swoosh open, and silence greets me. The recent change has been the most off-putting part of seeing Victor in his element. Victor used to sing along to his playlist, but he changed it to music the person on his table might enjoy. For the last year, it's been quiet.

"Hello, Detective Steele. How are you doing today?" His voice fills the surrounding void.

"Surviving. How are you holding up?" I walk over and lean on his immaculate desk. Another unsettling recent change. "How's the home life?"

"Same as you for both questions." He leans over the table and uses his forearm to tap the button on his microphone before dictating his findings. He hits it again to stop the recording. "What brings you down here?"

"I needed a break. Is there anything I should know about our victim?"

"I already emailed you my preliminary report. All the signs point to strangulation. I sent samples to Doctor Brown for analysis. I will complete a full autopsy later."

"Understood. I was hoping for some insight beyond the obvious. Did you have a moment for gut instincts to take over? Suggestions or theories?"

"I appreciate your inquiry, Detective Steele, but did you read the attachment or are you asking me to step outside the parameters of my position?" His curt question catches me off guard. I know we've all been under constant intense pressure for the last few years, but Vic always shared his thoughts on victims in the past.

"If I'm being honest, I gave notice to next of kin and walked over here from the precinct. I haven't been at my desk to check emails."

"Have Sydney put it on your phone."

"It's bad enough you all insisted I upgrade to this monstrosity of a phone; I'd rather not have the barrage of email notifications here. Texts are sufficient until I get back to my office."

"As long as you can entertain yourself and waste the time of others, that's all that matters, right?"

This conversation is heading down a path I have no interest in walking. I know Vic's been struggling, but we all have. I try not to take it out on my closest friends, but I guess that's not the case with him.

"I will read the report once I return to the precinct. Since I'm here, could you please enlighten me on Deidre Boxletter's visible injuries? I will maintain communication from this point via email for further questions or updates regarding the final report." My mother's angry voice erupts out of my mouth like second nature at this point. The coldness of my tone no longer surprises me. It's something I'm trying to work on, but we've all developed defense mechanisms. Why get rid of it when it's the only thing that works?

"Fine." He snaps off his bloody gloves, yanks the microphone off his ear, and lets it hang on his chest. His frustration flows through his fingers with each key punch and mouse click. "Ms. Boxletter presented with all the common signs of strangulation. She presented with petechiae in both eyes slightly bloodshot in appearance. Her lips were blue in tint and swollen. There was significant bruising around her neck, chest, and armpit area. I took several images and uploaded them into the system. They're attached to the file for your perusal."

He hits several keys before placing the earpiece back in, slipping on a clean pair of gloves, and going to the body open on the table.

"Maybe the assailant sat across their chest for support. Could you garner any information from the spacing of those bruises for an estimate for height, weight, or both?" I know I'm pressing my luck by asking for more details.

His expression is calm, but it feels like his eyes are burning a hole through my chest. "If I was going off my years of experience, I could deduce that if the individual in question used that position for leverage, I would consider them above average height for a female and average if male. But again, that is going on past cases I've examined before. I'll look deeper into it when I perform the autopsy."

"Considering the victim presented with nylons wrapped around her throat, could you differentiate the bruising to see if the perp used their hands as well? If they did, would you be able to identify hand size? That might go a long way in determining a physical profile."

"Detective, while the pattern could be within the deep bruising, I couldn't tell you which came first. The images attached to the file might allow you to make your own conclusions. As I've said previously, I might have more information for you when I complete the full autopsy." Vic taps the microphone with his forearm to record again. "Bullet fragment pierced the heart and lodged in the spine at approximately the T6 position. Sending to ballistics for further investigation." He hits the button again to turn the thing off. He grabs what I can only describe as a long scissor-like instrument with tweezers at the end. My stomach rolls as he maneuvers them inside the body cavity and pulls out the offending metal object.

"Grab that bag for me."

I know exactly what he's talking about and bring him over a small evidence bag. He drops the bullet inside, snaps off his gloves again, seals it, and fills out all pertinent information. Back in the day, he wouldn't have thought twice about leaving his gloves on during this transfer process. Another reminder of new protocols or stricter versions of the originals. Either way, the world is different.

"Were there any other visible injuries?"

"She fought back hard. Her index and ring fingernails are missing. Whether they broke off or ripped off needs further investigation. I did scrape underneath the remaining ones and sent the samples off to Doctor Brown. She would have more information for you."

"Considering her state of dress, could you deduce any sexual assault?"

"There was no evidence of bruising. However, there was a dried substance on her inner thighs. I sent that off to Doctor Brown as well. I'll be able to ascertain if she was assaulted—"

"After a full autopsy, I know."

"Look . . . just let me finish up here and I will get your victim on my table immediately. I'll call you with any findings and let you know about any other samples I send Doctor Brown's way."

"I'd appreciate that. I'll head over to Lillian's office and see if she and the team dug up anything."

"One last thing. Beyond the stamp on her forehead, there was a piece of paper lodged in her esophagus. Detective Locke has an image."

"I assume trace has that as well?"

"You would be correct."

"Thanks for your help, Vic." I push off the desk, and the doors swoosh open.

"When at work, please refer to her as Doctor Brown. While we all might be co-workers and friends, our relationships must remain outside of these walls. Professionalism needs to be heeded." The words stop me cold.

"Professionalism? How—" The confusion I feel instantly turns defensive. "I don't know what's going on with you, Doctor Hayes, but showing human connection within these walls has never been a negative thing, nor does it violate any rules in our manual. If there is something you wish to share with me, I'm all ears. Until then, I will continue to perform my job to the best of my ability in the same way I have always done."

"Headstrong doesn't work anymore, Jasmine. You should know that by now. The new rules, protocols . . . whatever the hell you want to call them, the higher-ups will use them as an excuse to reprimand anyone in this facility. We're expensive, and we have to prove why we need funding. There's a lot riding on this new version of the NYPD. So, please, as a favor to me, just refer to us as Doctor Brown and Doctor Hayes."

The sadness rolling off his body melts my defenses. "I miss hearing you sing down here. It always made the darkness feel less bleak. Like you were performing for the victims in their worst moments and promising to speak for them. What happened to that, Doctor Hayes?" I ask as another detective walks into the office, his eyes darting between Victor and me.

"If I'm interrupting, I can come back." The detective points to the table. "Was just checking in on the case."

"Protocols." Victor answers me softly before turning back to the other detective. "I'm almost done with the autopsy, but I believe I found the cause of death."

Once again ignoring the elevator, I walk up the stairs to get back to the main floor. The walk back to the office might help me focus on things and sort them out. I keep holding on to the year the world stood still as if it was this lifeless entity that held us captive. But as the years go on, its tendrils continue to reach far beyond itself, effecting the current day and age. The new societal rules implemented for the better were never the issue, for me at least. It was always the response to ensure safety among the masses.

The renewed scrutiny on an individual's jobs, rules, and what people perceive them to be . . . that is a constantly changing dynamic. One must question if they simply put these recent shifts in protocol in place to satisfy the promises the higher-ups guaranteed, even though those same powerful people refuse to implement a proper course of action to promote a lasting change. If this is the case, the decisions would cause more unrest within our walls and lead to the loss of good people to the private sector.

Either way, we cannot lose our humanity in the process of trying to find it.

***

A text message from Detective Locke forces a deviation in my plans to visit Doctor Brown. I haven't heard anything from Karina about our office, so I reroute to Sydney's lair instead.

The tech floor has a different feel since Logan's passing. Each time I walk through the doors and out into his former domain, there's an overwhelming sense of grief that sucks the air out of my lungs. The questions surrounding his murder and what we could have done to prevent it still linger in my mind. No matter what evidence we found at the scene, nothing was conclusive enough. It was a reminder that no matter what you find, arrests and convictions we get, the pain of loss never goes away. Victim's families get closure, but how good was that really? I still felt like my heart had a hole in it without my friend being around. I still felt cheated and no number of years on a sentence would take that away.

Regardless of my emotions surrounding Logan, Sydney has done her best to fill in the void he left behind. The staff, although overworked, seem content with the changing of the guard. They expanded beyond their normal scope, upgrading systems and digging deeper into social media realms.

Their most recent work assisted the FBI in uncovering fake vaccination cards. Apparently, a ring of medical professionals sold the cards with real dosage lot numbers to the anti-vaxxer crowd. The price, starting at two hundred dollars, made them money in the hundreds of thousands. Many in the office are still running down cards and arresting every individual who bought one. According to Sydney, only those in specific states are being held accountable for their actions.

While that's appalling, it isn't surprising. Back in the day, Logan warned the department of localized false information campaigns designed to use social media to spread the word. He and the team created new algorithms to highlight the false claims and see if something was actionable. Unfortunately, the majority were not within our jurisdiction, but the NYPD was coming around to the idea before his untimely passing. Since then, the programs he helped design are being implemented statewide.

His legacy lives on in the people in this department and the code in cyberspace.

Even with this new advancement in her career, Sydney seems to have drawn the short straw. The authorities chose to run the department with two individuals as equal partners, but right away that was not the case. While their workloads might appear the same, Sydney is the only one allowed to work on the dungeon's cases. Their argument was that her former connections to our department would facilitate a smooth transition.

It was utter bullshit. We all thought this new division was the start of something new. Instead, they sold a bag of lies. The worse part is if Sydney isn't free to assist us on our cases, the department turns a blind eye until her return. We truly are the lost cause section of the precinct. I knew that we'd get cases no one wanted going into all of this, but had I known this was my ticket to retirement before my twenty years were up, I would have refused the change.

"Hello, my former boss!" Sydney's chipper voice radiates out of her office. "How have you been feeling? You doing better? I assume you're here to talk dirty about the laptop dropped off this morning?"

"Lots of questions before my brain can catch up." I flop down into the welcoming comfort of the plush chair in front of her desk. "Simple answers: Not dead yet. Some days are better than others. If you have anything to share, that would be awesome. Now, how are you holding up down here, and why are you being so informal? Aren't you subject to all the new rules and regulations down here too?"

"Truthfully, this is a dream come true. I loved working as a detective, but using my degree, working with some of the best people in the state, that's just a whole new level. I never thought I'd get this chance, let alone help run the department. This is everything I needed that I never knew I needed. You know?" she answers with a broad smile on her face. "Plus, getting access to all the latest available technology . . . Man, Logan was so right. Once you get to use this equipment, going home to your laptop is a bit of a downer."

"I don't know. Logan once told me all about viruses, scams . . . all that stuff. Made me more afraid of my phone and no desire to upgrade it." I grab the offending device from my pocket. "Speaking of which, Victor insists I have you put email on this thing." I drop it on the desk.

"I thought you didn't want it."

"I don't, but I would also prefer less drama from my boss for not having access. At least this way, I can check it as needed."

She grabs the phone and starts her magic to make it work properly. Her computer setup with two monitors on a floating arm system is a change from Logan's ultrawide monstrosity. The wall screen behind her houses several media outlets airing the latest news. Her mouse and keyboard scroll through a wave pattern of colors.

"Done."

"Didn't you need my password?"

"Steele, I set it up for you. Memorized yours. Just in case." She hands me back the phone as it buzzes with all my unread emails.

"I needed you to fix it." Sydney knew me too well. "Thanks. Now, about the Boxletter case."

"Okay, if I go too fast or there's something you don't quite understand, just ask and I'll clarify."

"Syd, if it's technobabble, you'll have to slow down. Other than that, I'm fine."

"Frankie said—"

"You don't need to treat me with kid gloves. I might have to write stuff down, but I'm fine. Please don't treat me like most people are around here. I'm not broken, just still healing." My intention to sound firm and honest comes out more like begging or pleading. It's been hard to be back at work after my illness. I've followed all the proper procedures, been cleared on all fronts to return to duty. I would have liked to score higher on my assessments, but I've always demanded perfection from myself. No matter what my result, I'd still desire a better one.

"Okay, but know we're only trying to help because we love you."

"Only when I ask for it, deal?"

"Deal." Her demeanor changes to full business mode. "First, her laptop will take a bit more time to dig through. I'm currently running several algorithms and testing processes. They should be complete by this evening, so I'll send you a note if something pops up. A deep dive into Doctor Deidre Boxletter resulted in a number of interesting things. The obvious ones—school degrees, job information—are all important, but nothing out of the ordinary. I verified their authenticity and can officially say Doctor Boxletter was authentic in her work persona."

"Theoretically, that might eliminate medical malfeasance. What about the sex business?"

"That came up during my investigation into her financials. They were bringing in high six figures each year with their Toy Box & Whiskey website. Beyond the monthly subscriptions, they sold merchandise and charged extra fees for requesting positions or activities. If you wanted a private video session, there was an even higher fee. These ladies had a well-thought-out business plan, and it was flourishing. They also reported everything to the state and Feds under their business entity. From what I could dig up, they managed to use aliases when registering. I have no clue how they managed that one."

"No one would be able to deduce that these women were behind the company?"

"Well, not exactly. We have access to these databases, so our tools can bring it up right away. For anyone without our clearance, a simple search would come up with the company name. If a lawyer requested the information for court proceedings, they'd find it during disclosure."

"We need to find out if any requests were made."

"On it." Sydney types on her keyboard and a search begins behind her, replacing a news channel. "She didn't have the subscriber list on her laptop, but there were some communications. It seems like it was a pure streaming and website building machine. I did find their Discord channel."

"Their what?"

"It's a private group messaging system that allows their clients to talk to one another, not just to them. There were rules in place—everything from not sharing images or personal information to making requests within the forum. I scanned it for a bit, but the biggest issue I came across was their clients' desire to see their faces. Boxletter seemed to reply under *Woman One* and Tazlia under *Woman Two*. Very innocuous."

"Any name they chose could lead to personal discovery. They were very thorough."

"The ladies made it clear they were never going to cave to the demand and requested people stop asking. It seemingly worked. Overall, the chat was cordial. Most conversations between the patrons discussed their desires, taboo sexual position,s and relationship help. If someone overstepped in any capacity, they closed ranks and knocked the person back in line. Felt like a safe haven more than anything else."

"Can you grab names from their accounts?'

"I sent a request to the district attorney for a warrant. Discord can be difficult when releasing information. All of those social type platforms are."

"Even if you can get one, their lawyers will have it buried in legal limbo for eternity. They're only interested in protecting their bottom line. Is there anything else we can work with?"

"Once I thought the business angle was a bust, I dug into her personal stuff. It was all pretty average information. She's posted her thoughts on new treatments, images of patient success stories, holiday parties, all the things you would expect a doctor to post. Again, nothing that jumps out or screams 'murder me.' But then things got interesting." Sydney stays silent for a dramatic pause.

"Explain, please."

"So, I told you this laptop has no personal or financial information on it, right?"

"Yes. You said it was a streaming and website design thing. I'm assuming you found something else?"

"She had a password protected folder in her documents. After some due diligence from our program, I was able to survey the documents inside. The woman was a model doctor and partner. There's nothing to suggest otherwise. She had a firm belief system. Boxletter had another Facebook account using a fake name and different email address. We know the victim was rather busy between her two jobs. There was no evidence of her scheduling posts via apps or the website, so I correlated her work schedule around the new account's posting habits."

The screen behind Sydney lights up with several highlighted numbers. When the good doctor was not clocked in at either job, the posts were more frequent.

"Are we sure she only used this computer? There was no evidence on her cell phone?"

"Based on her post history, I don't believe so. Normally it indicates which device she posted from, but there's nothing there. It seems as if this profile was kept hidden from everyone in her life. I mean, why password protect a file with the login and password of social media accounts? Especially if you're in a long-term relationship with someone?"

"I don't know Frankie's passwords. I trust her. Was there evidence of an affair? You also mentioned something about a firm belief system. What did you mean by that?" I continue jotting notes and thoughts down as my mind runs faster than my hand can write.

"She was devout in her thoughts. Like there was no budging or compromising with anyone else. She was part of a few groups that we have flagged for their misinformation campaigns. In those situations, she appears to have been a lurker . . . um, a person who just reads but doesn't really interact or post."

"I know what that is, Syd, but thank you."

"When we look in this one group though, she was very active. It's restricted to the tri-state area for members, but the amount of vitriol in here borders on grotesque. They bully people, post about kids in schools to out them . . . Boxletter even posted about overturning gay marriage. Said that it was a farce of a decision."

"Even though she's a member of the community?"

"I don't claim to understand why people say things that go against who they are or how they live. To me that's like voting for a candidate that goes against women's rights, kind of defeats the purpose... as a woman. Regardless, I forwarded one post to the FBI. Boxletter wrote about overturning abortion rights and forcing the death penalty on those who violate the law. She continued further that if the government wouldn't do it, it was the God-given right of protestors to proceed with what she called purges. It's rather terrifying shit."

"See if the captain will clear Frankie to assist us with this. We need a more detailed profile on who we're dealing with. It's a long shot, but contact the district attorney about a warrant for the list. I doubt we'll get it, but let's tug on every lose thread we can."

"I already made the request. Some of the bullying cases yielded defamation lawsuits on the books. I couldn't find the status or their outcomes, but people in that group were mum once the legal system got involved. All of it leads me to believe someone would have found out who Boxletter was eventually. You can try to cover your tracks all you want, but techs like me eventually find you. If someone was angry with her profile, they might have been responsible."

"And with so many posts attacking various people, we have a suspect list a mile long."

"I'd say your small list of suspects ballooned to a list the size of Manhattan's population. You need to be careful. These groups run with a mob mentality. They're unrelenting in their assaults. If you come after any of them, you risk all of them changing the narrative on you."

"Great. You know we can't just pick and choose what we handle, Syd. What do you suggest I do to fight this possible misinformation campaign?"

"You can't." Sydney clicks a few more buttons and the screen behind her loads the previous news channel. "I wanted to get all that out of the way before I hit you with the big stuff."

"Like that wasn't enough to make me cringe?"

Sydney turns one monitor around so we both can see it. A video plays of Boxletter's murder. "The killer live streamed the entire murder to the viewers logged in that evening. They made sure the victim's face was in view the entire time. I sent you and Agent Marlow an encrypted link to view the footage. It's . . . difficult."

"Understood. Did anyone report this?"

"Doing so would require using a phone or email that could be traced. I don't know if they hide behind VPNs or something similar. In my mind, it would make sense to ignore it."

"When does the recording end?"

"It doesn't."

"What do you mean?"

"I mean the police presence, you and Agent Marlow . . . all of it was recorded."

"Could anyone save the video?"

"Screen recorders, screen captures . . . yeah, totally possible."

"Get the captain on that as well. We don't need this leaking to the press in any capacity. Anything else on that drive?"

"They recorded everything and backed it up to cloud storage. I've managed to remove the one of her murder but everything else is still there."

"How many clips are we talking about?"

"Twenty or slightly more. I only scanned over the ones the day of her murder. Everything seemed normal until that last clip."

"Okay." I look down at my notes, trying to sort through all the information. "Is it possible this group got wind of her relationship status or of the after hours company she ran? Could that be why they live streamed her murder? Did they want to expose the doctor's sinful side?"

"Not that I can tell. I was compiling a list of her most-liked posts, but there are just too many to count. I'm hoping the private correspondence she had will allow me to narrow down your search. Just don't count on it, okay?"

"Now that we covered all of that, what about the image on the paper in her esophagus? I assume Vic sent it over, yes?"

"It had the Theta symbol on it. It's part of the Greek alphabet for the number nine, but a search on Ancient Greece references it as the symbol for death. I found more details but can't verify the sources. It said in 1291, they used the Theta symbol as a hot iron branding for criminals."

"Regardless of the meaning, it proves premeditation." My watch buzzes with one of the many alarms Frankie insisted I set up. "I've got to run. Let me know if you find anything else out. You're doing a great job, Syd."

"Thanks, boss I'll forward everything to Agent Marlow."

"Don't forget to eat and stay hydrated! Can't have you passing out again." As I stand, my motherly tone comes out as my old body complains.

"I got my mini-fridge of energy drinks."

"Not good for your heart, Syd. Just ask Victor."

"Not for your old ticker. Mine runs on high octane! I'll put your order in so you can pick it up on the way home."

"How'd you know?"

"You have a set schedule, Steele. Now go before you upset the wife."

"You're too kind to me, Syd. Thank you. Truly."

She simply waves me out of her office and lowers her head back to the job at hand.

Each step to the main floor reminds me of the minor challenges we've all had to overcome lately. All of us found our way into this hodgepodge of a family. We learned about one another and flourished with support and love. Now some are missing completely, while others seem to be moving on. I'm not sure why it bothers me so greatly. Change is inevitable, but to accept things is to make them real.

That might be why this case has crawled beneath my skin and found purchase there. I've faced many criminals over the years, but to have someone who so openly cares for human beings be the one with to so savagely attack people online is still alarming. What is the rationale for doing that? Was she trying to antagonize people? Or was she truly that person the entire time?

Walking out to the main floor, I notice an old man we once knew as a regular visitor. Not for being in cuffs as much as for his frivolous complaints. Captain Zeile shakes his head and walks away from the scene, bumping directly into me.

"Hey, Cap. What's Larry in for? Are we allowed to arrest him on false complaints?"

"No, some kids drove up Riverside Drive. They sped up alongside his car and tossed some fast-food barbecue chicken on it. According to him, the acid from the sauce would destroy the paint on his car and it pissed him off. Witness says the kids were laughing, cell phones out, making jokes at his expense. Apparently, he'd had enough, found the kids and killed them all."

"Jesus, how many victims?"

"Six. He stopped and reloaded before ensuring they were dead."

"I don't remember him having a registered firearm."

"According to Larry, the police were in on it, useless, insert conspiracy theory here. So, he went out of town and bought one at a gun show. The kids were streaming the assault live. The parents saw it all before we could even identify the victims. Sometimes, I wonder what the fuck is wrong with these kids. Why antagonize someone to the point of murder? If they just left him alone, none of this would have happened."

"Larry's not innocent in any of this, sir."

"Of course not. He's going to prison for the rest of his life. But this allure for viral status madness has gotten worse since the pandemic."

Zeile walks past me to his office, probably to prepare for a press conference in a few hours. I walk in the opposite direction and out into the warmth. The fear of Chase's online presence climbs up my spine, resting in the back of my mind. We're raising him to the best of our ability, but once he's out of the house, it's out of our hands. Online and out the door, it's the Wild West. We must trust him.

One day at a time, Jasmine. That's all you can focus on. I can hear Doctor Preston's words from our last session. It's moments like these when I lean too much on chocolate and wine. Both of which my doctor told me to stay away from.

Chapter Five

Last night's dinner was the first one in a long time that felt somewhat normal. Chase's laughter was infectious. Frankie appreciated her personal pizza with the abomination of pineapple littering the top. Hank also enjoyed some of Frankie's concoction, though she denied sliding her hand down to feed him bite-sized pieces. The two of them split Frankie's dinner while Chase and I ate the bacon and cheese masterpiece I picked up. It was really a calm evening.

And you know what they say about calm.

An early morning text from Karina alerting me to a last-minute meeting gave me an inkling of how the day would proceed. Doctor Lillian Brown's name flashing across the seven-inch car stereo screen, interrupting one of my favorite 80's tunes just added to my dread.

"Hello, Doctor Brown. To what do I owe the pleasure of a call?"

"Detective, I have information regarding your case."

"Gotcha, what are we looking at?" I slow the car to a stop at a red light and try to tune out all the enthusiastic honking as pedestrians meander across the active lanes. I'm already twenty minutes late for work because of traffic, and Karina is trying to hold off our bosses from noticing my absence.

"I wish I had more positive news, but I ran every test I could think of and came up empty. Every sample, fluids, epithelial cells, scrapings from under the victim's fingernails all of it matches your victim. There was evidence of gloves being used, but the leather fibers were generic. While we know the perpetrator was in the room due to the video, forensically, it's as if they were never there."

"Nothing on the computer system? Glasses?"

"No, I'm sorry. I've already spoken to Detective Locke and walked her through my process and results. She's aware her department is now the lead in finding useful information for this case."

"I appreciate you rushing to get the results to me."

"You're welcome. I've emailed the official report. If there's anything else you need, please don't hesitate to reach out." Her professional tone is as monotonous as my old high school biology teacher's. She disconnects the call before I can continue the conversation.

Once again, we're facing a criminal who has studied how we operate. They seem equipped to combat our practices to uncover their identity. I believe there's always a sliver of skin, a fiber, or hair lying around . . . something to get a glimpse into the human being behind the heinous crime. I doubt the individual could just throw on coveralls and walk around the neighborhood.

I could argue there had to be a witness, but who really pays attention to the people passing alongside them on a street? We say we notice others, but truly . . . do we? The truth is, even if a witness came forward, we'd face the possibility of the mind twisting the actual experience into something the individual's brain could process. That's before we go into the explanation of what they saw and if it could hold up against cross examination. In the end, having evidence to support the eyewitness account is ideal. The defense still attacks it with vigor, but the jury sees the testimony with a renewed trust. Sadly, thanks to the internet and television, perpetrators are well educated in destroying or just not leaving any trace of themselves behind.

But another concern comes to the forefront of my mind. Did the victim know their killer? Was it personal? That would explain how easily they entered the apartment, but not the lack of evidence. Nothing adds up as my brain sorts through what we have.

I fumble with the buttons on my steering wheel, but somehow manage to call Sydney. After the third ring, she picks up.

"Hey, boss. Where—"

"I'm about to run into a meeting, but I had a quick question."

"If it's about the laptop, I know I promised I'd have it completed by now, but there was more to dig through than I previously thought."

"No problem. I know Lillian reached out and told you trace was a complete bust. Is it possible to check if there are red light cameras at the end of the victim's street? I think I remember a bodega on the corner. Would you be able to scan the footage if we can get our hands on it?"

"I can check the area, sure. Anything specific we're looking for?"

"Not sure, but the area is a quiet, community based section of the city. If someone walked around covered in blood, they would stand out. Maybe they wore coveralls or changed clothes in the bathroom? They couldn't take the subway like that. Driving? Either way, you can isolate the clips by time of death. Should be in Victor's full report."

"I'll take care of it. Talk soon." The call disconnects as I turn into the basement parking garage for the Jacob K. Javits Federal Building. Pulling into the first available spot, my eyes dart to the time. Officially, I'm thirty minutes late. This was not how I planned on making my first impression with the FBI going, but here we are.

The elevator showed pity on me and arrived within seconds of me pressing the call button. The speedy flight to the twenty-third floor forces my ears to pop. I run through a list of viable excuses, but I doubt any will stick. I left as soon as I could, leaving ample time to arrive. I didn't break procedure by using lights and sirens to bypass traffic. Yet here I am . . . late to my first meeting with Karina's people.

The doors slide open revealing a frantic woman pacing and mumbling to herself. Her head snaps toward me, her eyes wide as she pounces before I'm even out of the elevator.

"Are you Detective Steele?" My nod must be confirmation enough as she grabs my arm, leading me out of the elevator. "Everyone's in the conference room, waiting."

"Could you specify who everyone is?"

"The entire team assigned to the case."

That one statement confuses me even more. I was under the impression that Karina and I were working on the case with the support of the NYPD. There's been no indication the FBI is sniffing around our caseload at all. If they were interested in this murder, Karina would have warned me, right? That's what partners do.

Several turns later, she grabs a door handle and yanks it open. The low muttering I heard in the hallway comes to an abrupt stop the moment I enter the room. The woman who led me here wasn't kidding when she said everyone: Karina, Captain Zeile, Sydney, two men in black suits, and one heavyset male in business-casual dress next to Frankie. It put me on edge immediately.

"Sorry, traffic was a bitch." I sit across from my wife, trying to convey my confusion at her attendance. She barely meets my gaze. The sound of shuffling paper fills the room. Frankie still won't look at me. It's as if she's angry, but I can't tell why. When she finally looks up at me, she smiles, but it doesn't reach her eyes. I can feel the fear rolling off her. The chill creeps up my spine like a spider stalking its prey. This meeting won't end well for me.

"Glad you could finally join us, Detective Steele. I'm Assistant Director Tody." The man with the navy-blue tie and black suit waves at himself. "This is Special Agent Thomas Chalet." The man wearing a black tie and black suit nods his head. "The gentleman at the end of the table is Doctor Lewis Grayson."

I wait for him to acknowledge me. He doesn't. He leans closer to my wife and whispers something in her ear that makes her shake her head. His entire demeanor screams snake oil salesman. I blame Chase watching *Inside Out* for the image of little emotions screaming danger in my head as they run around for shelter.

"Pleasure to meet you all." My eyes remain focused straight ahead, my brain running through all the ways to get the man in front of me to stop fawning over my wife like she's a piece of meat. Frankie ignores my attempt to get her attention and continues allowing his advances. Maybe it's the lack of sleep or caffeine this morning, but I want to put space between the two of them. "Again, I apologize for my tardiness. Would you mind filling me in on what you've covered thus far?" My mother would be proud of my professional tone, with a wee bit of *fuck you all* built in.

"We were waiting for you to arrive to begin." Director Toby closes the folder in front of him. "Agent Chalet?"

"Director Toby and I handed this case over to the NYPD, specifically your department, for several reasons, including your success rate with limited resources. While it is to be commended, the publicity of some of your cases has created a less than favorable view of you two from the public. Specific social media posts regarding you both were brought to our attention. At the time, we felt it was best to keep things in house and monitor the profile. We were unaware this would be an avenue for the account holder to publicly admonish you."

"Someone called us out? How? Why? Agent Marlow and I haven't made any public statements regarding this case. Hell, we actively avoid speaking to the press." My voice rises as a fire ignites within me. I've always hated the social media landscape, and this is precisely why. While it gives people a voice, that same access can be used for nefarious purposes.

"We understand that, detective. The perpetrator set up social media accounts long before this case came to our attention. We've been trying to find the source of these profiles, but you know how impossible that can be. In today's day and age, a simple email allows you to circumvent the law for most things said online, regardless of whether they are harassing or defamatory."

Captain Zeile cuts in. "Detective Locke, please stick to what we need to know."

"Sorry. Whoever's behind these new accounts started posting random police images at first with occasional statistics intermingled here and there. In the last month or so, they've been uploading images of you and Agent Marlow. Most of them are much older images, some are press clippings, but they all question your work ethic and ability to catch killers. They insinuate you are merely puppets for the men behind you pulling the strings. They also made a serious accusation that neither of you listened to a victim who needed help. They said you shuttered their case before they could even file it."

"We've been scouring the databases to determine which case they might be referring to, but we haven't found anything on file. After serious discussions between our departments, we felt it was best to put you on the front lines to showcase your abilities." Zeile looks innocent enough, but his phrasing could use some work.

"So, catching Garrison wasn't enough? Hadley's stalker? We both have rather public records of our work. There's no need to *showcase our abilities* when we've been doing our best our entire careers." My defensive side pours out, and frankly, I don't care. The small scoff across the table makes me flex my hand in a tight fist. "Do you have anything to add, Doctor Grayson, or are you just here to take up space?"

"Jasmine!"

"It's all right, Franks." Grayson lays his hand on top of hers and once again I question who the hell this man is to my wife. "What would I need to add? Well, you wrongfully assume your history of successes should lead you to the promised land. *What have you done for me lately* is the way of the world. To say it simply, in case you don't understand, people want to see what you can do now. Not years ago. So, the NYPD and FBI worked together and put you on a case that could help eradicate this unpleasantness you and Agent Marlow are a part of. I'm sure you follow up to this point. Unless you forged your reinstatement evaluations." His smirk does nothing to calm me.

The spider sinks its venomous fangs into my neck and the paralyzing poison hits hard. Grayson's tone, the people in the room ... a chill creeps up my spine as the images of a setup fall into place. Why else would they trap Karina and I into a room with them? Sure, they explained about the public implications of this press, but they still want us to do our jobs for the sake of the departments success rates? Reputations?

"That's an egregious statement, Doctor Grayson. Be that as it may, I proceeded through the steps of reinstatement with great care. Including my recertification at the range. While I might need to jot down notes every now and again, my aim is still true." The dark undertone of my statement rushes forth before I can stop them.

"Is that a threat?" Grayson seems enthused by my words, almost like he's playing a game of chess.

"Now, doctor, why would I do such a thing? I assume you read my file fully before coming to this meeting as to be fully prepared. You also understand the ramifications of verbally stating falsities in public. One has to question if you are ill prepared, don't know or understand the law well, or just throwing around accusations to lift yourself up. Either way, it means nothing to me. Let's just focus on the case at hand, yes?"

Grayson's smirk slips to a flat line, his eyes darken as his body tightens leaning back in his chair. Frankie's glare forced me to stop, but there's an obvious history here I'm not privy to. Regardless, she should be more respectful to the team and shut down this man's antics.

"What my colleague meant to infer was that this was a calculated risk. Both departments consulted with Doctor Grayson and me. We felt if we put the two of you back out there and got the press involved, it would put a positive spin on whatever these profiles are showing. If this is an obsession of sorts, it's risky to pull you two off the beat. In fact, it might cause more disruptions if we removed you." Frankie's eyes plead with me to calm down, but Grayson's arm hangs behind her chair, and it infuriates me.

"And how did that work out for you?" Karina cuts in. "If we're sitting here, I doubt it went well."

"Unfortunately, you're right. It didn't work out the way we expected." Frankie clasps her hands together in front of her as she leans away from Grayson's arm. I can tell she's trying to reassure me and calm my jealous streak. We're at work, and we both need to focus. I nod slightly in agreement, but it doesn't mean this conversation is over.

"When we noticed the profiles and the subsequent posts, there was no active case for you both to handle. When the Boxletter murder hit our desks, we mutually agreed it would benefit us to have you both lead it. Our PR departments all felt this could alleviate the negative comments and threads online. Apparently, we did exactly what the perpetrator wanted us to do." Director Toby nods to Sydney.

She taps away on her laptop keyboard before spinning it to face the two of us. The feed of one account has a pinned post for all to read, along with an image of Karina and me staring at the body of Deidre Boxletter.

The post read: *Inept officers could have prevented the BRUTAL MURDER of a young woman. I warned you they're corrupt. More to come.*

"At least they had the courtesy to blur out the victim's face." Karina leans back in her chair, and I can tell she's ready to do whatever is necessary to stop the onslaught. "Where do we go from here?"

"Both profiles posted something similar, but one also insinuated you prefer to help people after death to bolster your careers."

"Wait, first we're just puppets for the powers that be, and now and now we're bolstering careers? People must see through this drivel, right? Otherwise, the press would blow up my phone requesting an official statement."

Sydney ignores my comments and continues. "They say the living have no value to either of you. That you're narcissistic, among other colorful things."

"Frankie?" I turn the conversation back to her, hoping for a different perspective and the beginning of a profile on the individual behind all of this.

"I know everyone here would like some clearer answers, but right now we have none. This is a complex issue. On the surface, the individual appears to have a vendetta against Detective Steele and Agent Marlow. What that is or why remains unclear. We can assume the blurring of the victim's face was for one of two reasons: compassion or the ability to post it to social media. If we're postulating that the poster is the murderer, the lack of bragging behavior leads us back to square one. They want to portray our colleagues negatively but control the entire narrative from start to finish. Doctor Grayson? What are your thoughts?"

"If the person posting is the killer, and we are assuming they are, this is going to be a public relations nightmare. This will spread to the far reaches of the globe and will continue until they feel justice is served. We have no idea what that looks like from their perspective."

"You've got to be kidding me. Karina and I have done nothing wrong. Why not release a statement saying so? Do an independent investigation into both of us. Neither of us has anything to hide!"

"Both your closets have skeletons. The department would rather stay quiet." Zeile speaks again. "It's also well beyond that point, Steele."

"What does that mean?" Karina sounds genuinely worried.

Sydney pipes up. "You've both been doxed."

"We've been what?"

"Internet sleuths posted your personal information, emails, cell phone, address, etcetera. We've approved security for both of your families for the time being. We must operate on the assumption that your cell phones have been compromised. Please turn them over immediately. Sydney will provide alternatives until further notice." Director Toby's voice was firm, but there were hints of a fatherly compassion within it.

"Have you found out who released it?" I ask the entire table, but the lack of a quick reply gives me the answer.

"Some of the people behind the accounts that posted or reposted put the information on other blog sites. We traced those individuals and are currently surveilling them."

"Arrest them," Karina growls at her director. "We both have kids, and this violates their safety."

"I understand that, Agent Marlow, but understand the optics it would present. People calling out two individuals who they deem criminals and the government comes down on them?"

"So, we just . . . what? Play nice while these lies permeate online?" My calm exterior unravels as the situation continues down the path of hopelessness.

"The fact is, detective, you both need to put on your big girl pants and play your part. Keep up appearances that all this negative press is just a flash in the pan. You said your record speaks for itself; then allow it to. There can be no deviations or attempts to counter punch these points. You'd be screaming into the void." Grayson might have a point, but I have no desire to agree with him at all.

"Everything has always been by the book, doctor," Karina spits through clenched teeth.

"Sure, that's why you're here and not in Seattle."

I can tell my partner is doing everything in her power not to leap across the table and punch him in the face. I'd gladly hold him down to get a few swings in. This man is a prick.

"Doctor, please enlighten me. Is it normal for a psychologist to make accusations regarding guilt or are you to be a simple observer and offer insight into situations? If that's the case, you can recuse yourself. Between Doctor Ryan and myself, with my lowly master's degree, we can handle it without your snide remarks. Now if you behave this way to bolster your ego, might I suggest a leave of absence for assistance with—""

"Jasmine, that's enough!" Frankie smacks the table for maximum effect. "I think we're all in agreement. We need to work as a team and not as individuals with defensive posturing. We owe it to the people we serve."

The rest of the table continues to talk while I stare at Grayson. I don't know the man at all, but how can one human being be so callous right away? He seems like a person who raises his nose at the people he deems below him. Mainly, Karina, myself, and my team. His theories seem to be rooted in something other than reality. Maybe it's his own personal bias or something else, but I will figure it out.

Special Agent Chalet's shrill voice brings me back to the present. "I'll be lead on this case from now on. Steele, Marlow, I expect you both to bring me up to speed after this meeting." Grayson continues leaning into Frankie talking against her ear. It's a disgusting display.

"That is all." Assistant Director Toby stands and walks out of the room with Captain Zeile, both of them deep in conversation.

Sydney walks around and holds her hand out. Without saying another word, my partner and I relinquish our cell phones to her. In exchange, we both get some high-end burner phones, complete with flip top and physical keys. Texting is going to suck. Before I can say anything, she grabs her things and leaves. I guess my attitude was less than appreciated by my friends in the department.

"If you'd all excuse us for a moment." Frankie's tone leaves nothing up for discussion.

"Steele, I'll bring Chalet up to date. Meet me in his office when you're done here. Out the doors, turn right, fourth door on the right. Got it?"

I nod in response, but I can't take my eyes off of Grayson leaning into Frankie's personal space. He motions her closer, but Frankie waves him away. His lip curls up as he catches me watching. I don't know who he is outside these doors, but his egregious behavior should have been stopped. If not by Frankie, then by any other high-level individual in the room.

I can file a complaint with the bureau, or I can let my wife handle things. Either way, it means trusting he will take the hint and back off. If he's like this to every female client he works with, then it might become a bigger issue that Frankie doesn't want to pursue. If I rise to the challenge and put him in his place, he can twist the narrative to say I'm an individual prone to violence, just like this anonymous online person. Perception is everything.

"Jasmine, are you even listening to me?" I blink and look around, realizing Frankie and I are alone. I take that moment to move around the table and sit next to her.

"I didn't mean to ignore you. I'm trying to wrap my brain around all this information. It's a lot to process . . . and there's a lot I don't quite follow."

"I know, love, but that's not what I want to discuss with you." She takes my hands in hers, and I wait for the sucker punch to come.

"I could feel the jealousy pouring off you in waves. Lewis is just a friend, nothing more."

"He didn't act like just a friend."

"Jasmine, he's an ex, and you put a ring on it. He's a stupid flirt, but I've learned to deal with it. I'm asking you to trust me."

"You said ex . . . right. Okay. So, he's someone you dated who continues to invade your personal space without your permission and degrades your wife—"

"I'll handle that. He's got a twisted sense of humor, but please, trust me."

"I don't like him." My pathetic, childlike tone makes her smile. "I love your smile, and I trust you. I can't promise to keep my mouth in check . . . and if he oversteps or makes you feel uncomfortable, I need you to tell me. I'll handle it."

Frankie's laughter warms my terrified soul. "I'll file a formal complaint with his bosses. With your support, of course." Her hand cups the side of my face, and my body naturally leans into it. "I know we're not . . . things are strained right now. But I love you. I married you. I *chose* you. No matter what the world says, we are forever."

Her soft lips press into mine, but just as my eyes close, she's moving away and out of the room. Frankie has a profile to work on and patients of her own. It's moments like this that make me miss what we had before the world ended. My thumb plays with my wedding band as I walk out of the room.

My brain speeds up as the door clicks behind me. Once we human beings get some kind of foundation underneath us, Mother Nature reminds us how fickle we really are. We destroy things for sport, for views or likes. We kill one another over differing opinions but crave social interactions as if they were the blood that fuels our body. We hurt those we love but desire their approval. All of my education fails when I pose a rationale for this behavior. Because there isn't one. Is it possible to fix the damage already done? At what point to you just give up, burn it all to the ground, and rebuild it again?

***

The meeting with Chalet was short, thanks to Karina's quick summary of the few details we have. My alarm on my watch reminded me I had a mandatory appointment, so I ducked out with the promise to meet up in our dungeon.

Sitting on the leather couch, I wait for my therapist, Doctor Preston, to notice anything new. It took me some time to feel safe within these walls. Once I reached that point, I found myself more open to processing my past trauma. Now these meetings have become something I dread. Each one results in a report to my bosses about any mental or physical concerns that have come up during the previous week.

Every appointment, we run through a checklist. Doctor Preston, one of the best therapists in the city, pushes truthful answers as she jots notes.

"How have you felt this week?"

"Still struggling to sleep through the night. At this point I expect it to be a lifelong issue. Memory is fine. Notes have helped mitigate other issues."

"How's the brain fog?"

"Much better. I find it happens more in the evening than any other time of day."

"Stress level? Any difficulties in processing it?"

"Nothing more than before my illness. The case we're dealing with right now is pushing me to my limit, but nothing some video games can't help."

"Have you tried meditation?"

"Too quiet."

Lightning flashes across the darkened sky. Slivers of light fight through the storm to create a perfect blend of gloom. I've always loved the windows in Doctor Preston's office. They're calming when nothing else in the world is.

"You know I dislike these check-ins as much as you do. I'd much rather be assisting you to move beyond the pandemic. But here we are."

"I know, doc."

"Then you understand compliance is paramount. You chose to keep me as the psychologist overseeing your recovery. You could have used the department-appointed individual. If you fail to answer or force my hand, I'll have no choice but to recommend desk duty. Now be honest. How are you really feeling?"

"I expect nothing less, doc."

The rain rolls down the windows in random patterns. The bolts of electricity bounce around the sky before they land somewhere, probably the Empire State Building. The rumble of thunder follows several seconds later. It reminds me of the darkness that lingers in the back of all our minds. Like a roach waiting for the daylight to diminish before it crawls out, allowing negative thoughts to rule our bodies.

"I've got my moments. Physically, I feel leaps and bounds better. I don't think I could run down perps like I used to, but that could be me getting older as much as long term side effects from COVID. Docs said I could be back to normal tomorrow, a week, a month, maybe a year or not at all. Karina and the rest of the team have been helpful to a fault. It drives me crazy sometimes. But I appreciate it."

"How about Frankie? Have things changed?"

Have they? While we had an amazing dinner, it feels like there's a massive gap between us. "I figured out some new triggers for my anger," I answer. diverting the question to something more manageable emotionally.

"Care to share?" The leather squeaks as she shifts in her chair. The back of my neck tingles and I assume she's glaring at me to continue.

"Idiocy is the biggest. People thinking the world revolves around them without a care about their fellow human being. That lack of compassion gets me. But it feels weird. I feel angry, but also helpless. I can't help either of them."

"Many people have those same triggers. I'd say that makes you human. When have you started feeling helpless?"

"Always, I just hid it better. Kept going to work trying to do my best to change things. If I could get answers for one victim's family, then maybe, just maybe, it would make a difference. Now . . . especially after today . . . I wonder if it's all worth it."

She stays quiet, waiting for me to finish my thought. The case flashes in my mind. The victim, her position, the lack of respect for her life. The accusations and lies spread for the masses to interpret. All of it moving around me like a hurricane bearing down on lower Manhattan. The waves beating the shore, but the storm remains at sea . . . The worst is yet to come.

"Look at all those people walking in the park. The storm's raging all around them, but they soldier through, maybe hoping to get home to dry off. None of them know what tomorrow brings, let alone the next moment. Every step they take could be their last, yet they walk on. They travel to work to earn a living. They head home to their spouses and kids. Each person making decisions, living life to the best of their ability. Yet, one lie . . . one fabrication or narrative switch from a small percentage of nefarious people can blow up everything like a tornado. You could prepare for it, but you don't really believe it's happening. You've never consciously hurt anyone, so why would they come after you? Why would they hurt others and blame you for it? Yet they do."

"Maybe because those individuals are going through such negative things, they have to lash out. It's easier than facing the reason behind their barrage of attacks," she answers as another flash has the rumble almost on top of it. The wind whistles outside as the sky gets impossibly darker. "Since you've been sick, I've noticed you've been more philosophical than before."

"Facing death tends to do that to a person." I shrug, watching the force of Mother Nature cause the people below to run for cover.

"You were dead on the table before, detective. What makes this any different from the past?"

"Marcus Aurelius said, *It is not death that a man should fear, but rather he should fear never beginning to live.* I'm questioning everything, doc. How many people did I leave in unsafe situations because there was no place to move them during the heart of it? How many people have I failed when I've been unable to solve a case? Now I have this person trying to destroy my reputation online with falsities because . . . what? They can?"

"You're struggling to find meaning in things?"

"I have my family. I have my team. I know that, but the purpose . . . the meaning of it all . . . feels hollow. What's the point when the cycle keeps repeating?"

"You can't hold yourself responsible for all the things that happened. The world was a different place. It changed everyone." I can hear her thinking. I've come here long enough to know when her breathing pattern changes, indicating her mentally processing things. "Maybe you need to discuss this with Frankie. Take some time off, go on vacation together as a family. Reconnect with your wife and son. Maybe things will be clearer upon your return."

"I wish I could, but the grip of a vengeful spirit holds me in the game. Even when I don't want to play."

The rest of our appointment passes by in silence. Me watching the storm, working through her words, and the doc filling out her forms. What would I do if I didn't have this badge? Who would I be?

Chapter Six

The crisp morning air causes slight bumps to form on my skin as I watch Chase run down the length of the lacrosse field. His rapid breaths form puffs of white mist as his right arm spins the stick to keep possession of the ball. Like a freight train, he muscles through the players and launches it toward the net. The goalie, half Chase's size, misses it by mere millimeters. Frankie and I jump to our feet with excitement, spilling a small amount of hot cocoa on the plastic lids of our cups. Hank barks in celebration on the blanket next to us, his school spirit sweatshirt on full display under his harness.

I cherish these moments more than before. It's a slice of heaven amid the nastiness. We sit back down, awaiting the faceoff, when my phone buzzes in my pocket. My thumb flips it open, revealing a text from Sydney.

The account posted this morning on all platforms. It's bad, Steele.

My reply takes forever to type out. *Explain.*

How can a detective carry a gun when they had a COVID-related stroke? They're a risk to the community as a whole. No wonder Detective Steele is unable to handle cases solo. She's the precincts poster child for equality in the department, otherwise she'd be forced to retire.

Sydney's text stops me cold. The complete fabrication of my medical records is a step too far. It's also an egregious lie. While I might have minor lingering symptoms, I was never hospitalized for a stroke or anything close to it. In fact, doctors ran a battery of tests to rule it out. Those very results are the reason I was cleared to return to work. So, several questions now remain: How the hell did my medical records get leaked and what is the department going to do about it? Will I need a union representative or a lawyer to handle this all? How the hell am I going to explain it to my wife?

"Hey, Frankie . . ." My soft words barely register with her.

"Did you see that? He was so worried he wouldn't score all year. But he proved his fears wrong! That's what happens with hard work and all the practice with this new coach. I cannot tell you how much of a blessing Coach Thomas has been since Will left."

"I'm really happy about that too, but there's something I need—"

"Do not tell me you have to leave. The game's almost over, and whatever is happening can wait. You're supposed to have the morning off. Seriously, work can wait." The look in her eyes is only surpassed by the pleading in her voice.

"I don't have to go in yet, and I know it's not ideal to talk here. I just don't have much of a choice."

"Okay, now you're scaring me. What are you talking about?"

"Remember when I was sick?"

"How could I forget? You lived in the basement the entire time. I was distant, and I'm sorry for that. I was terrified of Chase being exposed. I know it was hard on you, us being isolated like that."

"It's fine. I understood your actions and expected nothing less. I know I responded poorly to it, and I know we need to talk about that, but right now I need you to listen carefully." I pause as the stands erupt on the other side of the field. Their team scored a goal, but they're still down by double digits. "The department required I be cleared by doctors and recertify."

"I remember."

"During my doctor visits, I stumbled over my words and had trouble. Because of that and my dad's side of the family, the doc was concerned I might have had a TI or something similar. He wanted to rule it out. Now, everything was clear, but you know I've got some symptoms that are lingering. I'm on top of it, and they are getting better every day. Overall, I am just as healthy as I was before."

"Why didn't you tell me? I'm your wife. I have a right to know." Her eyes stare right through me, confusion and pain radiating off her.

"Partly because I didn't want you to worry, and I thought it was no big deal. But also, you're Chase's other parent. If something was wrong, you wouldn't be able to focus on helping our kid during this home school Zoom stuff. He needed you to be clearheaded, and I needed to know you were both safe."

"I'll try to ignore how I feel your statement is riddled with idiocy. I have to ask. Why are you bringing this all up now?"

"The individual running those social media accounts posted an exaggerated version of it online." Without thinking, I show her the message from Sydney.

"A stroke? If all those tests were negative, where are they getting the idea you had one?"

"I don't know."

"Okay, so regardless of the decisions you made previously, they used your medical information to continue stoking the flames of fear. This can't stand though, right? The department will have to force the platforms to remove it."

"I want to know where they got all of this from. It's not like you can just log into my medical accounts and pull this all up."

"True, which is why there should be an investigation into who leaked it." She pauses, and I can tell there's something more she wants to ask me. I wait until she continues. "Would you have told me if this didn't come up?"

"In time, yes. Truthfully, I was scared about how you'd look at me. I know I won the genetic pool of issues, and I couldn't stand the fear. You've already been through so much with me, I figured if there was nothing to worry about . . . why worry? But I know you deserve the truth and access to my medical portal. I should have told you sooner, but here we are."

"Yes, here we are." Frankie nods her head, and I can tell the wheels are spinning in her mind. She's probably frustrated, maybe a bit furious at me.

The buzzer sounds the end of the game. I hear Chase's team cheer as the kids move to the middle of the field for the "good game" meeting between teams.

"If you ever withhold something serious like this again, I will ensure Hank defecates in all your shoes before Chase and I leave you alone, pondering the reasons why. Am I clear?"

Before I can respond, she shoves the flip phone into my chest and walks a few steps ahead in her trek to find our son milling about the crowd. I know her fear-fueled anger has no malicious intention. We both watched people pass from the disease that washed over the world. It was easier to keep things to myself because truthfully, what could she do?

Chase's voice wafts over the small crowd of parents searching for their kid. He's going on about his shots on goal, which ones he missed, and how he needed to work on things in the future. I follow the back of Frankie's head and the tone to see my son having a serious conversation with his coach. As I get closer, the more technical side of his statements hit my ears.

"I missed too many open guys who had a better angle for the shot. I've got to view the field better, coach."

"That's all well and good, but you have to remember you're in a fast-paced game. Sometimes you make a decision based on what you know in that specific moment. If you can't see your teammate on the other side of the field, you can't hold yourself responsible for missing that pass. We can work on ways to run through progressions, but don't blame yourself for what you did today. The team played well."

Chase has grown up so much during the pandemic. If I'm being honest, I wish he hadn't, but I have no control over it. Not to mention his growth spurts. His father, Henry, would be so proud of him right now. My brother would probably pat me on the back and tell me I wasn't the only athlete in the family anymore. Hell, Henry might even say I've been surpassed in my sports dominance in this family. Of course, I'd argue Chase needs to win a few championships before he can knock me down a peg or two.

I'd trade all of my trophies and accolades for one more day with my family long gone. Some days I just need a hug from those who can no longer give it to me. Frankie, sensing the change in my mood, reaches back, slides her hand in mine, and pulls me forward. I attempt to place my arm around Chase, but he shrugs out of my grasp. We've reached that age already.

"Excuse me, Coach Ali, great game."

"Frankie, how are you?" He fist-bumps my wife. "Glad you could make it out here today."

"Of course! This is my wife, Jasmine. Chase's other mother."

"Guardian," Chase pipes up, his arms folded across his chest. He's never called me that before. The confusion must be evident on my face since the coach is in my space in seconds.

"Mrs. Ryan, regardless of his brief outburst, Chase speaks highly of you and Frankie. It's truly a pleasure to finally put a face to the name." His handshake is firm, but not too strong or flimsy. His dark brown eyes stare at me with an intensity that causes my neck muscles to tense.

"Jasmine, please. You'll have to forgive me Coach Ali. Chase doesn't share much about lacrosse when I'm home. I have to admit, I'm very impressed with how the team played today. Considering the past few seasons, this team looks completely different than last year."

"They just needed someone to guide them more than their science teacher could. Budgets and all that stuff. Chase is wonderful and a genuine delight to have on our team. Between their desire to work hard, a new coaching staff volunteering their time, and parents willing to sacrifice theirs so these young men can succeed . . . it's an amazing change. Gives them the foundation to do well on the field and in life."

I'm not sure how to take his statement. He could be just a really nice guy who'd make a great motivational speaker in the future, or was that a dig at my lack of presence at Chase's games?

"We're very proud of him," Frankie cuts in, breaking me out of my thoughts. "How about we all go to breakfast?"

"Frankie, you know the team has a tradition of a team breakfast after a weekend morning game. Team building and all that," the coach say offhandedly.

"I know . . . It's just . . . " Frankie pauses and looks around to verify if anyone is close enough hear. "Things have become a bit more complicated as of late."

"Frankie, Chase has explained as much as he could. I understand he has security, and it's been cleared with them. He told me it's not the first time this has happened, and it probably won't be the last, but I trust him to stay in line with us. I'll make sure he gets home by noon, if that's okay with the two of you?"

"That would be lovely." She kisses Chase's cheek pulls him into a tight hug. "I'll take your gear home. I don't want to hear anything about you acting out or causing a problem for your team. I know it's annoying, but please be on your best behavior. For me?" He squirms free from her arms. "Chase, do you understand me?"

"Yes, Mom." I stifle a laugh at his overexaggerated eye roll before he backs away.

"Hey," I call out to him. "No hug for me?"

He throws his arms weakly around my waist. "Thanks for coming, Aunt Jazz."

"I hate missing your games, bud. I'm gonna try—"

"I know. Crime doesn't sleep. Work always calls," he mumbles before jetting off to catch up with his friends.

"Eat a vegetable or two while you're out!" Frankie calls after him. She lifts his equipment bag and tosses it over her shoulder with practiced ease.

"That was different . . . colder than I'm used to. Is he already at the *hate your parents* age?"

"He's been a starter in the fall league all season. You've made it to one game and you want him to act like that's a gift? He knows you're trying, but maybe make more of an effort." This time I can tell her harsh words were meant to hurt as she gets a few steps head start back to the car.

"Wait up." It takes me a few long strides to walk alongside her. The security we both have hang back, giving us some space, but not too far away should something go wrong. "You want me to carry his bag?"

"Nope. I've been doing it all season. I consider it my exercise for the day."

"How about we go out to breakfast? Just the two of us, like we used to. Or I can make us some waffles. Or just eggs and bacon if we don't have any of the fancy fixings. Whatever you want, I can try to make it without lighting the kitchen on fire this time."

"It would give us some time to talk. You could tell me everything that happened during your fourteen-plus day isolation. I could walk you through giving me access to your online medical portals. It's not that hard, just a few clicks and an email," Frankie answers, giving me a glimmer of hope for the rest of the day.

"Technically you've always had access with the docs, just not the online portal thing."

"You're splitting hairs. I never called because I trusted you not to overly downgrade things since you were shot. Apparently, that is not the case. So, I'd like to see everything for myself. Please."

"I'll give you access to all the things, portals, whatever, as long as you don't make me eat something green with my breakfast." I laugh, trying to let go of all the stress this morning has brought us.

"There's nothing wrong with a spinach smoothie or some green juice with breakfast. I'd prefer to be around to play with our grandkids, not just be a picture on the mantle."

"Grandkids? You're aging me way too fast. Right, Hank?" I ask the pup at my feet. "Help me out here. Tell Mama she's moving too quickly for my liking." Hank barks right on time, making us both laugh.

My phone rings in my pocket, immediately killing any good vibe we had going. Both of our expressions drop at the intrusion. "Why do they always have to call you? Do you ever get any time off?"

I'd normally joke about how she knows it's work calling, but with the new phone, that's the only place it could be. It rings again. "I wish I did. Between the refusals to get vaccinated, layoffs, a murderer calling me and Karina out . . . take your pick, love. The department needs help, and unless I get fired, they're going to bleed me dry."

"Better answer it then."

"Steele." My voice cracks as I watch Frankie walk farther away from me. I really hate this.

"It's Karina. Are you still at the park?" she asks with sirens blaring in the background.

"Yeah, we're heading out now. What's going on?"

"I'm two blocks away. Zeile will handle your detail; they're staying with Frankie until we get back. We're needed in Jersey. Our perp left us another victim." Karina's emotionless response tells me everything I need to know. The call for us to go came from higher-ups. We've got no choice but to follow orders like the perfectly trained seals we are.

"I'll be waiting by the east exit." I flip the phone shut. "She'll be here soon."

"Then you better get whatever's bothering you off your chest now."

"I feel like we're being used as bait. They're making the calls for us, and we do as they say. We just creep closer to the edge of the ledge, you know? And if they need a scapegoat in all this, they cut our tether and we take the fall."

"You need to watch your back. I don't mean that simply either. It's obvious things have changed within the department for several reasons. The other members of my team are considering cutting ties with the NYPD, and I think you need to really take a hard look at your job."

"Frankie, this is all I know . . ."

"Jasmine, I know you're struggling, I get it, but you need to listen to me right now. You are a number to them. Sure, the people you work closest to are a family to us, but those who sit in their leather chairs could care less about you or your family." She takes a deep breath as we get to the sidewalk. She drops the bag to the concrete and pulls me to her. "I'm going to say something, and you need to really hear me."

"Okay."

"I know this case is important. I know your job is important to those who can't speak for themselves and for the families who deserve answers. I rationally know all of that, Jasmine. I still married you because I love you unconditionally. I know you live by a specific code of ethics and a level of integrity that I can't understand most times."

The sound of sirens hit my ears and I know Karina isn't far out. "I know you do, Frankie."

"Yet, you continue to cut me out time and time again. I'm an adult; I can handle it. I get it, even if it hurts like hell. But I know you, I know your heart. Our son . . . Chase . . . he didn't sign up for this. He didn't ask to be an orphan. He never asked for your career or mine. All he's ever wanted is to be loved and to be given some of your time. You keep fighting so hard for everyone outside our door, but you seem to forget who lives with you. How many cases have put us in harm's way? How many more details are we going to need?"

My silence is enough of an answer for her to continue.

"I need you to take a long hard look at your life and realize the family you lost is gone. The hugs you dream of having from your mom or brother, they're never happening again. But a hug from our son after a hard day or a well fought win, that is precious. A kiss from me should be worth more than the guilt you still hold onto."

Karina's car pulls up alongside the curb and she honks. I hold up my hand and beg for some more time.

"I need you to start fighting for this family as much as you fight for everyone else."

"Frankie . . . I . . . I don't know . . ."

"I thought therapy would help you."

"It has, more than you know."

"Maybe, but you're still doing the same actions and expecting a different result. I told you I would always put our son above everything else, and I have. We both love what we do, Jasmine. We both help others. The difference is I do put my foot down when it comes to family time. I demand a break from it all. You continue to put others before us, using excuses to buffer the pain. I want my wife back. Chase wants his mother back. Just think about what I've said."

Karina honks again. A security office picks up the bag and motions for Frankie to follow him.

"I'll figure it out, I promise," I yell to her as Karina screams out the window at me. Frankie catches my eye and nods in response. I slip into Karina's SUV and slam the door behind me. "You had to honk that much? Really? Couldn't wait two minutes?"

"Bosses don't care about personal stuff, Steele. They need us there"—she looks at the time—"like now. You okay there?"

"No, no, I'm not." I stare out the window blankly. "Unless you can give me a time machine or create more hours in the day, in which case I'd be better."

"Can't help you there, but whatever is going on, the universe has a way of working itself out."

Karina's words fall short. While I adore her as a person, she's in a different place than I am. Her kids are around a similar age as Chase, but she has her parents to help her. She's trying to prove herself in the bureau again and earn the respect of her peers. At the end of the day, those same peers think she's slumming it with a lowly detective. If push comes to shove, I bet I'd be the scapegoat there too.

Frankie's words bounce around my mind as we hit the highway. She's right about my absence and my desire to help everyone outside of our home, but she has one thing wrong. I would never put my job before my family. Every morning I wake up, I want to make the place safe for them to walk around in. Losing my family members, the fact that no one helped them . . . it fuels me to fight each and every moment for change. It's my responsibility to protect them, and this is how I know to do it.

Every crime scene elicits a unique response from law enforcement. The location, parties involved, victim's name, and status in society are all factors in how the situation can be handled. Preconceived notions based on years of experience prevents us from seeing everything as a clean slate. It's never malicious, but the science and statistics of these things rarely, if ever, changes. I wish it did.

"Shit, Chalet is here," Karina mutters as we pull up alongside another police vehicle. "I know we have our way of doing things, but this is not in our control today. Seriously, Steele, we need to follow the book exactly as Chalet and the others say it's written. Got it?"

"Karina, you know reality doesn't follow an instruction manual. What happens if we notice something out of place? What if we have a gut response that warrants a follow-up but the departments won't sign off on a wild-goose chase? How many times have your instincts solved a case when the higher-ups wanted you to ignore it?"

"Too many to count, but we don't have that luxury right now. Got it?"

I don't have a say in the matter, so I drop it. I look out over the mixed crowd of people pushing against the crime scene tape connected to streetlights. The perfectly manicured lawns of suburbia make every home look the same on this street. It feels like the beginning of a random drama or horror film, where generational secrets thrive, and people die behind the ideal façade. Just like anything else, though, there's a grain of truth to it.

"Detective Steele, Agent Marlow, if you'd both follow me," Chalet says, leading us away from the horde of people.

My eyes scan over as many people as possible, noting some minor differences among them in case it proves useful later. It's my experience that some killers like to view the response to their handywork. Sydney tells me that the digital media age has changed that. Now someone can hack a camera system or set up a small bug and watch from the safety of a secluded area. While it leaves a trace, by the time we get to the location, the perpetrator is long gone. So, I take my notes just in case.

"Victim's husband found the body when he flew home on the red-eye from his business trip. According to him, the kids spent the weekend at his parents' house. Thankfully, they weren't around to witness the attack." Chalet hands each of us a set of slip-on booties. The blue shoe nets snap in place with little effort.

"Is there anything we should know before going in, sir?" Karina sounds like a rookie just out of the academy. I get what she's trying to do, but by the same token, it's coming off so fake, it's painful to watch.

"Agent Marlow, you don't need to ask permission for your every move. I assume you know what you both need to do. Just keep it by the book." He forces us to stop directly in front of the main entrance. His demeanor feels off as we stand there. The sound of camera clicks hit my ears. I can see the press to the side of us.

"It was less asking permission and more a question regarding the scene, sir. Considering the team was here before us, is there anything we should know before we walk into the devil's den? Whatever you provide could be useful to our investigation." The words hang in the air, and Karina's expression is a mix of humor and fear. Truth be told, she looks sick.

"The entryway was clean. No tracks or trail from the front door into the main living area. There's no sign of a forced entry into the residence. The team fingerprinted the relevant areas and gathered several full prints. Based on the lack of damage to the front door, we can assume the prints are from the victim or other family members."

"I assume exclusion prints will be provided?"

"Of course, detective." He moves again as the camera clicks continue again. Karina and I are keenly aware of the situation we're in. The way the press hangs in perfect position to take images of our faces with Chalet giving us orders. It's all a show for the public to prove we have superiors and the departments are keeping tabs on their two unruly employees. It's degrading.

"So, basically, we're here for show." I wait for him to comment, but he remains silent. "If we were in the lead, beyond first responders, no one would step foot inside until we assessed everything. We'd be in the living room discussing our findings, a plan of action, and whatever else came to mind. Instead, we're outside in full view of the press being ordered around by a superior officer. Am I doing okay so far?"

"That's out of line and you know it. You have a job to do, detective. You have a choice to do it, but you can always tender your resignation and make this a whole lot easier on all of us."

"Respectfully, we both know that wouldn't be a smart move at this point in time." Karina tries to bring context to the conversation, but I can tell she's as disgusted as I am. "I'm curious about the optics, sir. We know you're the lead on the case, but for all intents and purposes, the viewing public believes we are in charge. Consider all the bodies walking through the crime scene before we even get to the location, let alone observe everything in its original state."

"Right, well, optics as they are, we arrived first since you both were otherwise occupied. Now, if you'll follow me." Chalet enters the house as the press point our way.

The smell of chemicals hits my nose hard and fast once I walk into the house. Whether it's from our crime lab or cleaning agents, I couldn't say. The gaggle of personnel in the living room with their alphabet jackets shows me all the agencies are evenly represented. The reason behind their appearance looms large over my head.

Seeing the full scope of invasion is bothersome. I've never been brought into a scene so late before. For all we know, everyone's had their hands on whatever evidence we have. Hopefully Sydney can make it all make sense instead of giving us an inconclusive answer due to contamination.

"This way," Chalet barks as he heads down the main hallway next to a small open kitchen.

"This place is a mess," I whisper to Karina. "Who knows what evidence they trampled on before we got here."

"Yeah," she replies, looking around. "But we've got a part to play. So, let's just do the best we can and solve this case before they strike again."

"The doors on the left are the kids' rooms."

"Has anyone—"

"They've been searched. They found some prints, but nothing appeared out of the ordinary." He stops at the only door on the right. "Bathroom is the door at the end of the hall, and this door is to the master bedroom. We've had a team scour the house and take samples from every viable location, but the bedroom has been off-limits. The husband, paramedics, myself, and the coroner are the only parties who've entered.

Once you clear it, the crime scene unit will go through the room. Doctor Hayes is waiting for you. I'll be in the living room when you're done."

"Why are all the other departments here?" Karina presses a question that's been floating in my mind.

"We're under a microscope, and our bosses felt having a series of checks and balances would ease the public's concern." He walks off without saying another word. His demeanor unnerves me down to my core. In the office, he's demanding, bordering on belittling, but at least you know what you're getting. Here, he's cold. His actions feel like a calculated setup. Nothing feels right about this situation.

"So, he's pretty much allowed everyone to enter a crime scene and is proud only a few people entered the bedroom? He might as well have the high school marching band enter while they're at it." My disdain rolls out with every word.

Karina knocks on the door before opening it to reveal the horror within the bedroom.

"Thank God you're finally here." Victor stands, looking behind us with tired eyes highlighted by dark circles. "I swear if that sorry excuse for a playboy comes back into my workspace demanding I do things his way, I'm going to punch him. He wants me to move the body, Steele. Before you got here to release it. That is not how I do business. You know this. Unless something's changed, you're still the lead here. Why would he ask me to break protocols they've been shoving down our throats for months now?"

"I'm sorry about all this. You did the right thing. We'll handle Agent Chalet. Can you fill us in?"

Karina closes the door behind us, allowing us to talk privately and at normal volume.

"I got a call early this morning about a body. I expected to see you both here, but you weren't. The FBI's most dubious egomaniac was running the show, demanding people set up a specific way. You know the outside was basically scripted, right? Everyone in here was mumbling about it. No one's happy."

"It's out of our control, Doctor Hayes." Karina waves him off. "Beyond all of that, what can you tell us about the victim?"

Karina's voice trails off while I take in the room. Given the length of the hallway, I expected the room to be much larger than it is. There's a dresser, three drawers wide with a large mirror attached to it, leaning on the wall next to the door. A few photo frames of two young children adorn the top on the left and right. A small, elegant jewelry box rests in the center. Looking carefully through the glass opening, it appears nothing was taken during the crime. Earrings and what I assume is the victim's wedding ring sits on a tissue in front of the jewelry box. I can assume these were the items she wore most often.

The queen-sized bed is against the far wall, between two doors. A large landscape photo of a beach during sunset hangs above the headboard. The wall is pristine, clean of any cast-off or any bodily fluids.

"Door on the left is the bathroom. The other one's a walk-in closet." Victor answers my question before I even ask it. "Before you ask, no, I didn't go in. Chalet had to clear the room first. He checked it out."

"Did he find anything?"

"Not that I know of, but the crime scene unit hasn't been in here yet."

I slip into my nitrile gloves and slide the drawers open. Each one is full of perfectly folded clothes and undergarments. It's almost too perfect. With no dust on the furniture, the mirror free of any spots, the room doesn't feel lived in. If there was a robbery, there would have been some kind of disturbance to the everyday setting.

Behind me, an armoire leans against the wall. The matching piece of furniture looks a little out of place with the door showing some wear. The knobs, specifically, have several scratches on them, and the paint looks chipped.

"Same stamp, *Paid in Full,* on the victim's forehead," Karina says from the bed.

"Let's hope our killer's done collecting on their debt," Victor replies as they continue to look over the body.

The two bottom drawers of the armoire hold various sweaters, sweats, and other workout gear. All folded, but it feels messier than the other dresser. Opening the doors, I see suits hang in their dry-cleaning plastic coverings, the name of the business printed on the white paper wrapped around the metal hanger. I jot down the information for a possible follow-up later on. The interior two drawers grab my attention.

A small amount of white residue covers the lip of the top drawer. Pulling it open, I see the undergarments and socks are in complete disarray. Buried underneath the mess are several empty pill bottles. All the labels list Paula or Peter Grubbs as the patient. The printed dates are staggered, but they give me pause. They're too close together to be the same narcotic.

"Karina, I've got some empty oxy bottles in here. The perp must have rifled through the drawer and found these containers. I can't say if they took the pills with them or not."

"Could that explain the pinpoint pupils and blue-tinged fingernails? Could this be a simple overdose?" she asks Victor as I finally walk over to the bed and take in the victim.

"I can tell you she has a white residue on her teeth and tongue, but I can't speculate if she took the pills willingly or not. I'll have Doctor Brown test is all when we get back to the lab. There's something shoved down her esophagus, but it's out of reach. Once I get her on the table, I'll be able to retrieve it."

A small amount of dried vomit lines the side of her mouth to the mattress below. "She aspirated."

"Yes, my assistant collected a sample and several photos to document it. Again, I can give you more context once I'm in the lab."

"Stomach contents, toxicology, and all of that?"

"Of course. I will pass along everything to Doctor Brown with a rush request."

There's a knock at the door before I can ask another question. Victor's assistant opens the door, revealing a gurney with a body bag on top in the hallway.

"Sorry to interrupt, Doctor Hayes. Agent Chalet released the body. We're free to take Mrs. Grubbs now."

"Did he say we were still in here?" I ask the poor man.

"He gave me strict orders to come in and remove the body. Nothing more, ma'am."

Victor waves him in, and the two work quickly to remove the victim's body properly. Karina nods as they exit before closing the door, preventing me from following.

"I know it's asking a lot, but I need you to play nice and let me lead. Please."

I don't know the reason behind her words, but I acquiesce to her request. She leads me out into the now-empty living room. A middle-aged man sits on the couch, his tie loosened and hanging off to one side. His eyes dart to mine before turning back to the wall.

"Agent Marlow, Detective Steele, this is the victim's husband, Peter Grubbs," Chalet says from the opposite side of the couch.

"Mr. Grubbs, I know this is very difficult for you, but we'd like to ask you some questions." Karina's soothing voice floats in the air, but I doubt the man is in any position to accept it.

"I've already told them everything I know." His waves his hand at Chalet. "He said I could go, but then you two come in. What more could I tell you that you don't already know? And please, stop patronizing me with the 'we understand' bullshit. You couldn't possibly know what I'm going through."

Karina holds her hand back as a warning to me. She knows I want to interject and ask questions, but I'm trusting her judgement here. She's worked with Chalet before; she knows his game.

Peter's entire demeanor screams rage and pain. His eyes are dark and hollow. His five o'clock shadow and stifled yawns let us know he's beyond exhausted. If he was standing, I'm sure he would appear physically imposing. Right now, he just looks broken.

"Sir, are you wearing the same clothing from yesterday?" Karina presses.

"Yeah, flew overnight, but no one will let me change." The wrinkles in his suit seem to back up his story. I'm surprised Chalet didn't have him go back to the precinct and collect his clothing there. Why leave him here for us to talk to?

"I should have been home." His voice cracks. "It's our anniversary, and my boss called me last minute to cover some bullshit meeting in San Francisco. I should have done it remotely. I knew I could have . . ."

"Sir—"

"Who would do this? My wife, she's the kindest, gentlest woman you'd ever meet. Why would someone want to hurt her?" He chokes on the last few words.

Before the pandemic, Karina or myself would have been next to him with a tissue or reassurance. But this is a whole new world where we still live in masks and keep our distance for the safety of our families.

A twist of the light reflecting off something pulls my attention away from the victim's husband. It was best to investigate it myself since I wasn't even sure there was anything there. I didn't need Karina or the team wondering if my brain was as messed up as the social media posts claimed.

But between some books, above the television set, rests a small security camera.

"Sir, you have a security system inside the house?"

"No. Paula wanted me to set one up outside because of the construction going on next door, but I never got to it. Why?" he answers, sniffling.

I slip two books out from their place revealing the wireless unit. Based on the dust surrounding the other novels, this looks like it was placed recently.

"Where did that come from? I swear I never set up anything like that in the house!" Peter yells, as if needing to defend himself.

My irritation forces me to look over to Chalet, who says nothing. He's been in this place all day with however many individuals and no one noticed a thing. It took the reflection of a random light from outside the front window to bring it to my attention. Then again, they might have noticed it and left it for me to find. Maybe he wanted to show our ineptitude?

"Anyone on the property who can bag this for the tech lab to analyze?" Knowing the camera might still be recording, I keep my voice neutral. We don't need any edited footage of a rampaging detective with no tact flying around the internet. I hear Chalet call something into his walkie as I look over the rest of the room. Again, nothing stands out, nothing disturbed to give an indication of theft.

A tech runs in with the proper items to secure the camera and rushes out the door with it. Chalet walks over to the entryway, leaning on the wall by the door. Karina's cheeks look red, her body language telling me things are about to get ugly.

"Mr. Grubbs—" she tries.

"What the hell is going on? The person who did this had a camera in here. How many are there? Was one in the bedroom? Have they been watching us? Have they been watching my kids? Why the hell didn't you notice is sooner? Trace that damn thing and find the person who killed my wife!" The words spill out with such speed and animosity it's hard to decipher what he means.

"Sir, is it possible for you to stay with your parents and the kids for the time being? We'll post a car out front for your safety until we know more." Karina's trying to calm the poor man, but we both know it's a Band-aid at best.

"Yeah, I can do that." He stands up, fixes his shirt, and stops. "What am I going to tell the kids? How do I tell her parents? They'll have to fly in . . . I don't know how to do this." His eyes fill with a fresh round of tears.

Chalet walks into the room and places his arm around Mr. Grubbs, leading him out of the house. The husband wobbles with each step, barely able to make it with the agent's help. The press captures the whole thing.

After a car door slams, we hear Chalet tell some officers to do a perimeter check, probably for the receiver end of the short-range camera. But they'd be long gone by now, if they were even here at all. I'm sure there'd be a way to rig it up to a cloud or something. Maybe Sydney could dig something up.

"You know that whatever they got is going to be online tomorrow sometime," Karina tells me, as if I didn't already know.

"Yeah. Makes you wonder why it wasn't removed in the first place. They had to see it, Karina."

"Maybe they did, maybe they didn't. We can't prove it either way. So, we focus on what we can work on."

"Going on the assumption she was murdered, poisoning takes time. Setting up the camera, the receiver, making sure everything worked properly . . . it takes a lot of time and energy. There must be some trace of it all."

"True. Not to mention how long were they watching the Grubbs? How does Boxletter connect to the new victim? All we've got are questions and an uphill battle to find any answers."

The press bellows begging for a comment as we exit the house. Each step through the throng of people is a gauntlet of flashes, screaming voices, cell phones, and accusations hurled our way. It's a shame that all these clips will be on social media or running through the news cycle without one ounce of verification to go along with it.

"They missed the camera, Karina. I don't know how much faith I have in the people we're blindly following."

"I wish I could say something different, Steele. We're stuck between a rock and a hard place." The car rumbles to life as Karina navigates the vehicle through some screaming stragglers and onto the main road.

"Elephant in the room . . . they pulled us in late. They pranced us in front of cameras for the country, if not the world, to see. We've got no experience working with the crime scene investigators and Victor was called in before us. If this were a crime movie, the audience would think we were being set up to take the fall. I don't like it."

"Could be. Could also be they're following orders just like the rest of us." Karina tries to lessen my concern. "But you're right. It doesn't feel good. There are several ways it could end. Best case, we get an unpaid vacation with our families. Worst case, we end up prosecuted and spend time in jail with people we put there. What could possibly go wrong?" Her nervous laughter tells me all I need to know. "It's the price of doing our jobs, Steele. We knew this when we signed up for this testosterone-filled field of police work."

Maybe she's right, but last time I checked murdering people is still against the law. It's our job to investigate the crimes to the best of our ability while keeping our integrity intact. Regardless of the plumbing my body showcases, I will never be someone's fall guy. Especially, when I've done nothing wrong.

Chapter Seven

The afternoon sun was nothing but a sliver of oranges and reds weaving through the tall buildings by the time we arrived at Sydney's office. Her pop music instrumental covers playlist filled the somewhat empty tech department. The skeleton crew doesn't seem to mind the noise intrusion as they bounce between their monitors as screens of data fly by. Their upper bodies are hunched forward, bringing their heads closer to the screens, probably to get a better look at the data with tired eyes. In my experience, it never helps.

"Steele!" Sydney pops out of her office, waving frantically. "You and Marlow, get in here toot sweet!" As quickly as she appeared, she slips back into her room as if sucked down into the depths by an underwater demon.

"I don't know whether to be impressed with her ancient colloquialisms or worried she's losing her mind," Karina whispers as we head into the unknown.

Sydney paces just inside the doorway. The music drowns out the mumbling as her hands wave about. Her head pops up, she freezes, and then raises both her arms in the air as if victorious . . . over something.

"My fellow earthlings!"

"Syd, I have to ask . . . are you okay? Taken anything we should know about? Maybe hit your head on something?" I hope my genuine concern for her well-being comes through.

"Oh. Yeah. Totally fine. Just been emptying my co-captain's fridge. We share things here, from jobs to what's inside that thing. Did you know he loves energy drinks? Like a lot of them. Since I had to work late, I figured why not try one or five?" Her hands wave over to the recycling bin overflowing with double-sized aluminum containers.

"Please tell me you didn't consume all of those."

"No, pfft, Steele. I'd be dead if I had that many. That's like . . . three days' worth. I mean if you consider each one is actually two servings, then I've had several servings, but nothing that made me lose my train of thought. Nope, I've been super clear on what we need to do."

She speeds away, stops by her keyboard, and begins tapping away. "Music off." As if by magic—or an AI device she has hidden somewhere in her office—the music stops.

"Is that allowed inside here?" Karina looks around the room for the offending control item.

"We created our own. Not like Alexa or anything; ours only works for the voices coded into it. I've been digging into Paula Grubbs. She's a pharmaceutical rep, wife, mother of two, and well-known in the community. Checked her work records. No complaints or write-ups. Doesn't mean there aren't any hidden away, just none readily available for us to find."

"That was quick," Karina tosses out as if looking for some nefarious reason for Sydney getting the information quickly.

"That's what got me. Like, this is all right there; no need for digging or pressing. It's all surface level, but it was still easier than normal to dig it up. So, I dug into their finances. Their marital assets and what not are all legitimate. Peter Grubb, the victim's husband, has several other accounts in his name only. I was hoping there would be charges or something leading us to a motive, but they just appear to be his private accounts. Nothing else."

"Okay, so our shot in the dark—hoping this would be a murder based on bad marital finances—is out the window. How are we doing with connecting our two victims? Beyond just a stamp on their foreheads."

"That's where it gets interesting." Sydney changes each monitor behind her to showcase different information.

"What are we looking at?" Karina appears as lost as I am.

"Okay, so here are Paula's finances." Sydney moves over to the first monitor. "There's nothing that would raise a massive red flag like donations to watch groups, but like clockwork, she made large withdrawals each week. Always the same amount, always during the same time frame. I dug a little deeper and found out those days her phone would ping off a tower here." Sydney points to the next screen with a small map.

"I know that area. Nothing but factories and industrial buildings. Everything is dead after six. Where could she go around there?" My eyes scan the map for any location that made sense for her to visit.

Sydney moves to the next monitor showing the website for Bernie's Bar & Grill.

"She travels all that way for a drink and a bite to eat? Why not stay local?" Karina looks over the map and the website. There's so much information, I fear it's getting lost in my mind, so I flip open my notebook and start jotting down trigger lines.

"I wanted to figure that out, so I kept digging. I found several email accounts attached to her name. The woman used varying versions of her own name, like an anagram, but she always used the same mailing address to verify her account. So, using that as my starting point, we could trace—"

"Wait, how did you get this without her cellphone or laptop?" I was seriously concerned if we could use this information to pursue the killer at this point.

"Let's just say I have friends who think you and Marlow are being wrongfully accused of negligence. They happen to work in high-level companies . . . and owed me favors. Leave it at that." Sydney moves to another monitor screen. "Anyway, once I got a list of the email addresses she used from my contact, I searched for them online . . . and found something. Most of them are throwaway ones for mailing list sign-ups and what have you. But I connected the last one to a phony Instagram account. It's a random happy profile that only posts positivity quote memes daily. She follows her kids, so it seems like she set this up strictly for spying or stalking . . . or bypassing the blocking process, but I digress. Since Instagram is owned by Facebook, I wanted to see if she attached the Instagram account to the other platform."

Sydney pauses, grabs the water bottle on her desk, and chugs about half of it before she stops. "That's when I hit pay dirt. Paula Grubbs not only had an account attached under the same email address, but she was part of several true crime groups. You know . . . the ones where they try to solve cold cases. Stuff like that. While there have been a few documented cases where these groups assisted law enforcement, that is obviously not the norm. In fact, several times they published the information of a suspect who wasn't even in the suspect pool."

"I've heard Cap talking about these people. Been a pain in his ass lately, but nothing to the point of murder. Was there anything posted or shared that would put a target on her back?"

I've seen documentaries on situations with the online true crime community. I've always believed it should be a last resort to get the public involved. Once you open that door, you no longer control how the information is handled or processed. The narrative swings wildly depending on the individual viewing it. Either way, it flies around the globe faster in the blink of an eye. Karina and I are experiencing the twisted version of it now. Once the opinion is out there, refuting it is futile. How do you fight the juggernaut of social media if you have limited money and resources?

"There could be. I mean, she replied several times, calling for arrests or investigations into people. To put it mildly, she let her opinions be known frequently. If there was a reason to get more sympathy or likes, it was on her feed." Sydney points to the profile on the monitor behind her desk. "At five o'clock, her posts become more nonsensical gibberish than anything else. Could be code to someone?"

"Or she's intoxicated." It would fit.

"But she posted about her sobriety a week ago. Paula was open about her addiction and the support group that helped her get sober."

"Could be, or she's lying for more sympathy," Karina adds, reading some of the posts on screen. "Based on what I'm seeing here, anything is possible with this woman."

"We need to visit that bar." It's a simple conclusion that the evidence has led me to make, but we could be stirring up a wasp nest. Especially if they're more people from the online groups in attendance.

"Wait, don't go running off just yet. I've got something else." Sydney changes all the screens behind her to a generic NYPD logo. She spins one of her monitors around, and the visual of the crime causes bile to burn up my throat.

"Did it air live?" The question tumbles out of my mouth as fear crawls up my body, digging its fangs into my chest. I can only imagine the new narrative alongside edited screen captures to back up their words.

"Based on the device Chalet dropped off, it doesn't appear to have that capability. Now if they shared a password or encoded the security footage to a set number of subscribers, it is theoretically possible."

"Well, I guess that's something, right?" Karina's words are barely above a whisper.

"I wish that was the end of it." Sydney spins her other monitor around. The latest social media posts by our perp are already live.

Before I can think better of it, I'm scrolling through the replies. Most are mundane ones screaming about our inability to do our jobs and a desire to have us fired. Others are darker and more threatening to our physical beings. How anyone can post thoughts about killing my dog all over social media and not have them removed is beyond me.

"Have they been reported?"

"Chalet ordered us not to report or flag any of them. He doesn't want the outward appearance of tampering, but they are investigating the most egregious ones. That being said, those who believe you two have been reporting them regularly. Sadly, they've told me the platforms consider these posts free speech." Sydney's hands wring together with negative energy.

"Investigating and reporting won't do a damn thing. People think they can do whatever they want online, and companies will protect them for the sake of their bottom line." The cynic in me crawls out of hiding. "Truth is, any replies people post in our defense could be detrimental in the long run. For example, if someone threatens to assault my wife in a comment and, the cops show up to the poster's house . . . it can be twisted that the post was a joke, freedom of speech and I'm harassing innocent individuals to make myself out to be the victim. Social media is a world with no context, where a paraphrased conversations destroy careers without evidence or validity. No matter what happens, we're going to lose this fight. That's what the whole meeting was about."

"Pretty much. I'm sorry. I really wish I could help you with this crap. The people that know you, that you've helped, they all know the truth. They're posting and defending you. You have people supporting you."

"Considering the volatility of our perpetrator, maybe that's not a good idea." Karina was right. It's not worth risking their lives and futures over this.

"Did you dig up anything on the posts threatening our families or Marlow and myself." I'm seething and trying to hold on to some semblance of control.

"Steele—"

"Sydney, we're collecting all information regarding possible suspects. As you have repeatedly proven, people rarely have one account to their name. Therefore, it is plausible to question if the original poster has other aliases they're using to bolster their diatribes. We could also find several associates the individual has enlisted to promote these posts. It could prove vital to our investigation. Worst case, if something happens to us or anyone else, you hand that list to the proper authorities. Not Chalet. Please."

I know this is a rather large ask, but I need to put things in play to protect my family. It's not pretty, but it's a contingency none the less.

"You got it. Just do me a favor and try not to put yourself in harm's way, okay? There's been too much death around here already."

The words hang in the air with a sense of finality. I glance at my watch once more before tapping it. My partner must understand my concern as she replies with a swift nod.

My phone buzzes with a message from Frankie.

Had dinner. Assume you'll be late. Be careful.

I shoot off a quick apology with a promise to be home before midnight and put my phone away.

"Smart idea about the list. Might even give us some leads." Karina and I both slip into the elevator. "Let's hope Sydney never has to pass it along. I'm telling you, Steele, I don't know how I'd handle it if this jackass goes after my family."

"You'd do what any normal human being would do." The elevator opens on the garage level. "You'd make sure that individual paid a heavy price."

"We might have different definitions of price."

"No. We'd both follow the law because our integrity runs deep. Beyond that, we'd end up in the gym beating the shit out of a punching bag to release all that anger. We don't have the luxury of doing anything else, Karina."

My thoughts wander to other things as the SUV pulls out into traffic. Why would a middle-aged woman want to take part in a true crime group? Paula had a solid career, a seemingly good family life, a roof over her head, and all the other creature comforts people strive for. Why get involved in cases that could put all of that at risk? A suspect or someone they wrongfully accused could file lawsuits, or worse, try to hurt them physically. What need does this behavior fill?

"I can hear the gears turning, Steele."

"I just can't understand why someone with a life people would love to have would get involved with these groups."

"There have always been these crime enthusiasts. It's just more prominent since the people were given access to instant information. Add to that the DNA and ancestry sites, and there's a lot of access for those who want to make connections." The GPS screams about traffic ahead. Our time of arrival creeps closer to a fully packed bar.

"You don't worry about those wanting their fifteen minutes of fame as much as the one who solved a case the police failed to close?"

"Maybe, but then you'd have to blame all the evil characters in movies with sad backstories. Truthfully, I don't know. Psychopath? Sadist? Frankie or that Grayson guy would know more."

"I'd rather not ask him anything." Just because I trust my wife doesn't remove the vile taste of jealousy from my mouth. "Regardless, if the actions of those in the group chat backfires—"

"Yeah, I hate to break it to you, but do people really think about that? How many people think before they speak?" Karina cuts my words short, but she's not wrong. We've gotten an influx of online-based complaints that should be actionable, but the law is far behind in cases like this.

"People should. Every action has an equal and opposite reaction. It's the big picture, you know? Sure, whatever the average person posts doesn't change the grand scheme of the planet. But you'll forever change the person your post mentions. Fabrications paint people with a layer of pain they can never wash off. To do that to someone innocent . . . it's reprehensible."

"Yeah, but sometimes they're not innocent, Steele."

"Maybe, but we live in an innocent before proven guilty society. If you go after someone out of revenge or what you perceive as a wrong, it changes everything. It will change people moving forward. The truth will be buried under the morass of fiction, preventing people from reaching out for help. If we're lucky, they'll talk to people around them who might convince them to talk to us. But in the end, society will falter and buckle under the weight of falsehoods. So forgive me if it doesn't seem logical to defame someone for your personal benefit."

"You're contrarian, Steele. You see the bigger picture with the long-term effects. Most people aren't like that. They think about instant gratification and the now. It's precisely why I don't want my kids having social media, but here we are. We'll figure out Paula Grubbs's motives when we get more information and evidence. Until then, we go one step at a time."

The conversation dies as Karina flips on the sirens to bypass the rush-hour parking lot to get to our destination. I wonder if people really understand the power they wield behind a computer screen. Do they know the next thing they tweet out could change markets or cause an uproar? Maybe or maybe not. I've always believed people were fickle. They go whichever way suits their best interests, desires, and wallet. It's not the most ethical or morally responsible thing to do, but that rarely stops them. I prefer to lean on scientific evidence. That is something that has yet to fail me. People fail me too often.

***

Bernie's Bar & Grill sits at the end of the block, with parking in the back. The streetlights have cameras on the poles, which is helpful. Looking at the brick façade and tinted windows with neon signs advertising a few beer companies, it feels like your average bar. I send Sydney a quick message asking her to investigate it further. Maybe she can cross-reference the footage from here with the clips we've taken from the previous crime scenes for something. Could be a long shot, but what have we got to lose?

"Quick Google search says it's a family-owned, respectable establishment." Karina holds the door open for us to walk inside.

"Could be, but what really defines normal?"

"You're a hard sell, Steele. Seriously."

It's not as packed as it could be, but still rather full. The mixed crowd of families, single, middle-aged patrons, and some teenagers laughing in the back near the pool table lowers my anxiety a bit. Maybe Paula just came here once a week to catch up with some friends. Maybe she wasn't breaking her sobriety. If she was getting blitzed, wouldn't this type of crowd report it?

"Can I get you folks something to drink?" The bartender smiles as he wipes down the table.

Karina holds up her badge while I show the bartender an image of Paula Grubbs on my cell. "Have you seen this woman recently? Maybe this week? Would you know if she was served alcohol during the time she was here?"

"I'm sorry. I don't think I'm at liberty to say anything." He dries his hands on a rag and motions to one server on the floor to cover the bar. "Let me get my boss." He walks away from us, down the length of the bar, before entering the back office.

"What's your take on him?" Karina leans her back against the bar, surveying the room.

"Just someone doing their job who's not up for rocking the boat." There's a one-way window behind the bar with the bar's logo. It's rather tacky, but it must make it easier to keep your eyes on the outside room.

"Same. Clothes are neat, form fitting, probably for more tips. No noticeable marks on his arms or discoloration of his fingernails. He's obviously taking care of himself."

"You investigating him as a perp or looking for a date?" The low chuckle breaks free from my chest before I can stop it.

"Investigating, Steele. That's just how I see things."

"You never describe female counterparts that way. At least not that I can remember."

The office door opens, killing our conversation right away. The same bartender walks out and lifts the small cutout down at the end of the bar. The half tilt of his head gets us moving through the opening and into the back area. The click of the door closing behind us echoes in the soundproof room.

The room feels smaller than it is. That could be due to the large file cabinets looming over us from the side walls and a massive wooden desk in front of us. Everything about the layout screams villain in a horror film. A middle-aged woman sits behind the desk, her hands folded neatly on top. There's nothing on the desktop, which seems abnormal. It's current working hours, the boss is in the office hiding, and there's not a shred of work being done.

"Malik said you have some questions about a patron?" she asks.

"Yes, I'm Agent Marlow and this is my partner—"

"Jasmine Steele, the lesbian detective who broke the Garrison case. I've read about you." That line and tone were more of a warning than anything else. Her body language is neutral, but the tone of her comment was not. If I wasn't more aware, I'd say she was a Stepford wife, complete with perfect smile hiding a more sinister intent.

"I wouldn't believe everything you read."

"What shouldn't I believe? That you're a detective that attempts to do her job or that you're gay?"

Interesting twist. "Within everything we read are embellishments to sell subscriptions. Someone needs to sort through the pork to ensure they find the truth, but that requires a desire to find it. I mean, most news broadcasts say they're entertainment in the credits." In a case like this, honesty is the only thing I can work with. The NYPD and press went wild with how amazing I was in the aftermath of Garrison. Awards, interviews

. . . It was fun for a week. After that, I hated all the hot air being blow up my ass. It's interesting how quickly the tides can turn.

Her laughter explodes within the small space. "Oh, that's so rich. I fucking love it. I might have to use that in the future. Until then, sit, please." She dabs the corner of her eyes to wipe away the tears from her laughter. "Seriously, you're a damn comedian, acting all serious with the 'media is bad' bullshit. Damn, I needed that laugh."

"I live to serve." My disdain for this woman continues to grow with every passing moment.

"Miss . . ." Karina leads, hoping the owner will fill in the gap.

"Dobbs, Evelyn Dobbs," she mocks. "Owner, bartender, and sometimes cook. But enough with the theatrics. What do you want with Paula? She's a wonderful human being, loved by everyone in this place. If you're looking for dirt, you won't find it here."

"We're just looking for some information." I can tell Karina's trying to calm the tension.

"What my partner is trying to say is Mrs. Grubbs is dead." I'm done trying to placate people. We need answers, and playing games has gotten us nowhere.

Evelyn's face deconstructs from the firm, defiant expression to one of loss and fear. "That asshole of a cheating husband," she spits out.

"What do you mean by that?" I've got my notepad out, while Karina pushes the conversation forward.

"Did you look up that freak? He's dipped his pecker into more pools than birds migrating south for the winter. Paula was talking about a divorce, taking the piece of shit for everything he's worth. We had a plan to expose all his fetishes for the world to see and more. If he found out about it, there's no telling what he'd do to cover up his . . . pleasures."

"I appreciate the information, but please explain this plan of yours?" I know exactly what my partner is doing. We have a sworn statement from Mr. Grubbs. If we have something that could blow a hole in it, then we have a suspect to investigate. I shoot a quick text message to Sydney with a 911 designation for expediency. If she finds something connecting Peter to Doctor Boxletter, then we'd really have something to go on.

"She had one of those tag devices hidden in his car. We tracked him to the airport on his trips, always in the same long-term parking lot."

"Mr. Grubbs was on a business trip."

"Yeah, but when we checked his travel itinerary, something looked off. The fool saved his passwords on his browser. Paula logged in as him and we found out the truth. There were a lot of business trips that he went on. For some of them, he had no flight information in his account. Now, I know the business flies him out, but he was always about the points. Paula said he convinced his bosses to reimburse him so he could bank those airline miles. Since he'd never met me, I followed him. I recording the bastard meeting some chick in a hotel lobby near the airport."

"How many times?"

"Three times a month that I know of. Couldn't follow him all day, every day. Just when I had coverage and Paula gave me a heads-up."

"When you followed him, did he always meet the same woman?"

"Yeah, why?"

"Normally, a full-fledged romance might require more attention than just a few meetings a month." I understand where Karina's thought process is, but I didn't think it was necessary to bring it up.

"I know what I saw."

"We'll take a deeper look into Mr. Grubbs, but we really need to know what your plan was to expose him." While the information about the affair is interesting, I'd rather have Sydney dig into factual details from the pieces Evelyn has shared. If we're going to point the finger at Mr. Grubbs, we need more than just speculation. We need to know what they planned to do, if he knew it, and if it was enough to warrant revenge.

"Paula and I met in a Facebook group. The two of us hit it off and chatted all the time online. We'd try to solve all these cold cases, just for fun. We never expected it to go anywhere. But when this stuff came up about her husband, she reached out to me right away. Peter's family never thought Paula was good enough for him, always ripping her down. We wanted to gather as much damming evidence as we could. Then we'd enlist the members of our group. They'd help us plaster it all over the internet, tag his socials, his job, his family . . . anyone and everyone we could."

"Was that the reason for her five p.m. trips?" I ask, scanning my notes for something that would help me during questioning.

"Yeah. That, some drinks, and company. Look, Paula was struggling a lot. She was a great mom; she loved those kids with everything she had. She worked her ass off in a job she hated to help give the kids a good life. I adored her, but Paula was so lost. Some days she went further down the bottle than the day before, but she was never out of control."

"Were you aware that Paula was in an alcohol support group? Did she ever bring that up?" The question is rhetorical. We both know she didn't. If she did, Evelyn would have knowingly contributed to the woman falling deeper into addiction. I'm sure Evelyn went into the friendship with open eyes, but her own personal desire for revenge . . . well, it blinded her to her hand in Paula Grubbs's destruction. The tunnel vision of the end goal regardless of the means is morally reprehensible.

But nothing warranting a meeting with the district attorney or jail time. Even if I wanted to pull their liquor license, I doubt it would be possible. The only ramifications people like this face are karma and guilt. If the latter is even possible within the human being.

"No . . .Paula never . . . I wouldn't have—"

"But you did, Miss Dobbs." Karina places her hand on the edge of the shaken woman's desk. "Is there anything else you can think of that might help us? Could she have other enemies that would want her dead?"

"Maybe the people online. They come to our group to proclaim their innocence, replying to our posts. A few of them stood out, and the moderators reported them, but it's still an open group, you know? That's why we have fake accounts. To protect ourselves from the crazies out there."

The irony isn't lost on me. "Maybe you should stop living online and start appreciating the real world." I toss the snarky remark over my shoulder as I storm out of the bar. I hear Karina asking Evelyn to call if something else comes up, but I don't expect anything more from the woman.

We walk in silence to the car. Logan once used social media platforms to spread the truth about Irving Garrison, effectively shining a light on his tendrils of criminal activity. He didn't fabricate anything and published everything we were legally capable of releasing. No lies, just cold hard facts. But that was then.

The police continue to use the new platforms as a way to bring attention to cases, potential suspects, and whatever else they need. Every notification goes out with the best of intentions, but like Karina and I know all too well, you can't trust anonymous people online. As the moments tick past, I'm struggling to see the value in any of it.

Chapter Eight

By the time my tired body fell through the front door, the house was dim and quiet. My hunger had fled Hangrytown station and transitioned to full on screaming-for-sustenance mode hours ago. Frankie must have known I would be starving at this point. Wrapped in tinfoil, with reheating instructions on top, was a plate of food. I know my wife well enough to recognize an olive branch when I see one.

I was worried our conversation earlier in the day left too many things unsaid. It was unfinished, rudely interrupted by the outside world. But coming home to this treat just affirmed we're moving in the right direction. I slept on our lumpy couch to ensure I wouldn't wake Frankie or Chase up. While my back protested this morning, my soul felt rejuvenated.

The house was barely awake when I returned from visiting Frankie's favorite bakery. Fresh coffee, donuts, and a Danish for my wife. In a wave of nostalgia, I snagged several plain rolls to go with seedless raspberry jam and butter. Just like Sunday mornings with my Oma, I shared it with the two of them. Much to my annoyance, my phone buzzed before I could wish anyone a good morning. I left a note and went into work.

The image of the breakfast spread at my house makes my mouth water as I chew on a tasteless soggy bagel from the cart up the street. At least my coffee is warm, albeit too hot to consume at the moment. Karina chuckles every time I take a bit or try to sip my beverage. She lips her designer reusable mug to her lips and moans at whatever fancy roast she's enjoying.

"Those sounds should be illegal," I mutter, begging my coffee to cool down.

"If you'd asked, I would have brought you some. If there's one thing to spoil yourself with, it's a good cup of coffee." Karina smirks as the elevator jerks on its way down to Victor's office.

"I left a perfectly good meal with lovely coffee at home. Because you texted me." Until I can get some caffeine into me, the sleepiness of my voice will remain. "But I would never turn down a coffee. So, tomorrow. Please."

"Nightmares?" Her question isn't out of the blue. We both know sleep has been hit or miss since the beginning of the pandemic. It's just the nature of the beast.

"First night of silence. You?"

"There's a reason I need coffee." Her voice seems almost sad, like she's alone this time. As if one of us is better for not hearing the wails of pandemic survivors' families.

"It was one night, Karina. I doubt it's gone. One step at a time, remember?"

The doors open and my partner puts on a brave face. Victor's lab is quiet, save for the loud noises of him eating his breakfast burrito.

"Ladies, thank you for coming in so early!" he says mid-chew, and it's rather disgusting.

"You made it sound urgent. What'd you find?" Karina diverts my attention from his chewing to the task at hand.

Victor takes a quick sip of his coffee before placing everything down on his desk. He pulls open drawer number five and slides the metal slab with Paula Grubbs's body. The y-incision looks pristine. I remember Victor demanding the best of himself as he learned his sutures. When Henry died, the accident did a number on his body, but the coroner's butchering was much worse. The Frankenstein-like stitching made my stomach turn.

I argued with Victor's boss. I wanted to know what he'd done to Henry and Belinda, why they looked so horrible. Their answer was cold and dismissive. It was because of metal, blunt force trauma, and more. He was not responsible for it. I filed a complaint with his supervisor, and Victor started practicing. He knew how difficult it was for me to see my family like that. At least something good came from the tragedy.

Once the man retired, Victor took over the department with a whole different outlook. Every person who came through those doors was to be treated with the utmost respect. The life might be lost, but there were other lives counting on the department doing a proper job. Even after years of toiling around in the basement, Victor continues to thrive down here. He still talks to victims as he runs through all the necessary procedures. I wish I had his temperament sometimes.

"I sent blood, tissue, and stomach contents to Doctor Brown for analysis. I noticed bruising around her chest, forearms, and abdominal area."

"Doc, are you suggesting she fought back?"

Karina continued to ask questions as my eyes scanned over the victim's body. The dark purple patches on her chest lead me to believe someone pressed down on the victim from on top of them. But without Victor's final report, I can't be sure.

"I don't know what the victim did before her passing, Agent Marlow. I can tell you the broken nails and bruising would lean in that direction, yes. Like we discussed at the scene, her pupils were pinpoints, and her lips were blue. I found white residue between the victim's teeth, so I swabbed her mouth and sent it to the lab."

"Can you give us a cause of death?" I scribble about the bruising in my notepad.

"Without toxicology, I couldn't make an official statement."

"Look, Vic, I know you don't want to make a judgement call, but it would really help us out right now."

Victor pauses, then looks between Karina and me before walking away from the drawer. "If I had to make a logical conclusion based on the blue tint to her pale skin and other factors, I'd lean on this being a drug overdose."

"The bottles at the scene would support that assessment." Karina's right on the money, but the bigger questions is if she ingested the pills willingly or not. "The defensive wounds might be mean someone tried to force the pills down her throat." My partner didn't miss a beat.

"When it comes down to murder, Agent Marlow, I truly believe human beings capable of doing unimaginable things. So, if you're asking if your suggestion is possible, I'd say of course it is."

"If that was the case, how long before the drugs would take effect?" If we're following Karina's train of thought, this would be the next logical question.

"That would depend on any number of factors." Victor grabs another bite of his burrito. I wait patiently for him to get the hint and elaborate on his previous statement. "We know the pills were orally ingested, but if the victim had a full stomach, the absorption rate would be slower. If crushed and mixed with something, it might disperse at a greater speed. Then we'd have to consider height, weight, tolerance . . . There are too many factors to make an honest conclusion."

Victor leans back on his desk as he munches away on his breakfast. I look over at Karina, whose eyes remain on the victim. My brain can put together what I think happened to Paula Grubbs, but several questions still remain. How did the killer get into the house? How did they get the medication in the victim without her waking up? If she was conscious and restrained, would that explain the bruise pattern? How did they set up the camera? The unknowns are piling up more than the evidence.

"What about the item buried deep in her throat?" At this point, the perpetrator is doing all the heavy lifting, from killing to connecting the two murders. I want to connect the dots to ensure we're not being led on a wild-goose chase. If nothing else, to rule out a copycat killer. I don't need Chalet and the rest of the FBI questioning the process.

"That detail I can definitely say was the same theta symbol." He crumbles up the empty tinfoil and tosses it into the garbage. "I can tell you the stamp was administered postmortem as well. I uploaded all relevant images to both victims' files."

Another detective enters the room and asks for Victor to step outside. I honestly prefer it right now. It gives Karina and me a chance to bounce ideas off one another.

"I'd say we can officially conclude these two murders are connected. If that was still up for debate, anyway." Karina watches the two men outside the glass doors. Their body language and arm movements show the tension between them.

"If the killer meant it literally, the stamp makes sense. Death is a form of payment. Considering Victor's statement about the time it was applied and the lack of smearing, it seems this was the last part in staging the scene. If they were fighting back, I doubt the two stamps would be as clean as it was on both victims."

"Not to go against the doc here, but if a person is incapacitated, it's feasible to stamp their foreheads as well," Karina counters.

"I don't know. Why would the killer knock them unconscious and stop? If you're trying to kill someone, do you give them the opportunity to wake up and possibly call the police? Unless this was some kind of torture scenario, I think they'd focus on finishing the job."

"Doesn't this one feel a bit over the top?" Karina walks around the body, pointing to various bruises and marks. "We have to assume she was a hostage for a good amount of time. The killer force-feeds her narcotics, holds her down until they take effect, and then waits for hours until death? It seems completely farfetched and just plain odd. Don't you think?"

"I don't know what to think." That was the truth. Doctor Boxletter's body left no defensive wounds. There was no forced entry into her home, but there were two glasses on the counter and the camera was hacked. The attacker knew the victim and the layout of her place. "They have to stalk their victims, but how?"

Victor storms in with the other detective hot on his heels. "Ladies, I apologize for the intrusion, but I need the office, please."

"Of course. Let us know if you find anything else." Karina heads out of the room.

I give Victor a worrying glance, but he waves me off. He grabs his cell phone while the other detective continues laying into him. Karina holds the elevator as I hesitate, leaving Victor alone with the barrage of attacks from the other guy. He finally drops his phone and answers the male in a calm, steady voice.

My phone beeps in my pocket. It's a message from Vic: *He's a dick, all good. Still on for game night this weekend? Lil's making her famous chocolate chip cookies.* I look back up at my friend, who continues his tense conversation. I make a mental note to check in on him later, but for now, Karina and I have work to do.

***

The familiar stomping ground of our rickety desks and old file cabinets normally comforted my mind during stressful cases. The new LED lights hanging from the ceiling give off vibes of an unrelenting sun as my eyes beg for sunglasses. It also highlights the dank environment we work in. But my body will adjust; it always does.

Karina digs through the files of our two victims. The FBI wanted us to use their fancy offices, but we couldn't be sure if the walls had eyes or ears. Instead, we chose our home, where we've got a positive track record for closing cases. The Feds protested profusely, but Karina shut them down quickly with a wave of her hand as the elevator doors closed.

We're not here to make friends with them, Steele. We're here to solve cases without interference from those trying to undermine our careers. My partner's words hung in the air the entire trip back to the precinct.

Karina scribbles *What We Know* on top of the whiteboard. She jots down the obvious information currently available to us. After a few minutes, she's filled in the victims' names, ages, locations, cause of death, and other minor details on the left side of the board.

I sort through a stack of printed pages, looking for the social media posts corresponding to the crimes. The magnets hold them on the board in order of release and according to which victim they correspond to.

"That's all we have at the moment?" Karina sits on the edge of her desk next to me. "That's really a crappy way to start, isn't it?"

I didn't need to voice a reply. She was right. This case was a supreme pile of nothing to work with. All these voices barking in our ear wanting a quick resolution to something with no shape or foundation other than bodies in the morgue and circumstantial connections. Nothing that the district attorney would appreciate if we presented it to her.

"Manner of death is different. Locations are different. Victims hold no physical traits in common. From a physical standpoint, these two cases feel like two separate attacks." I hope Sydney is digging into the bar, the affair, and other digital fragments. If we can't pinpoint a specific type of victim the killer preys upon, we need to understand the motive behind the attacks.

Karina walks over to the board and looks over the list under Paula Grubbs. "What about the alleged affair? Evelyn alluded to a stockpile of evidence that could bankrupt Peter Grubbs. Financial gain and hiding secrets . . . always excellent motives for murder."

"True, if we go on the assumption the cases are independent of one another. Considering the stamp on the foreheads, they could be connected or a copycat. If Mr. Grubbs planned to kill his wife and used Boxletter as a diversion, how did he know her? Did he subscribe to the online streaming service? How did he gain access to Boxletter's apartment when they rarely showed their faces or connected to customers beyond the digital landscape? Then there's the idea of a clean digital trace. How did he scrub his tracks?" The words hang in the air for a few moments. A thought pops into my head, one so obvious I'm angry at myself for not thinking about it sooner. I dial Sydney and put her on speakerphone.

"Steele, how are you? I don't have much time to talk. What's up?" Sydney doesn't sound like herself. Something's off.

"Syd, I need you to do a few checks for me. First, when the team searches through the video footage, can you have them start a week or two before the murders? Second, can you look through the video footage from both cameras again? See when the files started transferring elsewhere or just started recording in the Grubbs case."

"Of course, I'll tell you how that new sandwich place is. I'm headed out to lunch shortly, so I'll call you after." The call disconnects, leaving us confused. That didn't sound like Sydney at all.

"Either Sydney is on a sugar rush from those energy drinks or someone's watching her every move. The latter doesn't bode well for the two of us." Karina's words add to the bleak tension around us.

"How the mighty have fallen." The whispered words hang in the air. The department used us as poster kids for whatever they needed to showcase. If there was a fundraiser, Karina's or my face were plastered on promotional materials reminding citizens of our success rate. Tech event, Sydney's smile was a recruiter's dream. The same went for Will and the military outreach.

Or course, you're only valuable if the viewers think you are. With this new social media blitz, the NYPD looks like they propped up another shady officer who worked on several high-profile cases. The many posts Sydney sent our way not only called our ethics into question, but all our convictions as well. The added pressure on the court system made my blood boil. It was unnecessary and all because of one person's opinions without factual context.

"We need to focus on what we have in front of us." Or lack thereof. "We met Grubbs at the crime scene. His emotions felt genuine, even if he is a cheating piece of crap."

"Maybe Frankie should interview him. She might give us better insight into the man."

"No, she's too close to the situation. Sadly, we're going to need Grayson to handle this." I hate suggesting we use his expertise, but Karina knows I'm right.

Karina calls the man but spins around when Frankie's voice comes through the receiver. "Hey, Karina. Lewis is unavailable right now, but he told me to answer. You're on speaker."

"Um . . ." She puts her phone on speaker as well so the two of us can hear everything. I'm aware Karina doesn't want to get into the middle of an argument, but I'm wondering why Frankie is with him. "I needed help with an interview and was curious if he was available to handle it."

"Hey, Mr. Grayson, thanks for the breakfast. See you later, Mom." Chase's voice comes through loud and clear.

"I think your mother—" But the door slams before Chase can hear Frankie's reply.

The man is at my house. Early in the morning, and unavailable to answer his own phone. He can hear and reply but has no free hands to . . . I have to stop my train of thought before it goes down a really dark road.

"I'll be able to handle it later this afternoon. Hand me the jam, Franks." I can hear things moving around the table. The simple actions enrage me even more. I'm sure this is the response he desires, but I doubt Frankie would appreciate it. "Is that okay with you, Agent Marlow? Or do you need to run it by the detective first?"

"There's no issue here, Grayson. I'm happy you're enjoying breakfast." The seething tone burns up my chest like a dragon's fire. "Agent Marlow will send you the pertinent details about the individual. I'll notify Chalet and Toby that we're waiting on your profile before we can proceed. Have a good day." I hit the end call button once again, wishing I could slam a handset down for effect. Or stress release.

"That was a bit of a dick move. Amazing, but still a dick move. I'll give the bosses the details and ensure they're aware of Grayson's involvement. I suggest you call your wife and clear the air."

I press my thumbs into the top of my eye sockets near my nasal bridge. The eruption of pain begs for an ice pack or some painkillers. Neither of which I have with me.

"I know she wouldn't cheat on me, but this man is stepping over all kinds of boundaries, and I really want to knee him in the crotch . . ." I press my thumbs harder into my skin and focus on my breathing. "The conversation with Frankie can wait. Okay, the only connections we have are a stamp, a piece of paper, and social media posts." I continue the conversation, stopping my partner from leaving our basement dwelling.

"From the killer and our two victims, yes. But Sydney's team still hasn't found any correlation between the fake profile posts. Obviously, we're connected to it, but beyond the narrative, online crime solvers, and political pressure from outside sources, what connects our victims?" Karina's frustration pours out, and I can't blame her.

"Not leaving this room?" I ask, and Karina looks confused but nods her head. "Maybe we are the connection?"

"I don't follow."

"Well, it's like these social media groups. Everyone posts their opinion in a way where it might be true, but you're not one hundred percent sure. So, you follow it and do your own research. You dive deeper into the rabbit hole of information based on the one flawed account. Before you know it, all these pseudo-news places back it up and you can no longer see why you doubted it in the first place. It's classic cult leader tactics. They use a grain of truth, which could be what we're missing, and prey on genuine issues—actual fears. Man, Frankie would have a field day with the psychological trauma social media could cause."

"And you're saying we are that grain of truth."

"Maybe. Remember. we've been part of the governmental machine of success for so long, who knows where we've been led or misled. Hell, people sue private companies all the time because they're blocked, suspended, or whatever for speaking their lies. The world's gone mad, and people profit daily from it."

"I don't see who stands to profit by defaming us so publicly." Karina doesn't seem convinced, and frankly, neither am I. My thought was a stretch with no backing other than the original poster saying we failed them. Was that truth? Was it just close enough to where we're running down the rabbit hole making things worse?

"Everyone profits in this case. Blogs with ads, clickbait links . . . all of them post new, even more outrageous claims against the two of you. It makes them money and backs up the narrative." Sydney's voice cuts through our conversation. "Sorry for interrupting, but I was hoping we could talk before the big bosses get down here."

She drops into her old chair, flips her laptop open, and starts plugging away at things. Every now and again, she looks up at our whiteboard, but stays silent. Karina calls Chalet from the corner of the room, whispering. She's never done that before, but right now, I can't be concerned. I send Frankie a message asking about breakfast and if she's okay.

"She done or . . ." Karina asks me after completing her call.

"Gonna tell me why you were talking so low I couldn't hear? Not keeping anything from me?"

"You're being paranoid, Steele. You know we're playing good cop, bad cop with Chalet."

"Nope, wasn't aware. How did he take it?"

"Unhappy. He wants faster results, but he understands our desire to exclude Mr. Grubbs." She motions to Sydney. "Did she just meander over here to feel nostalgic? Change of scenery kind of thing?"

"No, I came here to help you two." Sydney cuts in. "Look, this case has a lot of circumstantial stuff, and everything's digital, so it might be hard to see the larger imprint. With Doctor Grayson's help, we built a digital timeline with several points of interest. I know you don't like him, but the man's a genius, Steele."

"Yeah, well . . ." What was there to say? Sydney's had more experience with the man. My phone buzzes with a heart emoji and a *thank you* message from Frankie. The simple acknowledgement calms my nerves. "Could I arrest him for being an ass?"

"Not last time I checked." Karina laughs. "Don't let him get under your skin, Steele. They're just colleagues."

"Didn't say they were more now, but they did date in the past. Just feeling insecure about it all. Plus, he ate the breakfast I got her. I wanted to have breakfast with my family."

"I say make a plan and have a day with the fam. If you're waiting for crime to stop to get a day off, you'll be in the grave before that happens," Sydney answers, staring at the screen.

"Okay, enough about that." I grab my notepad and flip through some older pages. "You said the killer must have used a virtual private network, right? Something about showing up anywhere in the world? I don't get it, but how does that relate to our case?"

"Yeah, better known as a VPN. In simple terms, when I want to watch out-of-state football games, I log in and make it appear as if I'm actually in Miami. If you want to watch something on streaming that is only available in the US, but you're in Canada, you just use your VPN to make it appear as if you're here and bam . . . Full access."

"How to be a criminal one-oh-one. Hide your tracks." Karina laughs. "Reason number whatever to keep my kids away from computers unsupervised."

"Normally, I'd be looking all over, but with the cameras and computers . . . I found this account was originally set up right here in the five boroughs." Sydney spins her laptop around. The screen displays some code, dates, times, and several other items that I can't decipher.

"What are we looking at?"

"I asked a friend of mine to do a bit more digging than we at the NYPD have access to. I know none of this could be used in court, but my buddy traced where the account was created to a small coffee shop in Brooklyn. I know it's not much, but maybe it adds to their local haunts? Or maybe a triangulation of where they hunt their victims?"

"Okay, so how do we use this to our advantage without having to prove where we found it?" I can't believe I'm considering this. "Considering our crime scenes were so far apart and no witnesses came forward regarding seeing anyone leaving the area, we could assume they drove to both locations. Parking in the city is rather difficult, but if you plan accordingly, you can get something up there. There was plenty of parking in the Grubbses neighborhood. So, we focus on vehicles."

"The team's currently scouring all footage like you requested." Sydney's words remind me the teams are looking for people on foot and any cars in the area at the time.

"So, have your buddy pull footage from around the Brooklyn location. It will help us narrow down the color, make, and model. Then we compare," Karina adds, jotting her thoughts on the whiteboard. "It's hard to get around without using tolls to get out of the city. Those cameras should be available to us."

"Sure there are, but it's easier to take tolls if they're the faster route," Sydney replies.

"Unless they want to be tracked." Both stop talking and look at me. "It sounds insane, but let's break it down rationally. Whoever is behind these murders continues to clean up their digital trail. It's not perfect, because Syd seems to find something, but for you and me, Karina, it works. We use all this tech to our advantage, but we're the boots on the ground. What if they want us to find where they're going or came from? Maybe they want to prove that we're so wrapped up in the higher end of technology that we missed the little things."

"Okay, calling cameras higher-end technology is funny to me. But I can see your point. Even if we found the car on all these cameras, we'd still need to prove the same driver was behind the wheel each time. Considering the tolls are all cashless now, the perp could disguise who they are." Sydney leans back, folds her arms, and looks lost in thought.

"True, but could they hide their profile? The way they sit in the car? The signature physical points you can extract from photos? You've connected dots like these before," I ask Karina, knowing the FBI worked on several cases like this in the past.

"We have, but it doesn't mean that people understand it or even believe it, Steele." Karina lifts her marker to the board and jots down the Brooklyn coffee shop. "But we have to try. Sydney, dig up whatever you can. I've got a friend in the FBI who might help."

"Do you have a warrant yet? If we find the vehicle, we can cross-reference it with subscribers and members of those groups." Her hopeful tone isn't lost on Karina and me. My partner pressed Chalet to investigate getting those lists, but he said he'd handle it. Since then, we've heard nothing.

"We put in the request, but we can't bank on it coming through." Karina's disdain for Chalet is clear, but what she plans to do about it isn't. She jots down a number and hands it to Sydney. "Just call that number, ask for Michelle, and tell her I sent you. In the meantime, we'll keep pressing Chalet for help."

"Can you have them go through all the group social media posts? See if there is one that both parties commented on? There has to be some crossover between those groups, right?"

"I'll try." Sydney turns off her computer and folds it closed. She pulls it tightly to her chest. "I'll keep you posted once I have more to share."

She's made it clear the conversation is over but makes no attempt to leave. It's as if she has more to say but is frightened to say it.

"Syd? What's going on? You okay?"

"I've been wondering how you two were doxxed, but no one seems to be doing anything about it. Like no one is showing up to your homes, following your kids to school . . . whatever. It just seems off."

"And this is a bad thing?" I fail to follow Sydney's train of thought. Considering the cases we've lived through, this is a blessing.

"Normally, I'd say it would be, but if this thread . . . this whole profile was that prolific, the outcry would be stronger than it is. Even with those fake news sites, blog posts, and all of it. It's too calm. In the past, they'd be outside the precinct daily, making noise. Your families would be in hiding. The response doesn't fit."

"Unless a lot of those accounts are fake."

"That's my thought. It could also be that the department has subtly stepped in. But what if someone on the inside released everything to the public?"

"Why would they do that?" Karina is invested now. I'm sure she's wondering if her serial killer of an ex-husband was involved.

"Only those with access to our files have access to our cell phones issued by the department. Normally, we give witnesses and victims our desk numbers. Your emails are readily available, and anyone searching the tax database can find out where you live, but the cell phones keep giving me an uneasy feeling. Since the Garrison case, they're unlisted."

"Can your friend dig into that a bit more?" Initially, I wasn't worried, but now that Sydney lays it all out, I need to know.

"Yeah." She gets up but remains in a protective stance. "I went to talk to the captain before coming down here. Special Agent Chalet, Assistant Director Toby. and some other people in suits were in his office. The conversation looked heated, and I came straight down here. I don't know if it means anything, but whatever was going on didn't look pretty."

"I'm sure it isn't." Karina turns her attention back to our notes as if they will change to something more concrete. "I'm sure public relations isn't thrilled with the two of us, either. We just need to keep working and focus on what we can control."

"Yeah . . . Your friends have your back, okay? We'll do what we can to help you both. No questions asked." With that, she disappears into the basement stairwell.

"I guess our time is running out." My heavy words hang in the air, strangling us both with reality.

"We'll get to the bottom of things." Karina's reassurance is cut apart by the loud ding of the elevator's arrival.

The doors bounce open as a swarm of locusts crawls out of the box. Their eyes dart back and forth between Karina and me. Choosing their next meal? Deciding which one of us is the easiest to take down? Considering the crowding of these pests violates the rules in place for the rest of us, it's not surprising. Those in power positions always do as they wish. The rest of us follow the rules or get fired.

"Detective Steele, Agent Marlow, I can see you've both used these offices instead of the Bureau's." Assistant Director Toby holds his arms behind his back in front of his gaggle of friends. Almost like a general waiting to give the order to attack.

"Yes, sir." Karina stands in front of our notes, hands behind her back, trying to keep their eyes focused on her. "We prefer the solitude, sir. Helps the thought process."

"I see. And how is the investigation proceeding?"

That's the million-dollar question, isn't it? Karina runs her hand over her writing of the coffee shop, smearing it before moving to the side of the board.

"As well as can be expected, given the circumstances, sir. Currently, we're waiting for Doctor Brown to return her findings regarding the most recent victim. Beyond that, our physical evidence is rather limited. Detective Locke continues to dig through the digital signatures, from the social media profiles to all the video we can find, but nothing stands out."

"The tech team is also scouring the toll cameras and local ones related to both crime scenes to see if there's any vehicle connecting the two crime scenes. It might be possible to find where the killer originates from. That would give us an area to investigate." I'm sure the assistant director is aware of these details, if not more informed. If I'm being honest, this seems like a test of our ability to work as a team.

"We live in a city with one of the most extensive public transportation systems. What makes you think the individual drove?" Chalet asks from his perch on the back wall.

"While your assessment might be true, it seems unlikely. While we are working under the impression the individual wants to be caught, that massive system doesn't extend into suburbia, New Jersey. If the person traveled via train to the nearest station, they would need to drive or walk to the second victim's home. That seems illogical." Karina's voice is firm but cordial. She's still trying to impress Chalet.

"While it might seem odd to drive uptown when one could easily disappear into the subway system, consider if they're wearing a full coverall? It wouldn't go unnoticed." I add to the conversation, hoping to get Chalet to move on to a different thread of evidence.

"You're both talking in riddles." Zeile is the first from my department to speak. He looks through the papers sitting loosely on my desk. "Steele, you've worked with less before. Why is this situation proving to be more difficult than any of your other cases? Agent Marlow, you've been with this team for some time now. There's no reason this one should have two of the best befuddled. What's the problem here? Is the killer correct? Are you two unable to function as a team anymore? Are you both burnt out and just needing some time away? What is it?"

The onslaught of questions does nothing to build our confidence regarding the case and interdepartmental support. If the department puts us on desk duty, paid leave or forces us to take our vacation, it'll be good PR for them. I can see the headlines now, NYPD and FBI suspend disgraced agents. They'll destroy our careers to protect the institution. Never thought I'd say that about the job I worked so damn hard for.

"With all due respect, sir, we're doing the best we can," Karina pleads.

"You're following a hunch and having an entire department scan hours, days, even weeks of video footage? That doesn't seem like your best, agent."

"If we had a warrant for the subscribers, we could cros- reference them with the online profiles. But our hands are tied here." I watch as my partner continues to present our case. She's not wrong, but the expressions of those within the room have already told me their minds are made up. We just have to live with whatever they've decided.

"Get me more evidence to support the need for one, and you'll have it," Chalet counters with a smug expression.

"A body used to be enough to sign off on such things. Or does that only work when you're trying to undermine me, Chalet?" Karina was close to losing control.

"Enough!" The assistant director cracks his neck and walks to the whiteboard. He scans our notes, pulls out a piece of paper from his pocket, and attaches it via a magnet to the right side of the board. "Did either of you hold an interview without our knowledge or permission?"

"No, sir," we say in stereo. Why would we hold any interviews? Other than speaking to Tazlia back in the early stages of this case, Karina and I have been silent.

"Then please explain why your conversations regarding the case have been posted online?"

"Wait, what?" Karina moves to the board and reads through the new information. "Sir, these were our private text messages sent through the phones you provided. We never even mention an interview."

"That's how they're being presented," Toby answers simply. He's right. "In fact, they're saying you harassed a potential suspect at a bar. They attached photos, so don't deny you were there."

"We followed up on a lead regarding Grubbs having an affair. Evelyn Dobbs owned the bar. We spoke to her and left. We never stepped out of line, and she was never a suspect." I'm so over the lies.

"In regard to this case, perception is everything. Out of context or not, the media is lapping this up. You say you followed the rules, they presented alternative facts and left it for the public to decide. When push comes to shove, authority never ends up on the right side of the discussion. It doesn't matter if you're following the law. This is a PR nightmare."

"Sir, if this is such a nightmare, why aren't Steele and I being bothered by reporters or citizens everywhere we go? Something isn't right here."

"You're not listening, Marlow. It doesn't matter." Chalet happily reiterates the assistant director's point.

"Both of you answer directly to me or Captain Zeile, effective immediately. You will show up at crime scenes to keep up appearances. While on location, you will not interact with anyone or investigate the scene. You will simply go inside and get out of the way. In the meantime, I expect you to turn over everything to Special Agent Chalet and his team."

"You're taking the case away from us because of some bullshit we can't control? I get it makes us look bad, but when have we bowed down to criminals trying to undermine an investigation? Are we as far along in the case as we'd like to be? Probably not, but it would be nice for some help instead of red tape and bullshit!"

"Detective, just stop before you take a step too far. We've given you both time to sort things out. Instead of making progress, you've regressed into a PR mess." Toby turns his attention to Karina. "The reason you're not being hounded is due to the tireless work of others. Be thankful they made sure the people behind those profiles didn't act on the information they have. It won't last forever, Agent Marlow. If we find more victims, the outrage will come to your doorstep."

They ignore the elevator and scurry into the staircase like scared cockroaches in the light. Zeile stands, patiently waiting for them all to leave.

"Cap—"

"I'm going to say this once, Jasmine. If you cannot comply with these rules, you'll be placed on administrative leave. A panel will assess the situation for punishment, which could include losing your badge and pension. If anyone works with you outside the parameters we've set, they will face the same ramifications. That includes Frankie. Am I making myself clear?"

"Yes, sir."

The doors open and he backs inside, never breaking eye contact with me. As it shudders closed, it feels like my foundation is gone. I went from having the support of a team, the trust of a new task force, to being tossed out like garbage.

"They might cut ties with Frankie, but they can't fire her from her own practice." Karina's attempts to comfort me fall flat.

"No, but they can ruin her reputation." We're literally watching someone do the same things to us right now. It's not farfetched to assume that both departments would do it to protect their best interests.

"So, as much as it pains me, we do what they want." Karina gives in easier than she ever has. To just toe the line and allow them to parade us around like fools doesn't sit well with me. "What else can we do, Steele? We've got families to think about."

"I know this sounds crazy, but why don't we clear our names? My union rep would love this."

"Steele, think about what you're saying. If you do that, there's no coming back from it. You'd destroy your career."

"Maybe, but I'm also thinking about my family. We need to hold people accountable for posting things like this. Last time I checked, defamation is still illegal."

"And extremely difficult to prove!"

"I know. Which is why we solve the case quickly and quietly. We do what they want on the surface and keep plugging away behind closed doors. Once the case is closed, we go after every single individual who commented and shared. Full stop."

"Or we get fired and laughed out of the courtroom. That's if we can even find out who's behind the profiles and put up all the money for lawsuits. Steele, your idea is such a long shot. It's terrifying. What would you do if it fails?"

"Get my resume together."

Chapter Nine

I went home after the bombardment in our office. Karina volunteered to deal with Chalet and Grayson about his discovery. We made copies of everything before handing it over to the Feds. It's still a meaningless pile of nothing. The only positive thing today is the snoring pup snuggled up next to me. His love is unconditional and has given me a foundation to process my anxiety before it becomes overwhelming.

"You're home?" Frankie asks from the doorframe. "I thought you'd be late again."

"Had an issue at the precinct and needed some time to think."

"Your doctor called me at work. Apparently, you missed a checkup appointment. She wants to make sure you're sleeping and eating properly. I told her both could use some improvement."

Shit. "I didn't mean—"

"I know. There's a lot on your mind. I'm trying to be patient, but your health is non-negotiable. You need to eat."

"I had what some people swear passes for a bagel, crappy coffee, and a protein shake. I'm good."

"That's not healthy, Jasmine. You have a stressful job, and it requires sustenance. And technically, you're still recovering. You need to be patient with your body."

The silence takes hold as there's nothing I could say to make my wife feel any better. I've been trying to put my health first, but there's only so many hours in the day. I have to sacrifice some things in order to do my job. Right now, that means less sleep and poor food choices.

"What's all that?" Frankie walks further into the room and scans the documents in front of me.

"The case."

"Jasmine . . ." The words hang in the air as she takes the seat across from me. "You know, Lewis called me today."

"Spending breakfast together wasn't enough?" Her body recoils in response to my negative comment. "I'm sorry. That was out of line."

"Apology accepted. I know we need to discuss the Lewis situation, but right now, I'd like to focus on these documents. Why do you have them when you've been removed from the case?"

Of course, Grayson would tell her what was going on. Was it to flirt and put a wedge between us or because he was genuinely worried about our well-being?

"Before you overthink it, he was concerned about you and Karina. Regardless of our past, he understands the social issues at play here and the psychological toll it takes on people. Now, please, enlighten me how a detective not on a case has the files on our coffee table?"

"Just the solving part. We're still the show ponies. Can't blame me for wanting to look into it. You know how I am."

"Yes, I do. But you're not a kid anymore. Maybe letting someone else handle things isn't so bad."

"Frankie, my name . . ." My throat tightens, as it isn't just about me. Frankie might go by her maiden name for her private practice, but all our documents have the last name Steele on them. "Our name is being smeared through the mud, and no one's protecting us. Sure, they said they've handled the doxing part and no one will come to our door, but for how long? I promised Zeile I'd play nice eons ago. I have. I've followed every rule, filed every idiotic report, sat for every interview. Yet here I am on the sidelines watching my integrity questioned because of a vendetta I don't even understand. How can I rationally stand idly by while this happens? How is that fair or just? We have laws on the books for everything, but anyone can post whatever they want on the internet with no ramifications. Maybe you can civilly sue someone for defamation. But who the hell has that kind of cash flow? I sure don't. So, what's the recourse?" Tears rolled down my face, my wall of strength crumbling as the helplessness takes hold. "Sydney said companies are refusing to remove the accounts, the comments, the replies, the re… whatevers. I have no control over this lie. I'm just supposed to take it, because it's considered free speech. How can a fabrication travel so freely when the truth is so easily found if you fucking use the tools available to you? Shit, Google would be a good place to start. But no one does. They just attack to get more attention for themselves. It's fucking sick."

"But that's human nature, my love. It's like when you come across a suspect that might have something to do with a crime and you look at evidence through that lens before something rules them out. It's just the nature of your job. People latch onto something they feel deeply about, and maybe they want to make it better. So they share the narrative they believe in so much that it has weight, and the truth is so jarring they can't accept it. It becomes a 'them versus me' scenario. You can't stop or change those minds. Even if you sue for defamation, even if they're found guilty of lying, it will never sink in. Those people are so devoted to their delusion, there is no escape. You can only focus on what's right in front of you. I'd suggest you talk to Captain Zeile and see what you can do within the confines of his rules."

"He doesn't want me anywhere near this."

"Then maybe that's for the best. We don't know the FBI team well enough to feel comfortable in their protection. If your investigation goes south, who do you think they'll use as a scapegoat?"

"Me."

"Exactly. We can't understand what's going on with this individual or why they're targeting you and Karina. But those who know you as a person and those you've helped in the past—they see the truth. This assailant, whoever they are, may be hurting, and this is how they lash out. We need to be compassionate about their situation to figure out the reasons behind their actions."

"I never thought of being kind to a killer."

"Love the sinner, hate the sin. Look, if you feel strongly about it, we'll sue to clear your name. We'll figure out the money side of things as we go forward. But sometimes people act in a horrific manner because they are in tremendous pain. The pandemic made that clearer than ever."

"I know you're right, but part of me is so enraged."

"And Doctor Preston can help you with that. But you need to let it go too."

"Rise from the ashes like a phoenix?"

"Yes, but until then, we work as a team to solve the case." Frankie walks around the coffee table and kisses the top of my head. "How about bacon and eggs for dinner?"

"Sold."

"I'm adding avocado to your plate. You need greens in there. No complaints."

"Fine." I feign a painful death if I have to eat it, but Frankie knows it's all for show. "We'll talk about Grayson after we eat, okay?"

My wife's smile warms my heart as her lips meet mine. Such a small action with an intense emotional connection.

"Am I interrupting?" Sydney's voice breaks the moment.

"Not at all." Her phone buzzes around the table like a wind-up toy. One glance at the caller identification and her expression shifts. Her smile fades, and she takes a deep breath before answering. She's out of the room before I can ask about it.

"Sorry, Aunt Jazz. I let Detective Locke in. I know her. I thought it was no big deal."

"No problem, kiddo. Can you do me a favor and take Hank outside? I think he could use some fresh air."

"Do I get pizza for doing this thoughtful task?" He's in that odd, almost teenager phase and has that adult look with a tinge of baby still in his eyes.

"Keep trying, kid."

"Chase, why don't you pack a bag for the weekend? We'll get pizza, pick up a ton of snacks, and game all weekend. Hank can come along and bark at all the squirrels ripping apart my yard. You in?" Sydney pleads with my nephew as if her life depends on it. She's probably stuck in the middle of a game on hardcore and wants his help.

His eyes fall on me as his hands wring in anticipation of my answer. I cherish these moments when he still looks like the innocent child we raised and hold onto it as long as I can before agreeing to let him go.

"Take the pup out first, and if your mom agrees, I have no issue with it."

I've never seen him run so fast outside with Hank before. "I've got the weekend off. I'll still be working from home, but nothing I can't do while he's playing some games or sleeping. I promise to keep him safe and away from all this noise."

"Syd, you don't have to do this."

"I do. Maybe I need more kiddo and puppy time too. It's been weird since Hadley left, and Logan . . . Look, I know I'm not his cool Aunt Hadley, but it might be good for the two of us. Plus, you'll be free to work on this." She slips something into my hand before I can argue her point. "Everything's password protected. Use my birthday, minus yours, no decimals and four digits for the year. Got it?"

"Yeah, but what are you doing?"

"Nothing major. I did some searching and found some things worth investigating. I tried to tell Chalet about it, but since it's not directly related to the case yet, he dismissed the information in the file labeled part one. The other folder has files for your eyes only."

"Karina and I are off—"

"It might be nothing, but my gut tells me it's something. I switched to tech thinking it would help my career, but it hasn't. I love it, I do, but I've been told to stay in my lane more times than I care to share. Point is, you trusted my instincts before. I'm asking you to do it again . . . on a few things."

"Syd, you're worrying me."

"I don't mean to, but I think there's more to the case than we know. If I'm right, it's not good, Steele." Chase bounds back into the room. Hank woofs from the doorway, while Chase hops back and forth in excitement, both adorned with matching lacrosse hoodies. Sydney tosses her car keys in their direction. "I'll be right there, and you're going to try pineapple on pizza tonight."

The young boy runs out of the living room, denying such an act will take place. Something tells me Hank wouldn't mind if the pineapple found its way to his mouth. That pug eats like a garbage disposal.

"Syd, you said there was something you found regarding the case, but what about those other files?"

"I just did some digging and found some information. With context it might be nothing, but it's worth looking at. And Paula Grubbs... Chalet has the information, but let's just say she has fake social media profiles as well. She and Boxletter are two peas in a pod." Without another word, she spun around and left me with more questions than answers. If the two victims were alike, then it's possible we had one killer with a vendetta. But I needed more information.

"Where's Syd running off to with our son?" Frankie wanders back into the living room, confused at the events taking place around her.

"Apparently, Chase is spending the weekend with his Aunt Sydney to have pineapple on pizza and game sessions."

"First, yum. Second, when did we decide this?"

"First, yuck. Second, we didn't. She just dropped off this drive, told me to look it over, and borrowed our kid and his trusty sidekick. I told him to see if it was okay with you."

"He didn't, but I'll get him back later for it. I'm sorry to break up our dinner plans, but that was Lewis on the phone. He's prepping for the interview you and Karina requested and wants my help."

"For someone who claims to be a leader in his field, he's not very good at it. He can't prepare for a simple interview or create a psychological profile on Peter Grubbs alone? You could do them in your sleep. He wants to spend more time with you, Frankie."

Her entire body goes rigid in a defensive posture. "Jasmine, he's a friend . . . more of an acquaintance who I used to date. There's nothing between us. Lewis loves to get under your skin. He was that way in college, and apparently, he hasn't grown out of it."

"You know I trust you fully, but he's a bully and I don't like it. I hate the way he controls your conversations or holds your hand—"

"Always in front of you. When we're alone, he never shuts up about how wonderful his life and career are. It's just who he is, Jasmine. There's a reason I broke up with him, and it wasn't about the plumbing. But he's in my field and we cross paths on some cases. This is one of those times. I'm going to keep up appearances and help him. Then I am coming home to my wife. Got it?"

She wraps protective arms around me. The instant warmth of her body and the strength of her arms are all I could ever need.

"There is more to this case, Jasmine. I can't share it with you, but after talking to Lewis . . . keep digging. We can't trust anyone but our inner circle with this. We'll handle whatever comes our way—together."

Her lips press against mine before she slips out of the room under an air of secrecy.

"Be careful!" I scream, hoping it hits her ears.

Once I'm alone, my focus turns back to the flash drive resting in the palm of my hand. After doing some math, which Sydney knows I despise, I figure out the six-pin passcode and enter it. It's obvious Sydney planned on my eyes seeing these documents because of her obsessive organization of folders. The main topic and then subfolders by year and if necessary, even more specific. Some of them I can dismiss right away, but several look promising. Those get transferred to my desktop for safe keeping.

My eyes continue down the laundry list of names until the air rushes out of my lungs. The title was a code that no one else would understand, but it burrows down to the core of my fear. It's something I need to share, even though all I want to do is run after my wife to keep her home. Instead, my thumb presses the second speed-dial on my antique phone.

"What's going on, Steele?"

"You busy right now?"

"Leaving the FBI building. What's up?"

"I know you want to head home, but can you drop by here first?"

"Steele, we're not investigating—"

"Yeah, I know. It's something else."

"Sure. I'm on my way, but you better order food. I'm starving."

"Chinese good?"

"Yeah. Be there soon."

After a quick call to secure dinner for the two of us, my mind switches back to Karina. She was leaving the FBI building. But why?

I send a quick text to Sydney. *Is Karina still on the case officially?*

The reply is immediate and damning.

Yes.

That one word places a heaviness within my chest. If she was there, was I being set up to take the fall for it all? Was her hand being forced by Chalet and the director? Worst case scenarios sore before my mind's eye as I stare at my computer screen. I've had many partners in the past; most have gone on to other things. Karina and I felt like a tandem that would last longer than the rest.

I adore Will, but that relationship started when he protected me from myself . . . and a madman. He was always the big brother and I his little sister in need of help. Our working relationship never had time to balance as crime never stopped. And now, we're apart. When Karina was brought in, we started on the same foundation. We both had flaws we wanted to work through, problems we needed to address. And we did.

Now it feels like the press conferences, newspaper articles, awards, and the politics of it all are being used against me to clear the conscience of the department. If Karina is with them on this, I don't stand a chance.

***

CHAPTER NINE

Time ticks by painfully slow as I wait for Karina to arrive. The food delivery helps keep my mind off that damn folder on the flash drive. So, I sort out who ate what, disinfect the containers to quiet my anxiety, and wait. A few sips of my beer later, the doorbell rings.

She stands on the stoop, her eyes dark and tired. Without saying a word, she slips past me and plops down into the chair with a covered plate of food. Before I've got the door latched, I can hear her moan in pleasure as she devours her meal. "How much have you had?" Her finger waves at the beer bottle on the table.

"Not much." The computer screen pulls my attention again. What could this all mean?

"What's going on, Steele. You say you're not intoxicated, but you're acting rather . . . abnormal."

"Why are you still on the case when Zeile gave us explicit instructions to stay away?"

Karina stops eating, surprised I'm aware of the change. "Chalet." Her one-word reply doesn't bring clarity to the situation at all.

"What about him? We've been partners for a while now, Karina. I think a little clarity isn't too much to ask for."

She says nothing but takes a few more bites of food. I know she's giving herself time to think. I'd do the same thing, but what is the deeper story that needs protecting? Why not just tell me the truth?

"I wish I knew. After the display in the basement, Chalet texted me demanding I meet him in his office to bring him up to speed. You and I both know he's fully informed on all aspects of the case, so it didn't feel right. I went there, relayed all the information to him, and even questioned how our information got leaked to the public. Of course, he didn't answer but sat there, almost frozen. I packed up my things to head home and he stopped me. It's then that he tells me to stay silent, tread lightly, and keep digging. I brought up Captain Zeile, and Chalet shut me down. He told me I was FBI and I answer to him. You were the NYPD's problem."

"Odd. From what you tell me, that man treats you like a criminal for your husband's actions but wants you to keep investigating? There's something wrong with—"

"I'm not lying, Steele. Trust me, it took me off guard as well. I don't know the reason, but it's what happened."

We both go back to eating. There must be more to this if Sydney left me that file folder, but what if it isn't true? This could ruin a man's career if I'm wrong. I'd be doing to them what's effectively being done to me. I need an outside opinion not blinded by my biases.

"Syd came over today. She dropped off a flash drive with varying cases for me to search through. She's approached Chalet with the information, but he wasn't interested. She's aware of my . . . distance from the current case, but these files could be promising leads."

"That's a lot of words for finding a roundabout way of investigating. She could lose her job over this."

"They were things we asked for and more." I spin the laptop around to face my partner. "But that's not all Syd and her friends dug up. I haven't looked at it yet, but maybe we should. Syd's gut instincts have held up in the past. I think we need to follow her lead on this one. That being said, I can't do it alone. I need your unbiased eyes to help me."

She glances to my computer screen and then back to me. Her slight squint and raised eyebrow reignite the nervous curiosity pulsing through my veins. "This . . . I mean, Steele, this is . . ."

"An extremely dangerous suggestion, if true. But until we read everything, we won't know if the department ignored complaints filed by citizens during the early stages of the pandemic."I chomp away at my meal. "We could let it die. Just do what we're told and clear any future investigations with Zeile and Chalet."

"We could. We could also open the files, scan things, and see if there's any validity to the concerns." Karina eyed the files as her hand hovered above the keyboard.

"But if we're not honest with our peers, do we not give credence to those accusations posted about ignoring the people we swore to protect??" The worry had crossed my mind. As detectives, we need to have the freedom to investigate within our means. Micromanaging and demanding answers when there are none doesn't work. It slows everything down and puts a microscope in the wrong place.

"From where I'm sitting, we've done nothing wrong. I'll be the first person to admit my mistakes. I screwed up with my ex-husband, and I took the ramifications in stride. It's what I needed to do. But no case is perfect, Steele. We've had to make gut decisions with no time to properly investigate. Some have gone well, others not so much. But through it all, we had the backing of our respective departments."

"But people won't see it that way." This conversation was heading down a road I didn't intend to travel.

"True, but in time, they might. It's a sad state of this country that the next horrible thing is right around the corner. We know the truth, and when we find the person behind it, we will fight to clear our names."

"What? You don't want to be associated with the loose cannon who chooses easy cases to solve to inflate her importance on the force?"

"I'm more concerned about you. I mean, being associated with an accessory to murder must be tough."

We'd both laugh if it wasn't our reality. Just because we've been home doesn't mean the posts have stopped. In fact, when word leaked about our removal, the original poster went on a spree. There were images of celebrations, and more posts demanding our arrests and prosecution. I'm still not sure what they legally could put us behind bars for, but people will write whatever they want when its anonymous.

"I think if we don't look into this, we're not doing our jobs. Forget all the noise. We never ignore a lead unless the evidence proves it wrong."

"What if this has nothing to do with the case?"

"Then we walk away." She shrugs as if it's the easiest decision in the world. "Until we find something, we do our due diligence. That's all. We let our bosses know we're looking into complaints filed, where citizen's requested you and I handle the case, that in turn never made it to our desks. The rest we do on our own. Is Syd looking for more?"

"She's taken the weekend off, but plans on logging in when Chase is asleep. After seeing what she's dropped in my lap, I think her willingness to babysit was deliberate."

"Okay, so just you and me. Maybe we can bring Frankie in the loop as needed."

That was the last thing I wanted to do.

"I don't think that works. Her connection to Greyson could put her in an uncomfortable position, especially if they turn out to be true."

"We'd hand the defense a perfect strategy for an acquittal." Karina leans back in acceptance of our silence. We both understand the consequences if things go south. It's like any other case we're dealing with.

One by one, we sort through files of complaints. The more we dig through them, I can understand why Zeile refused to send them our way. Some filings are for a completely different department. While we are more than capable of handling it, the other departments are specialized for a reason.

We narrow it down to five promising filings.

"I'll talk to Zeile in the morning. Let him know I'm following up on these complaints."

"If he pushes to ask why?"

"I won't lie. I'll tell him regardless of the connection, this will instill some good faith within the community. Either way, we can help these people."

"I'll have my team shuttle the others to the proper people."

"And Grayson?"

"I'll look into his medical license, patient history, and check if there are any complaints in his jacket. He's a weirdo, but that doesn't mean he's . . . Just, leave it to me, okay?"

I transfer the files to a different flash drive for Karina to take with her. Considering the sensitivity of the content, we want to ensure we have a copy and can keep Sydney out of it. It's only after Karina leaves that the adrenaline seeps out of my system. Then the fogginess, mixed with exhaustion, rolls back in. One moment I want another beer, the next, I just want to sleep.

Chapter Ten

My head was much clearer in the morning after four cups of coffee and some allergy medication. Frankie didn't come home last night, but I'm trying to stay calm. It wasn't so long ago that sleeping in her office was a better option if a patient exposed her to COVID. But knowing she met up with Grayson just puts me on edge.

The cell phone taunts me with the status *read* under the message I sent in the early hours of the morning. Frankie's never pulled no contact unless something was wrong. I can hear my mother's voice mentioning death and a ditch on the side of the road. She always had a flare for the dramatic, but my mind can easily imagine it. It's then that my phone rings.

"Frankie? Where are you?"

I can hear a bit of movement on the other end before I hear my wife's voice. "Hey, hon. I'm sorry. Things just . . . We lost track of time working on the profiles."

"Profiles? Frankie, you could pop them out in your sleep. What's going on?"

"Jasmine, I have to go, but I want to make something absolutely clear, okay?" She pauses. Muffled sounds in the background pull my ear, but they're too low to make out. "Let the team handle things. Please."

"Frankie, you know I can't do that. Our livelihood is on the line here. My reputation—"

"Jasmine, I'm not asking you. I'm pulling the spouse card. Accept responsibility and allow the team to process the rest."

"Frankie, playing this game could damage our entire future."

"We have no future if we can't learn from our mistakes and move on. I love you, but this needs to end. You need to sit with a therapist and discuss about why you have this . . . this savior complex. Jasmine, you run into buildings without backup. You continually put your family at risk and never once accept your part in any of it. If you can't support my decision, then my family was right not to come to our wedding. It wouldn't be based on respect or love."

Her words flow over my skin like melting glacial ice. The smiling faces from our family wedding photo stare back at me from its place on the mantle. Frankie's father smirked in most, but Waylon was happier than

I could remember. Her brother Wade refused to attend for personal beliefs, but that's not important right now. My wife knows I'm already seeing a therapist and her accusations are out of left field. Frankie's lying and she never does that. She's letting me know she's in some kind of trouble.

"Okay, I'll do as you ask. Just promise me you'll come home tonight. I love you."

"Ditto." It was the one word I begged her not to say when we started dating. That cheesy line from some classic romance movie she loved always bothered me. It became our code word to get out of uncomfortable or dangerous situations. Chase even used it to get out of a play date with someone who had been picking on him at school. In other words, she just activated a five-alarm fire.

It takes less than a minute to clear the line and get Sydney on the phone. "I know you've got the weekend off and are babysitting, but do you have access to your network of people from home?"

"Yeah." I hear a door close, a squeak, and then water running. "Okay, I'm in the bathroom, out of earshot. What's going on?"

"Frankie didn't come home last night. I need you to track her phone and whatever else your people can do. You once said you could remotely turn on mics and cameras. Do that and record it all."

"Steele, I'll follow you through fire, but if she's having an affair, I just don't want to get—"

"Syd, if I thought she was having an affair, I'd be on the phone with a lawyer. Frankie called and gave me her distress signal. I need you to trust me on this and just find out everything you can."

"And what if I find she's just cheating on you?"

"Like I said, I'll get a lawyer and bury myself in chocolate. I'm telling you, Syd, something is off, and I'm concerned. Yesterday, she was all up in defending my honor and our family name, but now she wants me to back off the case completely. Then she mentioned her family missing her wedding when only her brother Wade skipped it."

"That seems odd, but you might be overthinking things. Maybe she's just exhausted and wants a break from the mess. Look, I'll reach out to my people, but I wouldn't worry. Just remember none of this is admissible in court."

"I don't care about that. I want her home safe."

The sound of brakes outside pulls my attention. Press vans with their scandal hungry reporters pour out onto my lawn. "So much for the precinct leaving me alone."

"What's going on?"

"Someone must have spilled the story beyond social media. Bloods in the water and the sharks have microphones on my lawn. I'd prefer not to be dinner for some cheap ass ratings grab."

"Slip out before they're ready to shoot. I'll call when I have something."

The side door groans at the hinges, but I'm on my way to work before the news crews can set up. The question of why now lingers in my mind. Sydney told me our information has been readily available for a while now. No one's reached out for our personal comments. Now Frankie's acting out of character and the press is on my front lawn. This feels like a calculated move to keep Karina and me distracted.

***

The silence of the precinct adds to my already shredded nerves. I can feel my fellow colleague's eyes judging me as I shuffle through to Captain Zeile's office. One knock. Screw the people staring. They don't know the truth.

"Enter." My feet slip into the room with my body numb but attached. "Steele, what can I do for you this morning?"

"I know I'm off the case, but Frankie went to meet Grayson last night. She called me this morning and gave the signal she was—"

"Steele, she's an adult, and I can't let you back on the case. I'm sorry."

"Cap, please—"

"Doctor Ryan is more than capable of handling this case with the team. She's worked with us before without your help. There's nothing wrong with this situation."

"Sir, I know my wife is more than capable of working without me on this case. But she gave me the code word we have for distress. She's in trouble and for her to activate that alarm... she's scared."

Zeile leans back, and creases form on his forehead as he mulls over my comments. I just need access to Grayson's address, and I'll handle the rest, but I need permission or I risk losing my job. The cap can send me with another officer to do a wellness check for all I care. I'd have backup right there and I'd keep my promise to my wife. No running into situations without help and no involvement in the current case.

"Do you know the situation beyond her verbal notification?"

"As in severity? No, but if she's—"

"Then, I'll loop in Special Agent Chalet and we'll handle it. You are to return home and wait for us to reach out."

"Cap—"

"Jasmine, you don't know what the situation is. For all we know she's in an uncomfortable position and called you to come get her out of it. You didn't mention hearing her scream or someone threatening her... nothing to prove she's in danger other than your word. Now, in light of the public and our bosses being up our ass when it comes to you, jumping to conclusions would be detrimental. We'll get right on it, but I need you to keep yourself busy in the meantime. I can't have you trying to find Frankie. If she is in trouble, you'll put her in more danger. Go home, play videogames... do something."

I shift my weight back and forth as I contemplate the next part of the conversation. "Sir, I looked over the case again. Before you reprimand me, please let me finish." His eyes harden as he waves his hand for me to continue. "It appears the underlying issue in this case is a complaint that Karina and I never investigated. I thought it would be pertinent to see what those files entailed and look into them. If it gives us insight into the killer, great. If nothing else, it allows me to smooth things over with the community. I can direct any further action to the correct department or to you should there be something relevant. Maybe it's a waste of department time, but I'm being paid to sit home and worry about my wife. I think this would benefit us both."

He folds his hands in front of him as he shifts back on his office chair. "Close the door."

The click of the latch sounds and I turn, waiting in silence. Every noise feels amplified. The ticking of his clock. The creak of the springs on Zeile's chair as he shifts.

"How did you narrow down the cases? Hell, how did you find them?"

"Sir, I'm not looking to get anyone in trouble. I just want to help in whatever way I can."

"Steele, you're a pain in my ass, but you're one of the best detectives I've worked with. So, out of respect, let me say this simply. I know your team plans on helping you regardless of the FBI's or NYPD's insistence on your removal. As far as I'm concerned, yesterday's conversation was all for show. The Bureau keeps breathing down our necks like the department's responsible for the entire debacle. Maybe we have some part to play, and that's why I'll allow you to look over these files. But you keep me fully informed of your progress, and if it screams a setup, you walk away. Understood?"

"Yes, sir."

He turns back to the papers on his desk, signaling the conversation is over. I barely have the door open before he speaks again.

"I'm sure Frankie's fine, but I'll keep you posted the minute I know for sure."

Without a reply, I slip out to face the unknown. The usual white noise of the precinct that irritated me most mornings, gave me some level of serenity in the moment. My thumbs punch out a message of love to Frankie, hoping the delivery will trigger Sydney's computer to find my wife's location. With another annoying set of key presses, Karina's got a message from me with an update.

Every fiber in my being wants to run after my wife, but Zeile's right. If Frankie is in serious trouble, my involvement could make things much worse. But looping Chalet in doesn't raise the level of confidence within me. He gives off the *let Frankie die to punish Steele* vibes. But I do trust my captain. That has to be enough—for now.

Chapter Eleven

The late afternoon sun's warmth staves off the chilly breeze. Once it disappears behind the buildings, the cold should creep into my bones. I've covered so many steps along this journey but I'm further away than ever from my goal of finding clues to the killer.

The case files led me to different locations around our area. The complaints read differently, but the underlying message was always the same. Those filing felt unheard and forgotten. Some issues were minor in scale or scope, but the lack of attention to their plight deepened their pain.

So, I sat with them, trying to give them someone to talk to. The pounding in my head reminds me how many four-letter words and angry yells came my way. Sure, they'd let me know it indirectly wasn't my fault, but it still weighed heavily on my soul.

The scariest part of the conversations was discussing the outcomes. When people tell you they settled things through different means, your imagination takes over. It reminded me of my mother's brother. His alternative means usually got everyone around him in trouble. But he faced no ramifications. But it wasn't my place to judge when we failed them so egregiously. I just hope it wasn't something that would haunt them at night.

For those that still needed help, I called the precinct directly. Cap would give me the name and number of an individual who would handle the case. Before I left each location, I left the number to my direct line if something went awry. It isn't a perfect solution, but maybe it helps.

"One more file . . ." After that, there's no mindless work to keep me busy.

The small, two-story corner building might have been beautiful back in the day. Right now, it gives off every creepy horror movie vibe in the book. Broken glass riddles the path to the front door. The greenery is so overgrown, I'm lucky I can see a path at all. The dark, winding vines pull at the siding, digging below the surface, burrowing into the flesh of the house. The foundation looks sound, but the icy chill pulls me back to my childhood, desperately trying to stay awake after Henry subjected me to *Nightmare on Elm Street*.

"You from the city?" My bones leap out of my skin at the shrill voice of the neighbor. "We've been calling all the time. Owner won't clean it up, and it's a hazard to the neighborhood. People sleeping, partying, doing Lord knows what. It needs to be boarded up or fenced in. I don't care what, but do something!"

"I understand, ma'am. I'll document it and report back to my superiors."

"That won't do shit. Call them here now!"

"I can't do that, ma'am." My flip phone's camera sucks, so I'm forced to use my mini tablet. The video records the complete disarray of the property. My boots crunch with each step.

I'll get Sydney to look into the neighbor's calls. It might give us a better timeline of when the owner left the premises. If there was a bank lien or foreclosure, the fencing would be up already. So, one must assume it just hasn't been sold yet. I stop recording for a moment to dig out a pair of surgical gloves from my backpack. If nothing else, the interior could house a different crime or just gross things not meant for human contact.

The red light blinks on the screen as I continue the recording.

"This feels so wrong." That's the fear talking, I tell myself. "I should call for backup." For what, I don't know.

The next-door neighbor has gone quiet, but I can feel her eyes on me. Tilting my head, I wave to acknowledge her and ensure she's on camera before turning back to the door. It's locked, but that doesn't mean much as half of the door is glass. Reaching through the broken pane, I feel around and flip the latch to open it.

"Hey, you're not allowed to do that!" The same shrill voice crawls up my skin. "You better have ID before you go in there!"

I turn the camera back to ensure she's on video, say my name and badge number, and give a brief reason for being here. "Ma'am, I'm Detective Steele of the NYPD."

"Right, we'll see about that!" Her head drops out of view and I'm sure she's dialing the police to report a female trespasser. Part of me is thrilled. It saves me from calling dispatch and asking for help because of scary eighties horror film memories.

The door struggles against the rusty hinges, stuttering as it opens. The smell of human waste is overwhelming, forcing me to raise my N95 back over my face. I can only imagine what the neighbors had to endure if this building was in similar disrepair over the summer.

The light on the tablet illuminates the interior. Layers of competing graffiti images cover the walls, some more faded than others. Scattered throughout the room are beer bottles, cans, pipes, and more broken items I can't discern from the lack of light.

The small beam highlights the floor, giving me a clean path to walk along. It's hard to tell what condition the house was in before they left the home to rot. The crunch under my boot, accompanied by the top of the carpet moving, instantly makes my skin itch. The walls move.

"Indy's got snakes, I got roaches. Now all I'll be thinking about is those fuckers falling on my head." My cell phone rings, causing me to jump and stomp more bugs. God, this day was not going well. "Steele."

"Where are you?" Karina's insistent voice filters through the receiver.

"Checking out the last location on those missed complaints. What's up?"

"I got your text and spoke to Captain Zeile. I'm surprised you're not over here handling this yourself."

"You know I want to, but given the situation... I can't risk it. Cap says Chalet is handling it."

"He's headed out to Grayson's house now with a small team. They don't expect to find anything out of the ordinary, but when our calls went unanswered . . ."

"Prepare for the worst and hope for the best." Never thought I'd be using one of my mother's rules to live by to describe a mission to find my wife.

"Yeah... Look, Zeile's here running the meeting so I've got to go. Just keep your phone close and let me know if you find something. If it's related to the murders—"

"I'll call Director Toby if anything comes up. Just keep Chalet focused on Frankie, please." I'm not sure if Karina heard me or if my words just entertained the crunchy critters.

I should be out there looking for Frankie, storming the castle to save the princess like all those damn games I played as a kid. But sometimes letting the right people handle it, is the right decision. Karina won't rest until Frankie's on the phone with me. Then we'll laugh this off over a glass of wine and a bad movie.

Each step crunches beneath my boots, bringing me back to the current investigation.

The kitchen is no better than the rest of the main floor. Unfinished food, pizza boxes, and a ton of trash prove the neighbors' concerns. This house has become a den of debauchery. Each time the light passes over a surface, the shadows scurry away. The health inspector needs to get here and burn this place to the ground.

The railing on the staircase groans as it moves with the slightest touch. One at a time, I kick the back of each step and tap the top with my foot before putting my full weight on it. The idea of falling into a bed of cockroaches and detritus is not on my to-do list.

Pieces of a broken toilet sit in the main hallway at the top of the stairs. The light shines into a bathroom that has seen better days. The shards of the toilet, tub, and what might have been a pedestal sink sit in a jumbled mess on the floor.

The room on my left houses sleeping bags and other personal items. I assume squatters are using this place for a roof over their heads. If their things are still here, they'll be back before the freezing temperatures set in. Considering the number of sleeping bags laid out on the floor, I'm outnumbered if they all come back at once.

The room to the right of the stairs pulls my attention. Beyond the bugs, it's immaculate. No garbage or graffiti on the walls . . . nothing. The carpet has several dark stains under the broken window. Why, out of the entire house, would this room be left alone? Why not spread out?

The back wall gives me some sign of a reason. The two double closets no longer have doors, but the murals within them are fully intact. The design on the left showcases a young woman, smiling, with a puppy raised near her head. The design is full of bright colors and imagery in the background, giving the feeling of hope and innocence.

The one in the right closet depicts a darker image. It appears to be the same woman. The puppy is nowhere to be found. Her head hangs tilted as if a weight is pressing on her. Tears roll down her face as blood drips from her wrists. The dark colors fill the closet with the feelings of pain, loss, and fear.

The small strip of wall between the closets forces the air to flood out of my lungs.

YOU DID THIS

The edge of the faded, red capital letters look like they were finger painted. The person who created these must have been in incredible pain. I struggle to catch my breath because of the potent feelings they convey. Though faded with time, the entire mural is beautifully painful to view. The click of my cell phone's shutter collects some subpar images. Hopefully Sydney can figure something out. Either way, the haunting image needed to be documented.

I answer my ringing phone as my eyes move across both murals, transfixed.

"Where did you find those?"

"Last house. I need to know who owns it. I've been through the file a million times. The names are obviously fake. Seems like they knew we wouldn't get back to them."

"Okay, two shakes." I can hear her fingers flying across the keyboard.

"Kid okay?" Being in this house, knowing Frankie was out there, I needed to know Chase was okay. It was the only thing I had to hold onto.

"Yeah, he's playing Halo and is still in the dark about the current events." Her fingers stop and I hear her cheering at her speed. "Strat Markovich is the current owner. He doesn't live there, though. He's in a nursing home. I'll send you the address."

"Okay, do me a favor and get the health department and CSI in here. We need this house closed tight. Not sure there's any evidence that isn't contaminated, but this wall needs to be preserved."

"You got it. Be safe, Jasmine."

Syd ends the call as I notice some chicken scratches at the bottom of each image. It could be a name, so I grab some closer pictures on my tablet as the front door wails. Someone's here.

"This is the police. If you're inside, identify yourself and come out with your hands up!" a voice yells from downstairs.

Using the light on my tablet to navigate my way, I head to the top of the stairs, hands raised. "My name is Detective Jasmine Steele. I'm investigating a complaint filed with my precinct. I'm coming downstairs with my hands up so you can check my ID."

The officer must have noticed my gun, as his entire body tenses up. "Don't reach for that weapon!"

"Officer, I have no desire to reach for my weapon. If you—"

"I heard you! Keep your hands where I can see them."

My boots barely hit the main floor before the two men slam my face into the roach-covered walls. One grabs my weapon before the other roughly cuffs my wrists. I'm spun around and slammed back into the wall. The larger one holds me in place while he slowly slides his hands all over my body before pulling out my badge from my inner jacket pocket. Flipping it open, he sees my identification and badge. He tosses it to his friend.

"Where'd you get that from? Did you buy it from the local stores? Can't be too safe round these parts." He scans my badge for any markers proving it's fraudulent.

"I asked you a question!" The officer pressed his body into my back, his legs between mine as his stale breath brushed against my skin.

"Officer, I went to the academy. I worked my way up. Served under Captain Tyler Udall. I currently work under Captain Thomas Zeile. My partner is Special Agent Karina Marlow. You can call dispatch and prove it."

The larger one nods to his partner, who makes the call. It felt like an eternity, feeling little feet crawl across my flesh and a drunk on power man in my back, until confirmation came through the radio.

"Got to make sure. You know how it is," the one holding me pressed himself harder against my body one final time before standing upright and removing the handcuffs.

"There's never a reason for excessive force." I was ashamed I let these men accost me like that. The rage burned hot as they handed me my personal effects back. The crack along my tablet's screen didn't prevent it from turning on. It just looked like a spiderweb from the top right corner to the bottom left. The department was sure to be pissed off at me for the damage.

The tech team walks in, and I can tell the other officers are nervous and desperate to leave.

"Make sure you save the wall in the top right bedroom. The rest I leave in your capable hands," I rattle off to the investigators. I spin around and get several images of the two dimwits and their badges before I duck out the door. I can hear them yelling after me, but with the larger crowd, they won't do anything.

"Detective Steele?" A large man with a clipboard stands on the path to the door, spinning around.

"That's me. You the health department?"

"Yes, ma'am."

"Trust me, lock it down."

I send the images through my tablet to Zeile with a quick voice note of the interaction and where I'm headed next.

In the meantime, I must ignore the feeling of roaches on my skin and head to a nursing home. I send another text to Frankie in a desperate attempt to garner control over my racing heart. If she wasn't at Greyson's house, pinging off a tower would help triangulate her location. Call it a desperate act to feel like I was involved in finding my wife.

Chapter Twelve

I make my entire commute to the nursing home in silence. No word from Chalet or Karina regarding my wife. No one's replied to the few messages I've sent. Without the capabilities of newer phones, I have no idea if they've been received, let alone read. It just says *sent*. The only notification I received was from my captain approving my request to keep digging but advising me to tread lightly. Technically, I'm still off the case.

Visiting hours are closing as I drag my emotionally drained body across the threshold of the nursing home.

"Can I help you?" The receptionist sits behind the desk with her perfect teeth, plastered-on smile, and hair spray-defying hairdo.

"Yes, I'm here to see Strat Markovich." My badge hits the counter before questions about family, my purpose, or what have you pops out of her mouth. It might be part of the job, but I am beyond the point of no return.

"Detective, it's rather late and—"

"I understand that, ma'am. I don't mean any imposition, but it is of great importance that I speak to Mr. Markovich."

The glare of distrust is palpable as they grab the phone. I wonder if they can see the day I'm having reflected at them. Are there pieces of roach in my hair? The thought disgusts me more than the musty smell of this entryway. After several minutes of mumbling, she places the receiver down. She plops a large binder on the table and drops a pen on top of it.

"Sign in."

"Rather old-school, don't you think? I mean, plug the information into a computer system, maybe some cameras . . ."

"Detective, please sign."

I draw a line with an uptick for a smile at the end. Deliberately not my signature. She doesn't verify it or even look at it. She just slams the book closed and points down to the elevator bank.

"Fifth floor. Someone at the main desk up there will help you."

I take my badge, which I assume is my visitor's pass, and take the elevator to the designated floor. The small nurse's station directly in front of me is quiet. Even though it's well into the evening, visiting hours end closer to eight. There should be a number of people on staff until the evening crew comes in. Another reason I'll never be a resident here.

"Detective?" the only human behind the desk says, peeking over the lip of the counter.

"Yes, ma'am. I'm here to see Mr. Markovich."

"He's in common room two. Go straight down the hall. It's literally the last door on the right. Can't miss it."

"Is there anything I should know before I meet with him? Anything I should avoid?"

"Not really. He tires easily, so he might dose off during your conversation. If that happens, I suggest you return another time as early in the day as possible."

"Could you take me to him? Introduce us?"

"He's in a wheelchair with his name on the back of it. Usually stares out the windows all day, every day. Can't miss him." She turns her attention back to the computer in front of her.

"Thank you for your help." The sarcasm drips off my words. I knew these places could be horrible, but the simplest of tasks here feels disregarded for paperwork. *Be careful, Steele. Your tired, judgy side is showing.* I can hear Doctor Preston's voice in my head.

The stark white walls of the common room make it feel smaller, almost prison-like. Residents sit at tables, mumbling as they roll some dice or flip over cards. Others watch the television at what seems like maximum volume. But there's no employee within the room to help at a moment's notice if anyone needs assistance. They might be within vocal range but responding in those first few minutes is crucial.

I add the number of occupants allowed on the wall and compare it with the number of individuals in the room. Maybe the cap can pass along my concerns to those governing this district. The New Jersey District Attorney is running for re-election; maybe he needs a new platform to run on.

The wheelchair with the placard reading Markovich rests along a wall of dingy windows. The older gentleman, curled forward and buried under blankets, stares blankly through the cloudy film.

"Mr. Markovich? May I sit next to you?" My badge catches his attention, and his eyes slide up to me as if he's looking at a demon.

"Not like I can stop you." The weakness in his body is reflected in his wispy voice.

Taking that as affirmation, I situate myself close enough to appear friendly but not too close to his personal space. "I apologize for disturbing you this evening."

"What do you want, detective?" He coughs.

"I'm Detective Jasmine Steele."

"I know who you are."

"I was looking over an old complaint and came across an address. You're listed as the owner, but the house is abandoned and in disrepair."

"Yeah, it's mine on paper. Got offers to sell the land too, but I won't do it. It wouldn't be right. I'll leave it to Jamee to handle when I'm gone." His rigidly bent hand swipes at the tears forming in his eyes. "Either way, nothing for you to investigate anymore, detective."

"Jamee?"

"My daughter. She's the one that came to you for help. But you're a bit late for that. If you went to the house, you saw the images. My youngest's life depicted in two pictures."

"The murals . . ."

"My little Sadee." His tears fall freely now. "My eldest daughter, Jamee, she convinced Sadee to report it all. Promised that there were people who could help her, help with the collateral damage hitting all of us. But you never showed up. Sure, there are people out there hurting every day, and I tried to rationalize being ignored, but this was my family. Constant harassing calls to my job, my house . . . My kids weren't safe under the roof I provided. How's a father supposed to handle that?" His hands pound the armrests of the wheelchair as the sobs break from his chest.

"I'm so sorry." I wrap my hand around one of his for comfort.

He tilts his head toward our hands. He squeezes mine softly but doesn't let go. He's so quiet, but I imagine time has helped heal the gaping wound of loss.

"I wish you could have met Sadee. She, my wife, and Jamee were peas in a pod; it was them against the world. They'd always have their girl time, but Sadee was my everything. She'd run home from school and regale me with stories of her day. Her mama died when she was in high school. She suffered for so long, so money was tight. My youngest put herself through college and got a graduate degree to boot. But even then, my little girl still asked for advice about everything. I know she was just keeping her old man involved in her life, but I did my best to support her. I only wanted my daughters to be happy, you know?"

"Yes, sir. I do. I need to ask about the complaint. It doesn't go into too much detail. Your daughter was being harassed?"

His knuckles whiten as he tightens his grasp on my hand. "She really wanted this one position. Went through two or three rounds of interviews and eventually got the job. Gosh, she was so proud. Took me out to dinner to celebrate. Next thing I know, she's got herself a small studio apartment. Nothing fancy, but she was so proud of being independent. I warned her about sharing too much on those social places, but she'd just shrug it off. Jamee told me her sister posted some images at her new place, her office . . . just being positive and saying good things happen with hard work. From what I understand, she had so many comments congratulating her." His eyes stare out into the distance as if glazed over by a memory.

"I assume she received negative ones as well."

"You could say that. Her best friend Andi took a picture of Sadee's posts and combined them in this social media thing—I don't know what it's called—but she combined all these images with lies about Sadee taking the job from someone more deserving. Jamee and I weren't worried. We figured the two girls would sit down and sort through any drama. They'd delete the posts and it would blow over."

"But it didn't." It was the understatement of the century. Even if two central parties can come to an agreement, the people on the fringes who've riled themselves up continue the argument long after it's been settled.

"No, it escalated to a level we weren't prepared for. Kids she grew up with and considered lifelong friends ganged up on her. They kept posting things, fabrications mostly. Anything to keep the story going. They all believed Andi and that Sadee saw the job listing on Andi's phone. But I was there when the alert came through to Sadee. She asked if I thought applying was a good idea. I mean, she was slightly underqualified. I told her nothing ventured, nothing gained. So, she submitted her resume."

"I assume she tried to explain her side of things to this Andi . . ."

"Grace. Andi Grace. Yeah, she tried, but no one would listen. The two girls met in college and continued to grad school together. We let the woman into our house, to eat at our table. We treated her like family, and this is what she did to my kid? She was a lying snake. Kept posting increasingly outrageous tales, and people just kept eating it up. Ask her for proof and she'd manipulate text conversations between them, write a summary of an interaction instead, or give you a what about this or that? Nothing concrete or actual images of full conversations."

"Do you have the interactions between your daughter and Ms. grace?"

"No. Sadee was so hurt she deleted and blocked everything to do with Andi and her so-called friends. We called a lawyer, and they advised us to get the messages directly from the companies. So, we petitioned but got no response. Just like the social media companies refused to take the lies down because it didn't break their terms of service. So defamation was acceptable. Sadee'd had enough and deleted all her accounts. Then one day HR calls her into their office and shows her the social media frenzy. Andi and her friends tagged Sadee's job so many times they had no choice but to address it. They were being dragged down, and it was a public relations nightmare""

"They fired her." In my mind, that was a forgone conclusion.

"Yeah, they even posted they took the allegations seriously and that my kid no longer worked there. Lawyers and PR firms all said it would blow over and Sadee would be fine. We wanted to sue, but the lawyer fees .

. . I mean, who has twenty to fifty grand just lying around? We thought about moving, starting fresh elsewhere, but Sadee refused. She said it wouldn't matter where she went; it was out there."

"Sadly, the internet is forever, and the companies have no obligation to protect their users. If someone wanted to find that posting spree, they could easily do so." I add Andi's name to my notes to investigate later.

"Yeah . . . she lost everything. Moved home, told us she was a failure and brought shame to the family. We changed all our phone numbers and looked for a good therapist for Sadee. She went to a few sessions; we had Jamee go to him too. It helped for a while. Then one morning, Jamee calls me screaming through her tears. Took me forever to calm her down so I could understand her."

He shifts in his chair, his body tense and rigid. "Jamee found Sadee sitting on a chair by her bedroom window. She'd cut"—his voice breaks—"she ended her life staring at the beautiful blue sky that day. I couldn't protect my daughter ,and you want to know why I can't sell that land? That house is all I have left of my little girl. Jamee painted the closets, and I'll be damned if I let someone else just destroy them."

"Sir, like I said before, your home is filled with squatters. The police are there now cutting the closets apart to save them."

"You had no right!" His anger forces me to slide my chair away from him.

"Sir, the health department would just tear the place down. I'm making sure the walls will be protected, and once we clear this case, Jamee can have them."

"You lie. My Jamee lives there. She wouldn't let it deteriorate."

"Do you know where your daughter is?"

"You leave my kid alone. You want to talk to someone? Talk to Andi. Put some fear into that child for her reckless behavior. It won't save my daughter, but maybe it'll protect the next person on her list."

"I will, but I would like to speak to Jamee as well. If you hear from her, please let me know." I hand him my business card. "The health department should be in touch with you soon."

I hear him grumble obscenities as I walk out of the common room. I flip open the phone and search for Karina's name, but a call comes in from her before I find it. The pounding in my chest sores as my thumb presses the accept call button.

"Karina, let me get this out before you tell me anything. We need Syd to find the locations for Andi Grace and Jamee Markovich. Hopefully she can dig up who Jamee and her sister Sadee's therapist was. Could be connected to the bigger case, but right now it's still isolated to our sorted pile the precinct overlooked. Okay, hit me."

"Where are you?" Now I know something more serious is going on. If anything, Karina would acknowledge the information before replying.

"Jersey. What's going on? Is it Frankie?" Please don't be about my wife.

"We need you back at the Bureau immediately. Full sirens. Go."

The call disconnects and my singular focus is getting to the city before something gets worse. The elevator provides enough time to send a message to Sydney, but also see the lack of replies from my wife. In this moment I find myself making deals with the heavens. I'll do anything, just bring her back to me. We can handle the rest as long as we're together.

***

Storming into the conference room, a team of people surround a table screaming over one another. Karina is the first to my side, saying something that the pounding in my ears prevents me from hearing. My captain's expression is grim, almost fearful. Chalet and Toby stand in a corner with other suits, but two people are suspiciously absent from the room: Grayson and my wife.

"Did you find Frankie? Is she okay?" The whisper slips out of my mouth.

"Jasmine, let's—"

"Agent Marlow maybe we should—" Chalet waves his hands in my direction.

"Karina, please. Where's my wife?" The booming question knocks everyone into silence.

The seconds on the clock audibly click by as I wait for an answer. Zeile falls into a chair, his head in his hands. Chalet turns his attention out the windows as they all avoid eye contact with me.

"We don't know," Karina finally answers me. "Sydney and I were tracking her phone. We continued our attempts to get in touch with Doctor Ryan throughout the day. When our efforts went unanswered and the phone remained at Battery Park for a long period, I checked it out." Karina drops an evidence bag containing Frankie's phone.

"Is it Grayson?"

"You two, out," Toby says to the other two federal agents.

"But, sir—" one complains.

"Out." The two men drag their feet on the way out of the conference room. Once the door clicks shut, Chalet sits down across from me with a look of fear on his face.

"While on the surface the case has been about the victims, there was a second prong to it. One that Doctor Ryan was uniquely qualified to handle."

"Apparently, the Bureau had received complaints against Lewis Grayson."

Why are they going in circles? I just want to find my partner. "Karina . . ." I can't stop the painful sound of begging as my fists clench.

"The FBI's been working with Doctor Lewis Grayson for a few years. During this time, he's been a significant asset to the Bureau in all aspects of the investigations." Director Toby continues, undeterred by Karina's refusal to listen to his orders.

"If he broke protocol in any capacity, he'd make the defense's case for them." Karina piped up. I can sense her trying to calm my fears with every syllable.

"If they'd been complaints, there'd be some rumors swirling about him. Nothing's hit my ears or anyone in the department." I couldn't believe Frankie was in danger just yet. Panicking, yes. Ready to admit the truth, no.

"True, but before the Boxletter and Grubbs cases, we received an anonymous tip about Doctor Grayson. They claimed to be a patient and reported inappropriate behavior in their sessions. Nothing sexual in nature, but sharing information for profit and other nefarious behavior. Doctor Ryan has known Doctor Grayson for years, and we felt having her on the inside would assist in our investigation."

"She would have—"

"Jasmine, you know better than anyone that some things are best kept hidden." I know Zeile is referencing my desire to hunt down the entire Garrison family and bring the corruption to light. I kept Frankie in the dark about a lot for her own safety. "The team felt your ignorance, the natural jealousy you exhibited, benefited us. Grayson would read through you otherwise. You're good, but not that good." The director's explanation was sound, but it wasn't landing well. In fact, it just added to the anger and confusion mixing with the acid in my gut.

"You're telling me Grayson was just playing me for a fool?" Did I put my wife at risk?

"He's a narcissist, Steele. You were just fun to annoy." I'm sure Karina is trying to make me feel better. The pain in my abdomen screamed against her efforts.

"Doctor Ryan was never alone. We've had a team following her at all times for security. Doctor Ryan instructed the security staff that they should get food, rest, or what not while she was working on profiles. Apparently, both agents fell asleep, but there was no indication either left his house all night." His words explain the obvious, but one question remains.

"Then how'd her phone get to Battery Park?"

"We're working on that," Director Toby pipes up from the back of the room.

"This is all great information, but what aren't you telling me?" They glance at one another, but everyone avoids me. "Look, if someone doesn't start talking, I'll head to his house myself."

"Jasmine, Grayson's dead." Leave it to Karina to short circuit my brain into malfunction.

And Frankie's missing. The information seeped into my bones, weakening them as the words sank in. I know Karina's next to me, leading me to a chair but her voice is distant. Is this how she felt when I slipped out of our safehouse to confront the villains? Frankie was my rock, a foundation I knew I never deserved. I needed to find her.

"Detective, did you hear me?" Director Toby's face came into focus. My head tilted in his direction in acknowledgement. "I know you want to run out that door and find your wife, but you can't."

"What the director is trying to say is we need you to focus elsewhere," Special Agent Chalet cuts in.

Captain Zeile slides a piece of paper across the table. The names Jamee and Sadee Markovich, along with their pertinent information, stared back at me. "We need you to keep digging. Agent Marlow will accompany you—"

"No. I'm going to find my wife."

"Can I have the room, please?" Karina's question gave them all permission to flee the confrontation, which they do. "Jasmine, I need you to really listen to me, okay? Can you do that?"

"Yeah, sure." Not really, no.

"We have to assume whoever is behind these murders took Frankie because of her connection to you."

"Kind of obvious, isn't it?"

"Think about it, though. Why would they kill Doctor Grayson and kidnap Frankie? Why not just kill her? You'd feel the anguish and guilt from her loss. So, why take her hostage?"

There are many scenarios I can think of, but one glaring one comes to the forefront of my mind. "Barring evidence proving she was murdered and removed from the scene, I'd suggest this was a distraction. They know I'd do anything to protect my family, including focusing on their safety and backing away from the case. If that was their intention, they could proceed with their rampage and control the narrative of events."

"Exactly. So, we're going to let Chalet and the team handle finding Frankie. You and I will follow the evidence and get to the person behind everything."

"This is our fault. We missed it. If we'd just looked over the files before they were cast aside, we'd not be standing here now."

It's interesting how our minds try to take a higher road when the world nosedives. We use words like integrity, moral compass, and all that when our chest rips apart in a million directions. It's like trying to force our brains to do something when it needs time to process the trauma currently attacking it. Why do we hold ourselves to impossible standards when the rest of society doesn't do the same?

"We always do the right thing given the information we have, Jasmine. We might be wrong in the end, but we don't have the luxury of second-guessing things. This story has three acts, and we're only in act two. So, let them think things are in their control. Maybe they think they've got us against the ropes, but that's usually when they make a mistake. We'll find Frankie and the killer. There's no other option."

The fight flows out of me. "What do we do now?"

"Sydney sent me the address for Andi Grace. I say we pay her a visit." Karina picks up a duffle bag from the corner of the room. "And I'm staying at your place. Safety in numbers and all that. Don't argue with me; just go with it."

The two of us head down the long hallway to the elevators. I know there are a ton of things to do, but my energy is long gone. I want to go home, wash off the remnants of dead roaches, and sleep. I can only pray Frankie is safe until we find her.

Chapter Thirteen

I tried sleeping in our bed, but the smell of Frankie's shampoo kept my mind awake. I turned over on the couch, allowing the pain in my spine to wake up with me. Karina's soft snores from the air mattress on the living room floor nearby added to my inability to rest. I'd be lying if I said those were the only two things that disturbed the evening hours. Once we walked in the door, I called Frankie's family and explained the situation. Regardless of how they feel about me, they deserved to know the truth before someone on social media or the press got wind of it.

My phone's soft vibration signaling a call gives me hope for an update. "Steele."

"Are you okay?" The deep timber of Will's voice pierces my heart. "I've seen the news. What's going on? Are Chase and Frankie safe?"

I slither off the couch and move into the kitchen. Leave it to my friend to call when slivers of oranges barely peek over the horizon.

"Chase is with Sydney for the weekend. He's probably playing whatever games she has on that subscription pass thing. Thankfully in the dark about the situation."

"Frankie?" The word hangs in the air for a few moments. "Jasmine, please tell me the rumors I'm hearing aren't true."

I guess that depends on what rumors Will is referring to. I'm sure the internet is running wild with them. For all I know, they're calling me a cold-blooded killer for murdering Doctor Greyson because I was jealous of his affair with my wife. "What have you heard?"

"My daughters saw some crap online about Frankie being missing and you're involved. Nothing on the news, but it's still early for them."

The rumor mill still functions as advertised. "That's partially true, but I have nothing to do with her disappearance. In fact, they're following protocol and keeping me from finding her. Syd's helping as much as possible. The Feds and our team are on it. I'm still working on the other murders." The break in my voice betrays me. "Anyway, how's the family doing up north?"

"Nice redirection. Just know we're here for you, no matter what. I'm sure they'll give me some time off to help if needed. As for the family, girls are doing great. Everyone seems to love it here." The shuffle of footsteps and the telltale sounds of a coffee machine come through the phone. The deep sigh forces one of my own. I've worked with him long enough to know when he isn't sure how to touch on a subject.

"Just say it."

"I've gotten calls from news outlets. They're digging, Jasmine. I haven't engaged with them, but you know they're relentless."

Of course they have. These people are like wild animals, looking for dirt with dollar signs in their eyes. I doubt they even verify the information before they write about something for clickbait. How can one fight the promise of riches from the voracious masses demanding to be fed a fat meal of bullshit?

"I'll let Zeile know. They've been warned to back off."

"Yeah, but you know how they are. They won't stop until you give them something, Jasmine."

"And I will. I'll hand them the murderer behind the posts and let the department handle the rest. Will, you know I never wanted this name recognition or poster child crap. I just wanted to go to work, do my best during my twenty years, and go home to my family. That's it."

"The road to hell is paved with the best of intentions, Jasmine. We do our best to avoid all of this noise, but we can't control what other people write, discuss, or post."

"It's still too early for a philosophical discussion about what speech is and isn't protected. I say let the lawyers fight it out while I go about my business living my life."

"They'd bankrupt the country before we got an answer." Will chuckles on the other end of the line. "Seriously, as long as they have one thread of truth, it's going to continue."

"Don't tell me you believe—"

"Not at all. But it worries me. Is it possible you've been followed?"

"No, I've got a nice detail as per usual. I swear my life is more about my protection entourage than my actual job."

"Well . . ." The soft laughter warms my heart. It's been too long since I heard the jovial tone. "Is the department actively working with these companies to remove what they can?"

"Sadly, they don't see an issue with it. I don't know what's going to happen, but could you schedule some game time with Chase? He's going to need you."

"I'll call Sydney and work it out."

"Thank you."

"We're family. I'm sorry I'm not there."

"I know. You'll be back, though." The dead air on the other end of the phone brings up something I hadn't wanted to consider. "You're not coming back, are you?"

"I wish I could answer that. I missed the military life, but I miss being a detective in New York. I mean, I could do without being shot at, but you get the point." He halfheartedly chuckles. "But it's calmer. . . safer up here. And there might be a permanent position available soon. It's just an option. Can't be a cop forever, right?"

"Yeah." The whisper hovers over the rhetorical question.

"No matter what happens, I'm here. I know you're putting up a brave front and burying that fear, but my phone's always on."

"Thanks, Will." The pleasantries of his goodbye filter through as I hit the end button. The only thing keeping my anxiety in check is my belief in Frankie's ability to stay alive. That woman has stared down rapists and murderers from across a tiny table. Hell, she's raising a teenager. . . that has to be more terrifying than being held hostage. At least that's what I tell myself.

"Who the hell decided air mattresses were a good thing?" Karina's socks slide across the floor of my kitchen as she grabs her mug to down some coffee. "Chalet sent a message. He's got a lead, but he didn't elaborate."

The unknown doesn't help me. It makes me angry, unstable.

"Steele?"

"What?"

"Stop thinking about it. Nothing you could have done."

"I should have been there."

"Put aside all this guilt and think of Frankie and what she'll need when we find her. I promise you it won't be blaming yourself."

My leg bounces rapidly as I sip my morning coffee at the kitchen table. As a child, I always wondered why good people give up and walk away from life. Now, seeing everything going on around me, understanding swallows me whole.

"We'll grab something to eat and then head over to Grace's apartment. We keep our heads down and work this case until we get to the truth. That's all we can do right now."

A simple nod is all I have to give. The restlessness caused by no sleep and my swirling emotions make for a horrible combination.

***

The old brick apartment complex reaching into the sky with its twenty-two floors looks like all the rest. Dirty old bricks with little railings jutting out to give the illusion of balconies pockmark the side.

"Damn fools," Karina mutters, pulling open the door to reveal the lock covered with duct tape. "Homeowners have to know about this."

"Maybe." The second door slips open just as easily as the first. "Okay, why live in a secure building if you make it accessible to anyone off the street?"

"Not going to complain right now since we're gaining access to the building." Karina pushes past me and into the open elevator in the lobby.

Without saying a word to Karina, I find the recording option on the crappy work phone. People can present their own version of events, and I can release audio tapes if necessary. Slipping it into my breast pocket I ponder the legalities of it all but shake the thought away. If Andi Grace found the original thread and added to it, I'd have proof the narrative was false. I'm sure Sydney could use the recording to help protect my family's name.

Karina slips out of the elevator and down the hall with me hot on her heels.

"Here we are." She knocks on the door as I whisper my name and badge number into my chest.

"Dammit! I said leave it by the door! How dumb are you people?" The door swings open, revealing a rather irate woman, one hand on her hip and eyes focused on her cell phone. When neither of us answer her, she finally looks up. If we were in a movie, this woman would fit the stereotype of a spoiled rich kid with no manners. "You don't have my food. What do you want?"

I hold up my badge. "I'm Detective Jasmine Steele and this is my partner Agent Karina Marlow. We were hoping to speak to you about Sadee Markovich."

"Shit." Recognition splashes across her face. "You're those two idiot cops. You can stay outside. I don't want your negative energy anywhere in my place." She holds her camera up at eye level, I assume to take a picture or video to post online. "Hello, all my followers. Look who just showed up at my door. I'm airing this live so you all can see how horrible they are for yourselves. Now, what do you want?"

Streaming live. . . that was a new wrinkle I hadn't anticipated.

"As we stated, ma'am, we just want to speak to you regarding an ongoing case." Karina's honey-laced voice echoes in the hallway.

"They came here to talk about Sadee Markovich. Well, let's recap for you. She was my best friend, then she betrayed me in the worst way and killed herself before we could fix things. I'd rather not rip open old wounds and relive all that pain again."

"I understand that, ma'am, and we wouldn't be here if it wasn't important. We are hoping to bring closure to all parties involved. Could you shed light on the accusations of cyberbullying?"

She leans on the left side of her doorway, keeping it open with her foot as her cell phone blocks part of her face. "Not this again. No one ever bullied Sadee. We were friends, but she was overly paranoid and wouldn't do what was right."

"The online posts—"

"I posted the truth. I worked my ass off to get that interview, and they loved me. If not for all the other interviewees in the waiting room, they would have hired me. Then here comes my bestie, who only applied once she knew I interviewed."

"Do you have evidence of this?" Karina's question cuts to the heart of the issue.

"It was a logical deduction, Agent Marlow." Andi's sarcasm is clear.

"You both attended college and roomed together?" The silkiness of my voice sounds so foreign and fake.

"Yeah, they put us together freshman year. We got along and shared a lot of the same classes, so it made sense to continue the arrangement until we graduated."

"How was your relationship outside of school?"

"There was no *outside of school*. We were always together—traveling, working shitty retail jobs, whatever. We created a social media account for our college experience. Everything's there on the feed for you to dig into; don't know why you need to hear it all from me . . . again."

"Who has access to this account now?"

"I do, but I don't really post on it anymore. I just linked it to my professional account now. Like a funnel, you know?"

"Where did you submit your application to this job?" Karina tries to get the woman back on track.

"Online," she answers as if it was the most obvious thing in the world.

"Yes, ma'am, but was there a specific site?"

"The notification came through our school bulletin, but they redirected it to the company's main page. So, technically, I applied through their specific portal about two days after seeing it." In other words, it was a mass post with significant reach, and she has no way to prove her side of the story. "But I applied and then made a post about it for my followers along with a request some positive vibes for me to get the job. Sadee even commented on it, wishing me luck. So, you see, Sadee couldn't have known about the job until I put it on my socials," she sputters, defending her beliefs once again.

How can this woman be so sure Sadee saw the post and applied? For all Andi knew, Sadee was sincere in wishing her luck for a job she had already applied for. Maybe she was just being a friend and not cutthroat.

"Did you speak to her about your suspicions before you went public?"

"Yeah. I asked her why she did this to me. She swore she applied like the moment it posted, but she was lying. She has this tell, you know? Her right eye twitches when she lies. It's kind of obvious. Would you believe she even said she'd be happy if I got it? Like, no... no she wouldn't. She'd be just as angry as I was if the roles were reversed."

Or it was just a biological response? Why is everything assumed to be a conspiracy and not just a simple misunderstanding?

"When did you find out Sadee got the job?"

"Maybe three or four weeks after I interviewed. Her sister posted something about it. I was angry, so I replied and confronted Sadee. In the comments, people asked what I was talking about, so I put together everything and posted it for the world to see. Sadee was a horrible student and barely graduated. If not for me, she'd still be at the school begging for help. Yet, she got all the glory for my hard work. Sadee took that job from me, and the world agreed with what I said."

"Did the employer ever support your theory or contact you regarding the hire?"

"They sent me an email apologizing for the situation and offered me some other position I had no interest in. I turned it down. Why would I work for someone else when this mess gave me an audience? Now I'm my own boss as one of the top podcasters and influencers."

"Could you forward me that email please? Just so we can put this all to rest."

"Yeah, sure, as long as this all goes away. I don't need any of this drama. I'm happy now. I'm sorry Sadee's not here anymore, but I only posted the truth. I'm not responsible for hers or anyone else's actions."

No. Legally this woman couldn't technically be connected, but I can see grounds for a defamation lawsuit.

"We'd like to speak to the people that commented publicly on your post. Would you know any of those individuals?" Karina knows she's putting Andi on the spot, especially since she's streaming.

The young woman hesitates, her eyes darting around as if checking for another camera. "No. Like I said, I spoke out about the truth and people ran with it. I value the privacy of my supporters."

"We understand." I grab a card out of my pocket and hand it to her. "If you think of anything else, just give us a call." I nod and back away down the hall.

"Wait!" Her yell grates my ears. "Why are you investigating this, anyway? Sadee committed suicide. Unless you think she didn't?"

"We're just following up on an old filing, ma'am. Nothing to be worried about."

"Oh my God . . . you think I had something to do with it." She spins the phone around so her face is front and center. "You hear that? New York's finest screwups think I killed my friend! Sadee might have betrayed me, but I would never hurt her! You hear me, detectives? I wouldn't do that!"

Neither one of us respond to her bait. We just meander over to the elevator and bang the button, begging for a quick return. Andi continues to complain, but I assume she's inside her apartment as the sound has dimmed.

"I understand cell phones have played a crucial role in getting justice for victims, but there's a bad side to everything."

"Fifteen minutes of fame is an addiction. You fight so hard to get it that once you do, you can't let go. You become the very thing you hate, just to claw your way to popularity. I figure it'll be a reality show one day, if it isn't already."

"You're funny, Steele, but this is serious shit."

"My wife's missing and I'm barely hanging on by a thread right now. I could care less what that woman did. Besides, she's not the only one protecting herself." I stop the recording on my cell before slipping it in a pocket. "Having integrity doesn't mean giving up control. Fool me once and all that shit."

Our phones beep within seconds of one another. "Sydney?" I nod and put my phone away. "Message says she dug up something. Wants us to meet her at the precinct."

If she's at work, then where the hell is Chase?

Chapter Fourteen

The wave of negative energy hits me in the face the minute the doors open choking the life out of my body. The sorrowful glances from the other officers feed the helplessness swelling within my stomach.

"Don't let it get to you. Come on." Karina tries to calm my swirling fears as she leads me down to the captain's office.

Karina pushes the door open and shoves me inside without knocking or announcing our arrival.

"Agent Marlow, Detective Steele . . . so nice of you to join us."

"Captain, apologies for storming in like this, but—"

"Special Agent Chalet, I made a judgement call to bring them in." Sydney moves out of the shadows in the back corner of the room. "Chase is in your office playing video games, Steele."

"One that wasn't yours to make, detective." Chalet's harsh words cut deep. Sydney slinks back into her corner under his hardened gaze. "They're here now, so we might as well read them in."

"While you might have authority over this case, I will not allow you to speak to my officers in that manner, Agent Chalet. Are we clear?" Captain Zeile's fingers turn white, pressing into the top of his desk as he leans over. "My team is well aware of protocol, and if Detective Locke made a judgement call, I trust she did so with the case in mind."

The tension is thicker than the city humidity in the middle of July. "Enough of this. Doctor Brown, please share your findings." Chalet dismisses my captain's comment to take control over the room once more.

She hesitates, her eyes moving back and forth between Chalet and Zeile. I'm not sure she's met the FBI team, so her delay is warranted. As a precinct we answer to Captain Zeile, not someone from the alphabet departments. When he nods, she strides forward with the same confidence I've seen a million times before. Even if she presents minimal findings, Doctor Brown has such poise that one hangs on each word she utters. I'd be lying if I said I wasn't envious of her self-assurance.

"Evidence was scarce on both victims. The contents of Paula Grubbs's stomach confirmed the bottles found at the scene. Beyond the narcotics and alcohol mix, the victim snacked on some chips before her passing."

"Anything on the first victim?" Karina's question breaks Lillian's train of thought.

"No. Unfortunately, things were either degraded or just inconclusive. However, we did find something interesting regarding the piece of paper left in the victim's throat. We confirmed the material was normal paper one could buy at any supply store. The interesting part is about the ink . . . or the fact that it isn't ink at all. The chemical composition was positive for acrylic paint mixed with cremains. Before you ask, no, I cannot tell who the cremains belonged to. Just that they exist within the substance."

"Understood. Did your team uncover anything else?" Chalet rubs his eyes, and it's obvious the two cases are weighing on him heavily.

"Forensically, no, sir," Sydney says from the shadows. "We previously searched just using the theta symbol, but nothing came back. On a hunch, I searched for reports regarding this chemical composition. I got two hits. Each victim had a symbol on their skin, but after emergency personnel attempted to save them, they wiped it away or just missed it. We can't directly link them to our specific case, but it's possible."

Two more victims. The thought raises the hair on the back of my neck. Sydney isn't one to suggest a connection if her gut says otherwise. "You've scoured the internet posts, yes?"

"Of course. I've got two members watching for any reference to the victims or the other files I sent your way."

"Can you cross-reference a Sadee Markovich?"

"Steele, what are you doing?"

"Her job." Zeile's words, while nice to hear, don't add any confidence to my theory or train of thought. The team's belittling comments here and there have taken their toll.

I drop my backpack on the desk and pull out my cracked tablet and several files. "I followed up on those cases requesting Karina and me. There was one that seemed too on the nose to ignore."

"Detective Steele found evidence in the residence that was corroborated by the homeowner, Strat Markovich." Sydney drops images of the murals on the table as Karina takes the lead to explain. "According to Mr. Markovich, his eldest daughter Jamee painted them after his youngest, Sadee, took her own life."

"According to the father, the cyber-attacks on his daughter were nonstop. Sadee lost her job, apartment, everything. Both sisters entered therapy to work through the trauma. We're still searching for the therapist's name."

Sydney taps Zeile on his shoulder to get him to move. She slips behind his computer and attacks the keyboard. If I know her, she's digging into information on the two victims and seeing if anything connects them.

"We do know Andi Grace, Sadee's former best friend and roommate, posted the allegations online. Steele and I visited Ms. Grace and she all but confirmed her side of the story. She firmly states she is innocent of any wrongdoing, regardless of making leaps of logic without evidence to back her assertions. She live streamed our conversation and informed her viewers we consider her a suspect in Sadee's death. If unedited, the video should prove we said nothing of the sort."

My cell phone skids to a stop in front of Sydney. "I also recorded the entire conversation as backup. I don't need to add to someone's fifteen minutes."

"Forget that. She's an influencer with millions of followers. Her bio is something else. *Powerful woman who leads with love and shines the light on injustice everywhere.*"

"That's rich, considering her threats and lies on whatever platform she was streaming to." I laugh.

The sound of Andi's voice fills the room. First is the video of Karina and me with several comments posted below telling us to leave her alone. Some say we never suggested she did anything wrong and to stop lying, but they're in the minority. The next video promotes her upcoming convention appearance in the city.

"Oh, man," Sydney mumbles while looking at my tablet. "Poor kid."

"What is it?" Chalet pipes up. "Do we need to alert security at the con?"

"Not sure, but Sadee Markovich went through hell. The internet just ran wild with it." She slides the tablet across the table and turns her attention back to the computer again. "Every company has rules against this kind of behavior, but it's difficult to enforce. You can report posts, but they won't remove it unless it's clear-cut. They don't want to appear to choose a side, especially when people cite the infringement of free speech. They don't like the negative press. Beyond all of that, it's so difficult to trace these other accounts. Sure, they might have an email address attached, but you can spoof one, create a new one . . . Social media is a modern-day Wild West."

The posts on my tablet are disgusting. The comments are even worse. How these are still live and available for the world to see is despicable. It's just another reason for me to avoid this form of communication forever. Between Grace, Grubbs, and Boxletter, it feels as if evil has swallowed the goodness on the internet in one bite. Later comments about Sadee's suicide with smiling emojis and positive replies mentioning karma just support my thought process. These people have no remorse for being a part of it. In fact, their vitriolic replies make it sound as if they feel vindicated.

"Grubbs and Boxletter posted about Sadee Markovich, and it wasn't pretty. They went at her hard." Sydney shares another social media network, and the pieces come together.

"It's safe to assume Jamee Markovich is our prime suspect behind these murderers. Her father thinks she's been working and taking care of the house. She isn't. She painted the murals, and now we have acrylic paint with the possible cremains of her sister. It's all feasible." Karina's thoughts flow in line with mine. We need to find Jamee before she attacks again.

"Grace is going to be at the convention . . ." Sydney's words filter out as her gaze bounces around the screen. "It's easy to lose someone at a con. From experience, the crowds, the noise . . . it's overwhelming sometimes."

"In public? All the other victims were killed privately. It would deviate—"

"Karma." The word pops out of my mouth before I can contain it. "She doesn't want private. What if the others—the ones she felt were the worst offenders—were just the starting point? She had a plan, and if we caught her before she got to the top of the pyramid, it would prevent the big reveal. So, she watches them, studies their moves, and kills them at a convenient time. Andi Grace is the last victim, the last stop. She'd want the free publicity from people streaming when she confronted Grace. Even if she doesn't get the chance to kill her . . ."

"The internet has all the information and effectively does to her what she did to Sadee," Karina finishes for me. "It's convoluted, but plausible."

"How's this for convoluted." Sydney spins the monitor around. "Both Markovich girls were under the care of one therapist—Doctor Lewis Grayson."

"That might explain the viciousness of his murder," Victor says from behind Lillian. "Apologies, but unlike the others, this was violent. Twenty-seven stab wounds, sliced throat . . ."

"My team's still analyzing trace evidence found on his clothing and under his fingernails."

"What if he figured it out?" Karina's words quiet the room. "What if he called Doctor Ryan in for a second opinion and she witnessed it all."

My instincts tell me this could be one of two things. If Frankie arrived during the crime, one would expect the assailant to murder her as well. Unplanned, but necessary to keep things quiet. Conversely, she could also have opened the door for another game. It's that second thought that strikes fear in the hearts of most officers: their loved ones being used against them.

"Let's not jump to conclusions," Chalet chimes in as his phone rings. "Special Agent Chalet." His eyes lock with mine, and I immediately know it's about Frankie. "I'm on my way." He cuts off the call. "Captain Zeile, I leave you to handle the situation with Andi Grace. You'll have the full backing of the FBI in the endeavor. Agent Marlow, you're with me."

"Where is she?" The raw emotion in my voice surprises everyone, including myself.

"Detective Steele." Chalet stands in front of me, his arms cradling mine. "Jasmine, I need you to focus on this part of the case. We don't know what

Ms. Markovich is capable of, but I need you to put a stop to her criminal activity. Let me handle finding Frankie. Karina will be in constant contact, I promise. I can't have the public see a detective go rogue to save her family over saving the public. Not right now. Please."

A nod is all I can muster as a reply. I trust Karina, and she trusts him to handle this properly. That's all I can control. She places a reassuring hand on my shoulder before bolting out the door.

"Do we know what day of the convention Jamee might attack?"

"Tonight," Sydney pipes up. "It's the only night she's appearing. Her autographs and photo ops are all sold out."

"Then we have little time to form a plan. Are you all here, Steele? If not, we can leave you in the command center. I'll have someone—"

"No, sir. I've got this."

"Good, because she's seen your face. That might help us get her attention faster. For our part of the case, we want as much social media presence as possible."

Sydney jumps into the conversation. "If she's looking for attention, the autograph room makes sense."

"True, but they have security and handlers nearby. Photo ops might have a curtain or be completely open to viewing. Either way, the number of people trapped in the small room would have better audio for the confrontation. Not to mention those close in line to record an attack. All it takes it one person and a proper set of hashtags. Right, Syd?"

"Yeah." Her worried tone leaves me guessing. I'm not sure if she's proud of my knowledge or concerned about the case.

We have a plan in place after a few more minutes. But my heart fears for my wife. It's at this very moment I fully understand how she feels each day I go to work. She's received phone calls from colleagues regarding my injuries. She's waited with bated breath to know if I was going to pull through or not. Now it's my turn . . . and it makes me question everything.

Chapter Fifteen

The rain pounds the roof of the box truck command center. Sydney's working at the main computer while I stand back and out of the way. One by one the monitors come to life, showing the convention floor via their security feeds. Officers walk the grounds outside with bodycams, while others meander inside on coms.

Initially, we thought it would be a simple operation. After dealing with the miffed convention organizers, we learned there were three floors and multiple rooms for the event. In other words, a logistical nightmare we needed to process in the few hours we had before Grace's evening photo ops.

"And away we go," Sydney says, hitting the enter key. The screens pop up with dotted boxes around varying attendees. The facial recognition software should help us eventually, but I doubt they'll find Jamee in the crowd. She's avoided Big Brother from the beginning. I don't expect this to be any different.

"Steele, Locke . . ." Zeile's voice crackles in our ears. "Once things are running, give us locations of suspicious activity."

"Yes, sir," my colleague dutifully replies.

It feels like a waste of time. Checking all these people is a needle in the proverbial haystack. Sydney seems in her element, sliding from one keyboard to her laptop and back to the key computer systems. With the click of her mouse, cameras move, follow individuals as they move about, and zoom in for better access. Her movements are precise but quick, and I can barely track what person she's focused on next.

"Ever spy on Chase's social media accounts?" Her words break the silence, but not her process.

"No. I mean, that would be . . ." The lies form in my head, but the truth rests on my tongue, waiting to be shared. "I may have fake accounts on the same platforms. It's not him I worry about. It's people like Andi Grace and Markovich . . . all those people out there who post without thought or concern. They freak me out."

"I get it. You've got us all watching his back, but right now"—she hands me my old cell phone—"I need you to use those accounts and watch our perp's socials. If she follows the same behavior pattern, we'll see posts shortly for her followers to comment on."

"Serves to taunt the police that can't catch her and expose her last victim . . . unless she gets away with it."

"Then she'll become the vigilante the comments praise her to be. Here's hoping we stop this here." Sydney moves faster than before, as if she will single-handedly solve it all.

I stare at my phone, refreshing the feed repeatedly. Like a trained seal, I wait for the highlight of new posts to scroll through. Soon, several posts come to life. One after another, like a countdown, the images show different sections of New York City in route to this location. I know the path. It's clear to anyone who knows the city well.

"She's making it look like she's on her way, but there's no way to post every second. Could they be scheduled in advance?"

"Yes, which means she could already be inside the convention center."

"I'm headed inside. Keep us in the loop with everything." I place the earpiece in my ear before checking my cell phone for any communication from Karina. Nothing. Taking a deep breath, I grab my weapon, ensure the safety's on, and head out the door.

Sydney's calls fall on deaf ears as I storm out of the communication truck. My earpiece crackles to life with her voice warning the team I'm entering the field of play. Zeile seems rather disturbed at the slight change of plans, but it should allow him to divert more eyes to focus on Grace with her movements. We've got officers inside, ready to pull them out of line once she's close. If everything goes well, Jamee Markovich will be in handcuffs before Andi Grace even knows she's there.

"Any updates, Syd?" I'm hoping for a sliver of help in following these things. The generic images continue to post every minute or so. The path leads me through a back entrance and then up an escalator. But now, standing in a crowd, it's hard to make out the points of reference.

"Grace entered the back entrance thirty minutes ago. She's got security provided by the convention, but our officers are within range," Sydney informs the team. My heart rate increases. The game is officially on.

"Anything in my location?" The camera to my right moves until it stops focusing on me.

"Nothing came up through the system. No scans matching the DMV database for our suspect."

"Syd, is it possible to change your photo on those files?"

"Sure, it's been done before, mostly to expose the information of individuals in the New York State area. I've never read of someone hacking it to fool facial recognition software. I mean, that would be next-level coincidence, horror-movie-plot-driven-by-the-script crap." The speed at which the words tumble out of her mouth makes me wonder if she's taken a breath at all.

The crowd continues to funnel into the area as the security camera spins back toward the doors. Masses of people shuffle through metal detectors, scanning badges and pushing their way into the main hall. There are too many faces for the computer to scan them all. There has to be a better way.

Bringing up the map of the convention, I zoom in on the guest tables. Grace is on a panel first, then autographs before heading to photos. Her fans might recognize me from her last live session, so staying on the outskirts of the crowd is the smart way to approach it.

It's a medium-sized room, packed with attendees waiting for panelists to arrive. As if on cue, the lights dim. The crowd roars in approval as the moderator announces each participant. Andi appears and slithers across to the middle of the five chairs behind the table. Fans jump up and move to the two microphones on opposite walls. I assume those are for the question-and-answer segment.

Leaning along the back wall, a security officer tries to get me to sit down. I tap my badge and he backs away. Thankfully, Zeile and the FBI gave the security lead a heads-up. They know we're here and are allowing us to have the run of the place as long as we stay out of the way and show our badges when asked. Which is interesting, because I haven't seen people check attendees as they enter.

"Syd, once people are inside the building, are there any checks?" I whisper.

"Not that I can tell. Once cleared and inside, you have free range to visit anything. The only additional charges are for the autos and panels."

"Any hits with facial rec?"

"Two. Zeile sent some officers to check it out. Where are you?"

"Hovering over Grace like an obsessed fangirl."

"Hey, there's nothing with fangirling. I've had my fair share of convention experiences. But those stories are for another day. Just stay close to her. I'm not liking this."

I know what she means. This is too public. Too exposed. My flip phone buzzes.

Found Frankie. Leading a team inside. Once safe, will text.

Karina's words are a relief but also fill me with fear. Were there traps? If Frankie hurt? My thumb hovers over the call button, but the house lights come up before I can call. Andi waves to the crowd before she slips offstage and out of view.

I scan the social media feed to find a new post. There it is, an image of Andi onstage, smiling with one arm in the air, the words *"The truth will set you free"* posted above it.

"Syd, Jamee was in the panel room. You got any cameras scanning over here?"

"Hold!" I can hear her typing away. "Got her. She's headed toward the autograph table."

Zeile and the rest of the team acknowledge us as we converge on the main area. It's impossible to see over the swarms of people waiting in varying lines. I can barely make out the banner with Grace's face on it.

"Anyone have eyes on Grace?" Zeile's voice comes through. Negative replies follow.

"Syd, you have eyes on Markovich?"

"No, lost her in the crowd."

The main hall is a vast open room with vendors everywhere but confined to the side wall. Tables line the entire autograph area, security guards with each guest and some at the ends. Pushing my way through the crowd, I stop in front of a guard and flash my badge.

"Where's Andi Grace?"

"Ma'am—"

"No time for this. Where is Andi Grace? She's not at her table!"

He scans my badge quickly and radios, asking for Grace's location. "She's in the lavatory."

"Take me there." I don't care if she live streams me harassing her.

We duck through the black curtain as he motions for someone to take his place, glancing over his shoulder to verify I'm following close behind. The madness swarming around us makes it clear Jamee would go unnoticed sneaking through this. There are too many people moving about, and I'm sure individual security guards are only concerned with their specific charge for the day. He takes a sharp turn into a secluded area with two bathrooms. A guard stands outside the women's one. He glances over at us and nods. I assume he thinks I'm just another guest.

"Andi still inside?" He turned his attention to the man with me.

"Who wants to know?"

"She's a detective with the police department." The guard spun around to face me. "We good here? I need to get back to my post." Before I can reply, he's already on his way.

"She's still inside?"

"Yes, ma'am."

"Anyone else enter after her?"

"It's a public bathroom." In other words, he had no idea if someone was in there before she entered or after. What was the point of security if they weren't securing an area for a client?

The old metal door creaks as I push it open just enough to slip inside. Thankfully, the small amount of space isn't enough for the door to slam closed behind me.

"Welcome, my lovely followers of truth." Jamee's voice wafts from around the wall separating me from the main area of the bathroom.

"You've been so loyal, supporting my path as I serve justice to those who evade it."

A woman whimpers, and I assume it's Andi. I press my coms device to loop Sydney and the team into the situation. Peeking around the corner, I see Jamee has her cell phone propped up on a silver hand dryer attached to the wall. The mirror only shows three stalls in the bathroom. I don't know what weapon Jamee has or if Andi's hurt.

"Even though you've supported me, the biggest question I get is why I'm on this crusade. Well, here's the reason." I hear shuffling around and a muffled cry from Andi. "Andi Grace, influencer of the masses, was once my sister's bestie. But Sadee succeeded, and Andi here couldn't handle that. So, she tore her down by fabricating lies to garner sympathy and likes. Of course it went viral because no one ever took the time to actually read the entire thing. No one questioned why Andy here kept paraphrasing things and asking for money. That last bit should have clued you all in, but nope. You all just piled onto harassing a woman you didn't know. You made living so unbearable that my sister took her own life. People like Andi and mindless followers like you all . . . none of you care who you hurt as long as you get likes and follows. You trolls destroy human beings on a whim with no thought or concern for the life on the other side of the screen." Andi whimpers again. "Oh, you want to say something? Maybe tell them the truth?"

"I'm sorry Sadee's gone, but I didn't do anything wrong. She needed help."

"My sister was fine until you came along like a leech, draining her life force to feed your own sick games."

"Jamee, you don't need to do this," I call out from around the corner. "Let Andi go, and we can talk about it."

"We have a visitor, my viewers. Who's there?"

I could call out my name or . . . "I've got my hands up." My feet bring me in front of the two women before my brain can catch up. I just need to stall them long enough for backup to get here.

"Oh, wow. Detective Jasmine Steele finally graces us with her presence. I'm surprised you're here. How's your wife, Frankie? She at home, or have you abandoned her too?"

Don't take the bait, Steele. Just stay the course. Karina and Chalet have things handled. Frankie's going to be fine.

Jamee holds the influencer in front of her like a shield. A pocketknife presses against Andi's throat, a small droplet of blood on the tip where it broke skin. One wrong move and this goes south.

"I'm here." I step to the side, hopefully blocking the live stream. The world's already desensitized to violence, but these women have families. They don't need to see this. "I spoke to your father. He told me all about

Andi and what she did." I hear muffled sounds through the coms. The team must be in position outside.

"He did, did he? Did he tell you how hurt she was? How lost?"

"Yes. He's worried about you. Why don't you let Ms. Grace go and we can go see your father."

"Frankie said you'd try to stop me. Maybe even talk me out of this, but you're too late. The time to talk was when we filed our complaint. Not when my sister is gone and I walk around in hell. You ignored us—two breathing human beings in need—to focus on the dead."

"There was so much going on during that time, Jamee. It's not an excuse, just an honest answer. Sadee's complaint fell through the cracks. I failed her. I can't fix that, but I can help you."

Her eyes dart from the cell phone to me and over my shoulder. "Where's your partner, Agent Marlow? Hanging out in the hallway? Waiting to shoot me?" Jamee's tears roll down her face, but the rage behind them would raise the hackles on any K9.

"No, she's with Doctor Ryan." Her eyes widen and she smirks. It's unnerving, but I've let her know she won her game. I'm here and not with my family. Jamee Markovich has my full attention. "I know you blame Andi for all of this, and maybe you're right, but does she deserve to die?"

"All she has to do is admit what she did, then I let her go. If she doesn't, I'll let the lovely internet decide if she dies."

I can't let that happen.

"I didn't do anything! This bitch is a liar!" Andi bellows as Jamee presses the knife harder against her neck.

"Andi, you can stop the charade. The evidence you provided our tech team was fabricated. The company never offered you the job or any other position. The only reason Sadee was fired was because of online social media pressure. Otherwise, she was a stellar employee. In fact, the Markovich family spoke to several lawyers who all claimed they had an excellent case to sue for defamation, but they couldn't afford the cost to go forward with it. You lied, Andi. Not Sadee, you." I slide one step closer to the women. "While your feelings of betrayal and hurt were valid, the way you went about addressing them was not. We all need to accept our part in this so we can go home to our families."

"I didn't do anything. I'm the victim here." Andi screams as the knife presses harder into her neck.

"Jamee, please don't do this." She looks up to see the barrel of my gun. "You're streaming this online, so the world knows what she did. They'll hold her accountable. We can get you help."

"Like Doctor Grayson? He told me to talk to you. He told us your wife would help us. But no one did. Everyone lied, so I killed him too." A thought washes over her face. "Everyone lied to me."

She pushes Andi forward into my arms before slicing her right wrist.

"No!" I push Andi to the floor and rush over to Jamee before she can do anymore damage. Without thinking, I pull off my shirt and wrap it around the open wound, pressing down hard. I hear Andi's voice, but it takes everything within me to fight Jamee reaching for the blade. Her free hand and legs swing wildly. I slither behind her, wrap my legs around hers, and hold her right arm in the air. Every muscle in my entire body screams as she continues to struggle.

"Let me die!" Her wails break my heart. I say nothing as her body falls into shaking sobs. "Please let me see Sadee."

She collapses against me; her cries are the only sound my ears focus on in the room. Zeile and a team of paramedics burst into the room.

It all happens in a blur. Zeile hands me a NYPD sweatshirt as they wheel Jamee away on a gurney. Outside the bathroom, Andi gives her statement to officers while paramedics look at her neck. A few moments later, she's at her table signing autographs like nothing ever happened.

Zeile walks up alongside me. "You'll need to give your statement back at the precinct."

"Will Andi Grace face any repercussions, or will she be free to do it again to someone else she transfers her anger to?"

"Fame and fortune talk, Steele. Besides, what's the old adage? No press is bad press? Maybe she does it again, but I hope she won't. Remember, people end up believing their own bullshit so much that eventually they take it a step too far. Have faith in karma. It's all we have when the law hasn't caught up yet."

Maybe. That was the million-dollar word here. If someone gets away with something once, we usually believe they're bound to repeat it. Andi could have died, but part of me believes she'll use the incident to make more money. Like they say, when someone shows you who they truly are, listen to them.

"Steele!" Sydney runs through the crowd and grabs me by the arm. "Karina's been trying to reach you. I don't know any details, but they're at the hospital. I sent the location to your phone. Now go!"

Frankie . . .

***

Before I could leave the building, Captain Zeile insisted Sydney take me to the hospital. The ride was a complete blur as the sirens blared and lights illuminated the surrounding areas. I'd tried texting Karina during the entire ride over, but she never replied. I didn't know if that was a good thing, like she's getting Frankie's statement, or if it was a much more dire scenario. Knowing the evil that roams the world behind a smile, my mind leaned toward the latter.

It feels like I'm outside of myself when we reach the front desk. The words coming out of my mouth sound foreign. I feel like a marionette, as if my limbs all move according to the universe, tugging the appropriate string. The elevator takes us to a higher floor. Officers meet us by the nurses' station, rattling off some information to Sydney and verifying our credentials.

Karina is the first to reach me. Her icy hands hold onto my biceps as her mouth moves, and her eyes bore into mine. Nothing lands. The weird and warped reality I find myself in muffles all the sounds in the room. My head bobs in acceptance and my body moves through the small crowd of agents. Chalet's frame holds up a nearby wall, his face ashen and empty.

Once I see my wife, I understand his expression. She lies prone on the bed, her wrists a rainbow of bruising that dances up her arms. It doesn't take a genius to know the restraints used. Her right leg lays on top of the sheets in a soft cast. I can only sit and hold her left hand, praying she feels me next to her.

"Tell me." The pained whispers fall from my lips so low I'm not sure Karina even heard me.

"When the doctor gets—"

"I need to know what you saw, Karina." My jaw clenches tightly as the worst images possible flow into my mind's eye.

Karina rattles through the scene. Apparently, Jamee was squatting in an abandoned building near subway tracks. The noise drowned out everything around it, but there was barely a person within earshot anyway. Images of Karina's and my family littered the walls, our faces scratched out in rage. There was a hit board with images of people with the corresponding social media posts. Jamee sorted which ones were easiest to kill and which ones were more difficult, for whatever reason. The crime scene unit was still gathering all pertinent evidence.

"We found her in the back of the fifth floor. She's been beaten badly and stabbed in the leg. She's got lacerations and bruising all over her body. But the doc can explain it better than I can."

"If . . ." The question hangs on my lips. "How long would she have survived?"

"Considering the freezing temperatures, not long."

Is this what she felt like all those times my life came close to ending? This hollow emptiness that seeps into your chest, squeezing your lungs as you desperately beg for oxygen, feels so final. Like it will never end as the helplessness devours you whole.

"Sydney's going to take care of Hank and Chase until . . ." Karina's words trail off. What could she say? Until we're home? Until I'm ready to take care of him again? At this moment, they all know I'm in no shape to make any kind of decision on anything. "I've called everyone. I tried to keep them from traveling here, but Hadley and Will were rather insistent. She'll be on the next flight, and Will was on the road before I hung up. Apparently, his entire family was in the car the moment I mentioned Frankie's name."

"Vic? Lillian?"

"They were here before heading back to the precinct. Something about ensuring the evidence is processed correctly."

It's what they can control. I understand.

"Detective Steele? I'm Doctor Burlor. I'm in charge of Doctor Ryan's care."

I can only muster a nod in response to his introduction.

"I'd like to discuss your wife's case with you." Doctor Burlor kneels next to me, something I never expect someone at their level to do. Her voice lowers to a soft, comforting level, even though we both know what she's about to share is anything but. "She was unconscious when the paramedics rushed her in. There's swelling along her spine, but we feel that's due to her positioning. It should subside with time. While the bruising on her arms and left leg appears superficial, her left ankle is shattered. Your wife will need surgery to repair it. I'm also concerned about a concussion, but we'll know more when she wakes up."

"When?"

"I don't have an answer for you, Detective Steele. Each person heals differently. Doctor Ryan will wake up when she's ready to."

"When she's stable, fix her ankle. Don't need that healing improperly while she sleeps."

"Understood."

The shadow next to me fades away from my personal space. In that moment, all I want is to be home with my family. Thoughts of laughing over a board game or watching some random movie fill my vision. Of all the goals I've ever set out to achieve, that image is the most important. I don't want hospitals and lack of control. I never wanted that.

"Steele?" Karina's voice reminds she's still in the room with me.

"Thank you for keeping your word. Tell Chalet I owe him. Please?"

"Sure. I'll be right outside if you need me." I mentally thank her for understanding my need to be alone with my wife.

The moment the door clicks closed, the pyroclastic cloud of fear and pain rushes over the room, killing all rational thought in its path.

"I'm so sorry . . ." I sob into her hand, too afraid of touching the rest of her body. "I should have been there. I should have protected you."

In the back of my mind, I know the truth. There is only one person to blame for all the torment swirling across Frankie's body and mind. But rational thought is dead. There is only pain. Only guilt.

I did this. I put her here. If I never enlisted as an officer, maybe the requests for help would never have come. She'd be free from the darkness of evil, and this may never have happened.

I brought this into my home. I put her in harm's way. My love for her, my desire to provide for my family, put her in this bed. It doesn't matter who was physically behind it all. I gave them access. I am just as guilty.

Chapter Sixteen

Three weeks. That's how long I've been watching over my wife. Telling Chase was difficult, but he sat there as I spoke. I expected him to lash out at me, at the world, at anything. But he didn't. He was silent for a while. He just took the seat across from me, grabbed Frankie's other hand, and stayed there while she slept.

The surgery to repair her foot went off without an issue. She'll be in the cast for several weeks before starting physical therapy. Overall, they didn't see any complications in her future. She'd have to be careful and understand certain activities like skiing should be avoided.

It was the beginning of the second week when her eyes opened for the first time. It was a relief when the doctors cleared her of any neurological issues. We were lucky. Frankie rarely spoke to me, but entertained Chase every time Sydney brought him by. During his visits, I'd have phone sessions Doctor Preston to stay the course for my mental health. I knew I had to stay focused on it in order to be strong for my family.

Friends came and went, bringing us food or taking Chase home. Sydney snuck Hank in as often as possible. He'd lie by Frankie's feet and fight when it was time to leave. Frankie has a large amount of support around her, but her energy is different. The woman lying in the bed will hold my hand but rarely speaks to me about what happened.

Her angry scoff brings my attention back to the current moment. Against doctor's orders, Frankie has the news on. Their coverage of Jamee Markovich's case forces her blood pressure monitor to beep louder.

"She's as much a victim as those she killed." Her voice is low and angry.

"I don't deny that, but she has to answer for her crimes, sweetheart."

"Of course, but she needs professional help. I promise you, putting that girl in prison is a miscarriage of justice."

"She killed two people, possibly four, and left you for dead."

"I'm not excusing what she did, Jasmine. I'm saying she fell through the cracks. Had we helped her sister, would she have done this?"

"She cuffed you to a radiator and left you for dead. Frankie, I'm sorry but I can't—" My voice cracks.

"Hey, I'm here." She pats the side of the bed, shimmying over to make room. "Come on, get up here."

I slide into the bed and her waiting arms. I snuggle up against her, being careful so my larger frame doesn't hit her cast foot.

"I could have lost you."

"It's a horrible feeling, but it's the nature of our jobs, love. But I know what I'm talking about regarding Jamee. She doesn't belong in a maximum security prison. I worry that she'll never get the help she truly needs. I know you didn't like Lewis, but he was a good therapist with adults patients. But he was never good with teenagers or children. It's why he sought out jobs with the alphabet groups. If he hadn't taken these girls on as patients, maybe they would've gotten the help they needed. These two innocent victims slipped from place to place until the horrible happened. She deserves incarceration, but in a medical facility capable of helping her deal with her trauma. Not bars and throw away the key. It's not right."

"I trust your judgement." Her lips pressed against my forehead. "Doc said you can go when you're ready. But there's no rush. Whenever you feel—"

"I want to go home. It's better for Chase and Hank to have some stability. Coming to the hospital isn't good for them."

"They'll be fine, Frankie. This is about you." Even if it would be good for the kid to not come to this place again, if Frankie wasn't ready to come home, no one would push her.

"It's for me too. I need to see them at home, living life. That normalcy will help me a lot." Her hand squeezed mine.

"Okay. Sydney and Will installed a security system so we can keep tabs on the press camping out on our lawn. Will and Lillian offered to cook you anything you crave."

"Tell them I only require tiramisu and coffee." The small chuckle gives me a hint of the woman before the attack. It's a moment like this that gives me hope we'll get through this stronger than before.

"I'll let him know. I have to go to the precinct for a bit. Sydney's bringing Hank and Chase soon. Hopefully, the doc will have all your paperwork ready when I get back. Then I'll order your favorite pizza and we can head home."

"You'll order pineapple on pizza?" Frankie's left eyebrow raised in disbelief.

"Yes, a personal one for you and a normal one with bacon for the rest of us. Hell, I'll even try it if it makes you smile."

"No." Her seriousness caught me off guard. "I don't want to waste good pizza that way. I've been living off dry chicken for too many days to give away yummy food."

"Consider it done."

There's a knock at the door before Hank pushes his way through. "Sorry, but these two couldn't wait." Sydney apologized for the interruption.

I slip off the bed, pick up our pup, and place him next to her. Hank kisses Frankie before lying down against her side under her right arm. Chase takes over my side of the bed, showing Frankie Hadley's new movie he brought for them to watch.

"I'll be back soon, okay?" Frankie nods in reply as Chase slides the chair closer to her.

"I'll be here," Sydney says, patting me on the back.

Taking one last look at my family, I feel a sense of calm fall over me. I wish I could stay with them, but paperwork doesn't do itself.

***

Frankie's been home for a little while, and she seems to be healing better. Will's wife Mia has been a tremendous help. She and the girls come by when I need to go into the precinct to handle paperwork or sit through a meeting. Zeile and the Feds have given Karina and me space to handle things. We might have solved the case and brought a killer to justice, but the damage was done.

The minute we arrested Jamee, the NYPD released a statement regarding the posts and an investigation into Karina and me. A month later, they held a press conference discussing the changes they planned to implement. The first regarded the complaint filing system. Every precinct would create a rotational group of officers to investigate complaints that weren't clear-cut. If that investigation led to something more, the case would be routed to the proper individuals to handle it.

Jamee's court hearing came and went with little fanfare from social media or the news. Frankie testified for the defense, causing the victims' families to erupt in anger. As expected, they refused to accept the remorse and psychological defense. In the end, the judge saw the larger picture and how everyone lost. Jamee would face life in a mental facility.

After the judgement was released to the public, the FBI and NYPD suspended Karina and me for two months without pay. When the union detailed the grounds for the disciplinary action, I zoned out. With all the circulated fake news, there was no way to avoid this. So, I just accepted it and waited for the conditions of our reinstatement. When we return, we'll be on probation for another six months as we attend sensitivity training. None of it sits well with me, including the selective training that doesn't apply to the rest of the city wide force. Considering this was the first time anything negative was filed against us, it feels performative. But it's all about perception.

"Steele, come in." Captain Zeile pulls me out of my thoughts. The noise from the busy precinct rushes to my ears as I try to adjust.

Without saying a word, I walk into his office and relish the moment the door muffles the outside world.

"You wanted to see me?" His message on my voicemail had been pretty insistent. It's not that I was avoiding him, but my suspension wasn't up yet, and the call came out of nowhere.

"How's Frankie doing?"

"Healing. Still getting her strength back."

"That's good." He walks around his desk, slips into his seat, and folds his hands in front of him. He doesn't look happy.

"Cap, whatever it is, just say it." The dread washes over me as I prepare myself for the worst-case scenarios that perpetually run through my mind.

"I don't know how to broach the subject, so I'm just going to be blunt. What are your plans after your suspension?"

That was the million-dollar question. Would Frankie want to go back to her job? Would she be comfortable with me putting my life on the line again? Would Chase? To be honest, would I feel okay with all of this?

"I . . ." The confusion rolls off my tongue with one syllable.

"I spoke to the higher-ups and your rep. You've barely used your days off, and considering Frankie's condition . . . maybe you take some, if not all of it."

"Helps keep me out of the press too." Considering my name was still being sullied in the media, this wasn't a shock. It still made me angry. Even after the truth came out, Karina and I were still pariahs to our bosses. The road to hell is paved with good intentions and those with integrity. All the while darkness clouds the minds of the rest of the population. Maybe this world is just doomed to repeat the history they're now denying happened. It's sad, maddening and makes me want to travel to one of those science fiction multiverses.

"Well, indirectly, yes. Agent Marlow is being offered the same. She took leave for an additional month. With the families appealing the Markovich ruling, the media is bringing back up the accusations against the two of you."

There it is. Instead of standing in the truth, the precinct wants to shovel it, and us, under the rug. It hit me hard that this was never going to end. Nothing Karina and I do will ever fully clear our names unless we take the fight into our own hands. My instincts tell me even a judgement in our favor won't stop all of it. Who really reads a newspaper retraction? It's the original article that gets the most reads. Life is never going to be the same again.

"I know." The words weakly fell from my lips. These people were so concerned about their image or their desired outcome, but what about those of us on the other end? Have they thought of what these proven untruths are doing to my family? My career? No. Because all that matters is their immediate desire for vengeance. Like Frankie said before, people live in their safe bubble of a delusion. Who are we to knock them back to reality? Even though the justice system is supposed to do that, it fails. Repeatedly.

"The FBI has some cases out of town. They're cold... but maybe another set of eyes would help. You could consider that or the extra time off." Zeile's voice stops my downward spiral.

A cold sense of calm washes over my body. "I won't leave Frankie alone to heal while I gallivant here and there for the FBI. What happens if I want to jump back in right away?"

"I'd have to put you on desk duty until Agent Marlow returned and the appeal is concluded. That could be a few weeks or longer. But you could catch up on your paperwork and possibly assist your other officers with theirs. But you would be relegated to your basement office all day." The captain's face was firm, his shoulders tense. There was no room for negotiations, nor a union rep here to help me sort through it all. I was alone and meant to take a punishment they've all deemed necessary for the greater good.

My entire career is sitting on the edge of a cliff above oblivion. The sound of my badge and service pistol hitting the top of the captain's desk made my heart race. Frankie and I made a plan in case I was cornered. Hadley helped us find the right people and here I was, watching things click into place that I tried to avoid.

"Steele? What are you doing?" Was his concern for me and my family or how they didn't want to release another statement regarding my resignation? That might blow up with protests demanding my pension and more. The warnings from my lawyer's race through my mind. It's the first time I could vividly see what they were talking about.

"I don't know, but I have to put my family first and figure out where my career goes from here."

"I'll put in your vacation time. Use it all. Then we'll revisit this." He pushes my gun and badge back my way, but I stop him.

"No. You can hold on to them until I fully file my paperwork. But I won't take them back right now. You owe me this. Please." The lack of emotion hid the angry that flared below the surface of my skin.

Before I can blink, he's around the desk and pulling me into a warm embrace. "My door is always open." And I know he means it.

I sent a message to my representation before I left the parking garage.

***

I sent Frankie a quick message letting her know my decision to activate the plan, not about my resignation. That wasn't part of the big picture. Her response was swift.

We're in this together. I'll make the call now.

Will had said something similar, but what could they help me with? The water I found myself swimming in held sharks I wasn't aware of. It's a new territory that I have to navigate on my own. I was always willing to put my life on the line for someone else for the greater good. Sure, I knew Frankie and Chase dreaded a call from my boss during each shift, but I never understood it. Not until I saw my wife lying in a hospital bed, broken. It made me face some dark realities about myself.

My phone lit up with a follow up message from my wife. *Lawyer filing papers. People being served today. Press release sent to outlets.*

There was no turning back now. It was time to clear my name, protect my family, and stand up for myself. It would cost a lot of money up front, but if it ended up in my favor, that would be repaid easily.

Stopping by Frankie's favorite bakery, I grab several treats and four hot chocolates. Will stayed with Frankie and Chase while I was out. The boys immediately jumped onto the game system with some new title Will bought for the occasion. Amid all the pain, it's nice to see the two of them catching up again.

Hadley stayed with us for a week or two, but filming obligations pulled her away. She still calls and video chats, more regularly than before. One night, once Frankie finally fell asleep, the two of us hashed out our issues over a bottle of wine. I may have snored horrifically that night, but she promised to come back as soon as possible.

As I walk into the house, the boys' voices hit my ears right away. Walking into the living room, I see the big, bad Marine was sitting on the floor with Chase next to him. The two of them are closer to the television than they should be, but that's just the adult in me talking.

Frankie sits on the couch, a small smile on her face as she watches the two of them interacting.

"There's donuts in the kitchen and two hot chocolates for you knuckleheads." I laugh when they glance at each other before taking off in a mad dash for the kitchen. "I swear Will is a big kid."

"You're just learning this now?"

"You know I'm slow with these things." I hand her a hot cocoa and a small bakery bag.

"You spoil me."

"Mom always told me there was nothing a hot chocolate and a good pastry couldn't fix. In your case, a personal tiramisu cake from Francesco's. Sorry it took me forever to get here. The line was ridiculous, but here I am with bribery for the kids to give us some peace. Lord knows they've been playing all day."

She leans forward, her hands sliding along the back of my neck as her lips press firmly against mine. "You went into work today. I thought you weren't supposed to be there until the suspension was over."

"Yeah, Captain Zeile wanted an update." I sip my drink and try to ignore the elephant wandering into the room.

"And?"

"Karina's taking an additional month off. The Bureau's letting her use her vacation time for an extended leave."

"Well, that helps them too, doesn't it? I overheard Sydney talking to some of her team members. They're still tracking all those posts, and with the appeal hearing, all this comes back to the forefront. It's only natural they'd want to keep the two of you out of the public eye."

"Yeah. They offered me the same thing. Take some or all my unused vacation time to stay home, help you heal, then head back to work. Give us time."

"What did you decide?"

I take her hand in mine. My thumb runs along her wedding ring as I ponder over all the things we've been through. "I asked him to hold on to my badge and service weapon before I told you to have the lawyer handle it. I don't know if I can go back after this."

"Jasmine . . ." Her voice trails off as she brings my eyes to meet hers. "I'm so sorry you have to do this. I know it goes against everything you stand for, but sometimes the people who think they're right are terribly wrong. We're doing the right thing."

"I've probably destroyed my career with the NYPD."

"Maybe, maybe not. Those who know what's going on wouldn't fault you for doing this. If it can happen to you, it can happen to them. For all we know this opens doors you thought were unavailable to you." I really love her optimism even when the storm clouds rage above.

"But I brought this . . . I did . . ." I can barely keep the tears at bay now. "I swore to protect people, and I couldn't protect you, my own wife. I couldn't protect Chase. What kind of cop am I?"

"A good one." The stern statement stops my train of thought. "You cannot control what people do. Yes, you made mistakes in the beginning of your journey. Hell, your foolish actions almost got you killed. But you're still here, with us. You've learned, grown as a cop, a wife and a parent. Beyond that, you, Will, Sydney, Karina, Victor, Logan . . . you gave families closure. In my opinion, you've all done your best to keep this city safe. But you're only a few people in a city of millions. Even superheroes need help."

"Maybe, but the internet's forever. Those lies . . . they're not going anywhere. Whatever good I've done . . ." I can't form the words to fully explain the utter depression taking hold.

"No, they'll be there, but it doesn't tarnish your legacy. Our defamation lawsuit requires depositions from all parties. And we will not settle out of court. I want these people to come forward and be forced to speak under oath. Unfortunately, there might be some people who refuse to acknowledge the truth. They'll live in their own world, ignoring reality. No matter what they say, we know what we've overcome. And if the justice system works, they will be paying us for the privilege of their deception for years to come."

My wife's protective nature spills out with a soft voice and beautiful smile. My mother warned me the quiet ones were the most dangerous people on the planet. Seeing the fire in Frankie's eyes reminds me of my mother's protectiveness over my brother and me. In moments like these, I wish she was here for a reassuring word, a hug . . . all the things a mom does.

"But they'll just twist the outcome to suit whatever story they're spinning. How is that okay? How is that right?"

"It's not, but it's also not our problem. We can't police morality or common sense. We can just hold them accountable for their actions if illegal, live our lives to the best of our ability, and move forward."

"I don't want to lose what we have."

"I'm here, my love." She pulls me into a tight embrace. "We've survived before, and we'll do it again. It's a hard road, but we can do this because we have each other."

Her words lift my spirits as I pull back from her arms and look directly into her eyes. "I love you so much. You are my rock, my partner, my world . . . you and Chase are my everything."

"Even though I'm broken?" She lifts her leg for emphasis. "It's really annoying not being able to help you around here."

"I do it gladly. Plus, our friends help a ton." Hank barks from his perch at my feet, a bit of powdered sugar on his nose. "You too, buddy." I scratch the top of his head before he reaches for Frankie's treat.

"What we have, what we do . . . none of it defines us, Jasmine. How we get through this, how we live, how we raise our kid . . . all of that is our legacy."

"You're both my heroes." Chase's voice fills the room. Without saying a word, he rushes to squeeze us in a group hug.

I peek over Chase's shoulder and see Will with his cell phone, grabbing a quick image. He smiles at me before leaving the room. Even struggling through the darkest days, I know Frankie is right. The badge doesn't mean anything. It's a piece of metal, a promise to the people of the city I upheld. But this, in their arms, this is everything.

My phone flashes with a message from Hadley. The headline reads: *Detective Jasmine Steele files defamation lawsuit against news organizations, social media corporations, the NYPD and more.*

It was time to protect my family from the evil outside my house. The rest of society... they'd have to wait.

THE END

About Author

Kimberly Amato is the author of the Jasmine Steele Mystery Series and Enemy. Having won awards for a TV Pilot she co-wrote & produced, she dove headfirst into writing novels. Always creating, jotting down new ideas & unafraid to try new genres, Kimberly writes mysteries, crime, romance, sci-fi & more. Beyond that, she's a podcaster with her wife, Sheila, for the show Forever Fangirls reviewing TV and film on streaming services and in theaters. Kimberly enjoys keeping in touch with her readers. You can find her by using the links below or going to her website KimberlyAmato.com.

amazon.com/stores/Kimberly-Amato/author/B00RKJDIXA

bookbub.com/authors/kimberly-amato

facebook.com/thekimberlyamato

instagram.com/kimberlyamato

Go to the link below to stay up to date on new releases and more!
https://www.kimberlyamato.com/newsletter

Also By Kimberly Amato

THE STEELE SERIES

Steele Intent (Book 1)

Melting Steele (Book 2)

Breaking Steele (Book 3)

Cold Steele (Book 4)

Steele Shield (Book 5)

Steele Influence (Book 6)

STANDALONES

Enemy

Milton Keynes UK
Ingram Content Group UK Ltd.
UKHW040716141024
449705UK00001B/105